From: Delphi@oracle.org
To: C_Evans@athena.edu
Re: fashion designer, Sasha Bracciali

Christine,

That Teal Arnett is in the custody of Kestonia's new dictator is devastating news. Of course I am willing to help you! Athena Academy, and all that it stands for, means so much to me. For your next rescue mission, I've brought in reinforcements. I've contacted Allison Gracelyn.

It seems the Kestonian is hosting a gala for the international who's who, including Mafia contacts from the U.S. Thanks to his mob dealings, Sasha Bracciali's father may be able to get her in. No worries about her ability to go undercover. Yes, she's a fashion designer, but she moonlights as an FBI asset. And she's an Athena alumna. That says it all.

This time, Teal is ours.

D.

Dear Reader,

I recently took my first trip to Europe, mostly to research a time-travel story that takes place in Renaissance Italy, but we also spent five days in Rome as background for future books and because it has always fascinated me. I'll never forget my first glimpse of the Coliseum. Wow! I still get shivers. It was truly the high point of an amazing two weeks.

And so, when Silhouette Books asked me to write about an Italian-American heroine, my initial response was, Can she go to the Coliseum? Luckily, the answer was yes.

I hope you enjoy the visit as much as Sasha and I did.

Ciao!

Kate

Kate Donovan

CHARADE

ATHENA FORCE

Published by Silhouette Books

America's Publisher of Contemporary Romance

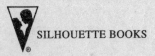

SILHOUETTE BOOKS

ISBN-13: 978-0-373-38974-2
ISBN-10:   0-373-38974-4

CHARADE

Visit Athena Force at www.eHarlequin.com

Printed in U.S.A.

KATE DONOVAN

has been dreaming up romantic adventure stories since childhood. *Charade* is the seventeenth of those to find its way into print, ranging from spy stories to time travel. In her real-life adventures, she's a wife, a mom, an attorney and a winner of a *Romantic Times BOOKreviews* Achievement Award for Series Romantic Adventure. You can visit her at http://katedonovan.livejournal.com.

This book is dedicated to the city of Rome
for being such an amazing inspiration
and for helping me get into Sasha B's point of view.

Chapter 1

Champagne in hand, Sasha Bracciali wandered through a late-afternoon crowd of wedding guests, enjoying the rays of simulated sunshine pouring down from the skylight in the domed ceiling of the Martino family's ballroom. This magnificent venue had been inspired by the ancient Pantheon, complete with marble floor and ornate columns. And like its predecessor, the room's circular walls were studded with alcoves that housed huge statues of Roman deities and Italian saints.

Sasha had played here often as a child, especially during wintertime, when don Antonio Martino had allowed his children and their guests to skate and ride bicycles and to in-line skate here, warm and secure, no matter how fiercely the Chicago blizzards raged outdoors. The place still gave her a sense of complete security, even though she now knew all about the dirty business that supported it.

She also knew what don Martino would do to her if he found out she was working as a confidential informant for the feds, so she was careful, as she moved among the beautifully dressed revelers, not to appear too detached or too observant.

Just let the bra-cam do all the work, she reminded herself, strolling over to the wedding cake so that the tiny lens embedded in the lacy bodice of her navy-blue waltz gown could get a clear shot of some nearby musclemen. Clad in black suits, these thugs weren't making any pretense of enjoying themselves. For them, this was business: protecting the bride, the family and the expensive wedding presents.

"Any sign of him, Camper?" asked a voice from the microreceiver in her ear.

Sasha raised her glass to her lips to hide her reply. "Lots of familiar faces, but so far, no zio Vincenzo."

"You're doing great," the voice assured her. "Even if the Butcher doesn't show up, we've got some valuable footage, thanks to you."

She bit back a smile, wondering how Special Agent Jeff Crossman always managed to sound so reassuring and appreciative when she was wired, especially since he was so suspicious and critical of her at all other times. As her handler, code name Summit, he had helped her through every one of her official ops so far, while tirelessly working in the background to get her fired.

If he ever used that sweet, sexy voice on you in

person, you'd have a vaginal meltdown, she teased herself. *Luckily, there's not much danger of that happening.*

She began swaying to the music, acknowledging that the love ballads filling the air were beginning to get to her. Nearby, a father was dancing with his toddler daughter, allowing her to stand on his feet to follow his steps. It stirred vague memories of Sasha's own father, and she imagined him—the powerful Franco "Big Frankie" Bracciali—behaving in the same indulgent way at weddings past.

It brought to mind one of Big Frankie's favorite stories, about the first time he took Sasha to Rome. She had been five years old, and when they had walked into the middle of the Pantheon, she had looked around, then announced cheerfully, "The Romans stole this idea from zio Antonio!"

Refocusing on the little girl dancing nearby, Sasha warned her silently, *Your dad's a hero to you now. I envy you that. But I'm also afraid for you, because if he works for don Martino, or any of these other Mafiosos, you're in for some serious heartache.*

"Heads up, Camper. A limo just pulled into the private driveway at the side of the house. Keep an eye out."

"Copy that, Summit." Grateful for the interruption, Sasha turned toward the entry hall that led to Antonio Martino's study just in time to see the bride—Gianna Martino-Barrett—dash through the columned doorways. The poor girl was probably sneaking out for a bathroom break, or even more likely, a quick drag on a cigarette. But there was always the possibility that her exiled uncle—Vincenzo "the Butcher" Martino—had shown up to kiss the bride, despite the multiple outstanding arrest warrants that bore his name.

"Summit? I'm going to check out the rest of the house."

"Negative, Camper. The party's in the ballroom. It'll look suspicious."

Sasha continued walking toward the hallway, murmuring, "Vincenzo won't show himself in here. Not with a crowd like this. They'll meet in Antonio's study for a quick hug and some tears, then he'll be gone. This may be our only chance, and I'm taking it."

There was a moment of silence, and Sasha was sure Jeff had muted the speaker so that he could fire off a couple of expletives about the "spoiled Mafia princess" he was being forced to handle. Still when his reply came, it was in Summit's trademark tone. "Don't take chances, Camper. Just get a shot of his new face, then get out of there."

"Copy that."

Relief flooded through her. Of course, she would have proceeded with or without his blessing, but it was better this way, especially given the number of times the words *willful* and *reckless* already appeared in her file.

And *always* in Jeff's handwriting.

"Pardon me, miss." A huge guard blocked her path as she reached the far end of the entryway. "Can I help you?"

"I need to use the little girl's room."

He motioned toward the alcoves at the east side of the ballroom. "Guest bathrooms are over there. The entrance to the ladies is behind Minerva. Gents behind Neptune."

Sasha pretended to pout. "I'm not just a guest. I'm an honorary member of the family."

"This part of the house is off-limits at the request of don Martino."

"I'm guessing you don't know who I am. Either that or you have a death wish." She arched an eyebrow, but only in mock reproach. "I'm Sasha Bracciali."

His brow furrowed. "Bracciali?"

"That's right," a man's voice growled from behind her. "She's Big Frankie's daughter, you moron. Get out of her way."

Sasha turned to give the bride's brother, Carmine Martino, a quick hug. "Finally! I was wondering when you'd notice me. Thanks for the rescue."

"My pleasure." The future head of the Martino crime family beamed. "Good thing you changed your mind about coming. I would've taken it personally if you didn't."

"It's all so complicated, isn't it?" She exhaled slowly and audibly. "I was afraid I'd run into Daddy and end up making a scene. But when I heard he could only stay for a few minutes, I decided I could time my arrival to avoid him."

"I figured it was something like that. Come on." Carmine took her by the arm and tugged her back toward the party. "Let's dance. You owe me one from the last time I saw you."

"At Bobby's wedding?" Sasha grimaced. "That was your lucky day. Remember how I left early with a stomachache? It turned out to be the mother of all flu bugs. Be glad you didn't get close enough to catch it."

"It would've been worth it," he murmured, his eyes openly scanning her body.

"You're so sweet. Stay right here, okay? I need to pop into the powder room for a sec, then we can dance."

"I'll show you the way."

She almost reminded him that she knew this house by heart, but decided it might offend him. Or worse, make him sentimental for the old days, when she had hung out here with his sisters—Gianna and Vittoria— while Carmine lurked in the background, wanting to hit on her, but afraid that her father would hear about it and have him erased from the face of the earth.

She even wondered if she and Carmine might not have ended up dating, secretly or otherwise, if she hadn't spent most of her teenage years at the Athena Academy, an all-girl prep school in Arizona. That experience had changed Sasha's life, exposing her to cultural and ideological influences that differed greatly from her childhood in Chicago—or more accurately, the Chicago of her honorary uncle Antonio Martino and her father, don Franco Bracciali.

Still, Carmine had been enough of a stud back then to attract her when she came home during school breaks. Sasha hadn't yet discovered the dark side of her family's business, much less the way it warped men like her father—and boys like Carmine—with its heady combination of power and violence.

In those days, all she had wanted to do was design dresses, fall in love and please her father—not necessarily in that order. Slowly but surely, the Athena Academy had shown her there was more to life, nurturing her academic and creative talents while also teaching her martial arts, weaponry and mountain-climbing—skills she never would have thought to acquire otherwise. That solid foundation had given her the strength to endure and succeed even after her mother's violent death during Sasha's second year of college, an event that might otherwise have damaged Sasha beyond repair. Even so, her subsequent estrangement from her father, whom she believed was responsible for her mother's death, had almost destroyed her.

Reminding herself now of the job she had to do, she allowed Carmine to take her by the hand and lead her into a second hallway, where she noted in frustration that the door to don Martino's study was closed tight. There was no sign of Gianna, and the room was guarded by two armed men.

"What's *that* about?" Sasha asked in a hushed tone. "I've never seen muscle in this part of the house. Not even during the drug war."

"We've got a very special guest," Carmine told her, adding quickly, "It's no one you know."

Noting a hint of wariness in his hazel eyes, she decided to take a chance. "I know everyone who's anyone, remember? And the more special they are, the more likely they visited *my* house at least once during my childhood to pay their respects to Daddy."

"I thought you needed to take a leak."

"I do. *After* I prove to you that I know your special guest. Unless he's so special that *you* aren't allowed in there with him."

Carmine laughed. "You haven't changed a bit. Still

gotta have your own fucking way every single fucking minute of every single fucking day."

Sasha laughed, too. "Why should I change? I'm perfect just the way I am."

"True." He licked his lips. "How about a deal? We'll join Pop and Gianna and the guest. If you know him, I'll wait on you hand and foot for the rest of the reception. If he's a stranger to you, we'll go up to my room and you can be my love slave."

Summit's voice intruded immediately. "Negative, Camper. Do *not* take that bet."

"Hmm…" Sasha sifted her fingers through her long, loose hair, then nodded. "Okay, handsome. You're on."

As much as Sasha disapproved of violence, she felt a tingle of anticipation when one of the guards refused to step aside on Carmine's orders. In an instant, her muscular escort had pinned the poor slob against the doorjamb with one hand while sticking a slender silver blade against his throat.

"If this wasn't my sister's wedding day, you'd be dead," Carmine assured him. "Now apologize to the lady, then move your fucking ass out of the way."

Sasha flashed them both a playful smile, then took a deep breath and tiptoed into the sanctum sanctorum, where she saw her friend Gianna crying in the arm's of a middle-aged stranger while another man stood nearby, also sobbing. Sasha would have known the second man anywhere, despite the fact that all the shades were drawn and the lights were dimmed.

"Zio Antonio!" She didn't have to pretend to be happy. "It's so wonderful to see you."

"Sasha?" He strode over to give her a bear hug. "My God, look at you. More beautiful than ever. And because of you and your God-given talent, my Gianna looks radiant, too. This gown you designed for her is a work of art. It should be displayed in the Uffizi next to the masters." He held Sasha at arm's length as he added, "What's this I hear about you refusing to let us pay you? If anything, I should double your usual fee for such a treasure."

"You got the family discount," Sasha explained. "I hope you don't mind, but that's how I'll always see you and Gianna. And Carmine, of course."

Carmine chuckled. "No, thanks. I'm looking for a different kind of relationship."

Sasha laughed, then turned back to Antonio. "Take a closer look at Gianna. I think *she's* the work of art. Don't you?"

"Of course."

"Thanks, Sasha," Gianna said, wiping away her tears. "And thanks again for coming. I was afraid you wouldn't. And you're the closest thing to a sister I have, now that—well, you know."

Sasha gave the bride a warm hug, knowing how much it would have meant to her—to everyone—if Vittoria Martino had lived to see this day. But Tori had died young, another victim of the mob violence that had plagued both their families for almost a century.

Wasn't that why Sasha was working with the FBI? To put an end to that madness once and for all?

Taking a deep breath, she directed her full attention toward the man with the unfamiliar face who had backed into the shadows, watching them in silence. "You must think I'm awfully rude, sir, bursting in this way and interrupting your tender moment. I'm Sasha Bracciali." Extending her hand, she walked closer to him, positioning the bra-cam to capture his face, and hoping that there was enough light for the image to be useful.

"You've grown into an exquisite young woman. More beautiful than even your mother, and she was a goddess." The stranger kissed her fingertips respectfully. "You may call me zio Dante. I'm not really your uncle, but I'm an old and dear friend of your father's, here for a short visit."

Sasha tried not to stare, but the effort was wasted. This was just too good to be true. The man's voice was familiar, but she had never seen that face before in her life. Rumors of Vincenzo "the Butcher" Martino's plastic surgery had abounded for years, and she was sure she was now getting confirmation thereof, not to mention, a huge coup for the FBI's Organized Crime Unit.

"Did you get a chance to see Daddy?" she asked him carefully. "He was here earlier, I'm told. But he left before I arrived."

"Big Frankie and I had a nice visit last year when he came to Roma on a business trip. I was sorry to hear about your mother's death, Sasha. She would be so proud if she could see you today."

Yeah, it's a shame Dad killed her, isn't it? Sasha challenged him silently. *But considering how many people you've offed in your time, I guess you'd be the first to understand why he had to do it. Caesar's wife and all, right?*

"Don't talk about her mother. It makes her sad," Gianna scolded the men. "This is supposed to be a happy occasion."

"The happiest day of my life," Antonio said quickly. "To see my daughter married—that is pure joy. And on that same day, to have both Sasha and my beloved cousin return to this house after too long an absence. It is more than a man deserves. We must drink a toast immediately. Carmine?"

His beloved cousin? Sasha's pulse began to race. *Vincenzo is one of his cousins! Isn't that enough proof of his identity to move in now? I hope Summit's getting all this! If the bra-transmitter lets us down I'll shoot myself.*

Carmine poured brandy into four elegant snifters and handed them out. Then he murmured, "To Sasha. She's as fucking stubborn as ever, but tonight, that's gonna work in my favor."

Antonio scowled. "What sort of toast is that?"

"Allow me." Sasha lifted her glass with a flourish. "To my family, not through blood but through choice."

The man who called himself Dante chuckled. "Any girl who can quote Sinatra deserves to be a Martino."

"To Sasha," Antonio agreed, raising his glass.

As the others echoed the toast, Summit's warm voice sounded in Sasha's ear. "Okay, Camper. We've got more than we need. I'm going to ring your cell, you're going to answer, and then you're going to tell them your best customer just called you in hysterics over some dressmaking emergency and you have to go soothe the ruffled feathers."

Her phone rang on cue, and she apologized, then stepped away from the group and answered it.

"Good girl," Summit whispered. "You've done an amazing job. First by designing that crazy bra, and now this. It's unbelievable. It's also over, so get the hell out of there. And if that horny bastard Carmine tries anything, tell him you'll sic your father on him if he doesn't back off. Got it?"

"For heaven's sake, Martha!" Sasha exclaimed. "It can't be that bad. Just calm down. I'll be right there, I promise. Just don't try to force the zipper whatever you do. We used the last scrap of fabric for the lining of the jacket. So *please,* just calm down. I'm on my way."

She could see disapproval in the eyes of Antonio and Dante, not to mention annoyance in Carmine's. "Sorry, I thought I turned that thing off," she said in apology. "But it's lucky I got the call, because my best customer is having a panic attack, and she's having it in her five-thousand-dollar business suit. I'm so, so sorry, but I've gotta dash. Forgive me?" Before they could protest, she walked right up to Dante and said, "I'll give Daddy your best. And next time I visit Mom's grave, I'll tell her all the lovely things you said about her."

He patted her cheek. "She would be sad to see you put business ahead of a family wedding. You should marry young Carmine here. Then you'd never have to work again."

"And we'd *really* be sisters," Gianna agreed with a

tearful smile. Wrapping her arms around Sasha's waist, the bride insisted, "You were so sweet to come at all. I know it was awkward, but it meant the world to me and that hunky new husband of mine."

Sasha gave her friend a teasing smile. "You'd better go find him. Last time I checked, he was dancing with Tessie Gallo."

"What?" Gianna scowled, then said to Dante, "Stay right here, *zio.* I'll be back before you leave so you can kiss the bride one last time. Or the widow, depending on what's going on out there." Grabbing Sasha's arm, she added, "Come on. I'll walk you out."

"No, I'll do it," Carmine told her, his tone leaving no room for argument. "Sasha and I have unfinished business. Right, beautiful?"

Sasha arched a disapproving eyebrow in his direction, and was pleased when he winced. Then she took Dante's hand and smiled sheepishly. "I made such a silly bet with Carmine. He told me you were an old friend of don Martino, and I thought I knew everyone from the old days, so I bet him that I knew you. Is it possible I'm just forgetting? Maybe you met me once, when I was just a baby. I *really* want to win this bet, so..."

Dante chuckled. "There was one time in particular. You spit up milk all over my brand-new suit. I'd say that binds us for life, wouldn't you?"

"That doesn't count!" Carmine bellowed. "Sasha doesn't remember it, so it doesn't count."

Sasha sent an inquiring glance toward his father. "I'll abide by your decision on this, *zio.*"

"Fuck that," Carmine muttered. "I won the bet, and I'm going to collect."

Antonio Martino's eyes darkened, but his voice was even when he announced, "My son is the loser here today, in more than one way. Gianna? Show our guest to the door, then go and pay attention to your husband. Sasha, take care. And Carmine?"

The son's expression had twisted with apprehension. "Yeah, Pop?"

"Apologize to Sasha for trying to take advantage of her. And to your sister, for ruining her wedding day. And then, if you are very, very lucky, I will allow you to apologize to *me*."

"So? What do you think the don did to him? Slapped him around, right?" Winston Lowe grinned at Sasha. "Man, I would've loved to see that."

"Yeah, but at least we got to see Carmine Martino cower in fear, thanks to Campie's brilliant tittie-cam," said his partner Chuck McBride, the third member of Jeff Crossman's Organized Crime team.

Sasha bit back a laugh. "Have a little respect. It's called a bra-cam."

"Too bad you can't find a way to have the lens implanted directly into your nipple," Winston said wistfully. "That way if some hotshot like Carmine ever gets you naked, we could still see the show. Er, I mean, collect the evidence."

"You guys are so immature." She glanced toward the special agent in charge, hoping for a nod of agreement. But Jeff Crossman was scowling.

Oh, fine. The honeymoon's over already? she asked
in silent disgust. *Even after I got you a photo of
Vincenzo Martino's new face? You're such an ingrate,
Crossman.*

Aloud, she murmured, "What's the problem, Jeff?"

"As if there's just one?" He exhaled in apparent ex-
asperation. "Fine. Let's start with that toast of yours."

"The Sinatra toast?" Winston asked with a wink.
"Did you really quote Old Blue Eyes, Campie?"

"Stop calling her that," Jeff warned him. "If you two
clowns want to participate in this debriefing, grow up."

"Sorry, Jeff," his men said in unison.

But Sasha could see that their eyes were twinkling,
so she threw them a bone by insisting, "I'm fine with
'Campie.' But I draw the line at 'tittie-cam.'"

"That's right," Jeff muttered. "Laugh it up. I'm still
waiting for an explanation."

"Of the toast?" Sasha shrugged. "It's just something
I've heard my father say."

"So you didn't mean it?"

"Pardon?"

"You said they were your family. By *choice.* Did
you mean that or not?"

Sasha stared into her handler's dark green eyes and
wondered if he could possibly understand, even a little,
the complex world in which she had been raised. A
world where family was everything, and sometimes,
everyone was family. And sometimes they weren't.
Sometimes, even your own flesh and blood weren't.

It was complicated.

And Jeff Crossman was a simple guy. Clean-cut.

All-American, both figuratively and Heisman Trophy-ly. With his six-foot-three athletic frame, his squeaky-clean background, his intact family and grass roots schooling—all of which had spawned a black-and-white view of right and wrong—he viewed Sasha's world through an amazingly clear lens, when in truth, it needed multiple filters if one really wanted to discover the truth.

Jackass.

She sent a warning glare in the direction of Tweedledum and Tweedledee, then told Jeff, "Yes, I meant it. They're family to me in one sense. But that doesn't mean I endorse their behavior. And it doesn't mean I'll protect them. They're criminals. The kind of criminals who rob innocent victims of any chance for a normal life. They robbed *me* of that when they killed my mother. And no one robs Sasha Bracciali and gets away with it."

She paused for dramatic effect, then assured him, "Go ahead. Put *that* in your report. I dare you."

"Did you ever sleep with Carmine Martino?"

She drew back, stunned by the question, and before she could stop herself, she answered with a resounding, "No!"

"Sheesh, Jeff. That's kinda rough, isn't it?" Winston murmured. "She just fingered Vincent Martino for us. Cut her some slack, will ya?"

Sasha laughed lightly. "My hero. Now if you boys don't mind, I'm going home. I've got a raging headache."

Jeff held up his hand. "Wait."

She cleared her throat, wondering if for once this

hunky marionette was actually going to apologize to her. "What now?"

He slid a picture of "Dante" across the table to her. "You're convinced this is Vincent Martino, aka, the Butcher?"

"Absolutely."

"Based on what?"

"Like I said, I recognized the voice, although I couldn't swear in court that it was Vincenzo. But he said he was Daddy's friend. And Antonio's cousin. And that whole thing about me spitting up on him. And his crush on Mom—ugh. That seemed familiar, too. So all in all? Yes. I think we've got our guy."

Jeff leaned forward, his gaze imprisoning hers. "And tell me again, just for the record. What is your relationship with Vincent Martino? Do you consider him family? By choice, not blood?"

Sasha could almost hear the accusation in his tone, but she shrugged it off. "My relationship with him? When I was a kid, he used to slip me a cannoli every once in a while when my mother wasn't looking. I *loved* him for that."

Winston grinned. "Slipped you a cannoli? Is that as dirty as it sounds?"

Sasha stared at him, speechless for a moment. Then she burst into laughter. "That does it. You're officially a pervert. But that's better than Jeff, because *he's* officially an ingrate." Grabbing her purse, she headed for the door, adding over her shoulder, "Nice working with you, fellas. I'm outta here."

Chapter 2

Exhausted, Sasha would have crashed into bed within minutes of arriving home, but she was anxious to follow up on a news story that had been taunting her all week despite her need to focus on preparation for the wedding op. Now that she had been debriefed, she could stop tuning out the rest of the world, beginning with the fate of two kidnapped girls.

Her favorite twenty-four-hour news channel was re-running a video of Representative Bryan Ellis of Arizona, who pleaded into the TV camera for the return of the two teenagers. According to Ellis, both victims had been students at a prestigious Arizona prep school for girls.

Athena Academy.

Thirsty for information about the status of her fellow

Athenians, Sasha fired up her laptop to check AA.gov, but the alumni Web site was strangely silent about the fate of the girls. It simply parroted what Ellis had already told the media: that the abduction had been bold and well planned, the families had been notified and the whole country was praying for the safe return of the students.

"Bullshit," Sasha muttered. "There's a lot more than praying going on. We have women in the FBI, the CIA, NSA—you name it. These creeps are gonna wish they'd never been born when they come face-to-face with pure, unadulterated Athena force."

Every fiber of her being wanted to call the school and offer to help, but it was the middle of the night. Plus, she knew that the Athena Academy had alumni much more experienced than she to tap. After all, Sasha's function with the FBI was to be a glorified snitch. An asset, not an agent. It made sense, given the nature of her work, but still it rankled her, even on a good day. And on a bad night like this, it truly frustrated her.

As if they're going to ask a Mafia princess for help on something like this? she mocked herself.

Immediately, she tensed. That was Jeff Crossman's viewpoint, not her own. Apparently he had really gotten under her skin with his doubts about her reliability. And while she knew it wasn't totally his doing—she had her own internal conflicts, especially in regard to her father—she still cursed Jeff for daring to speak them out loud so often.

Sleep, or even resting under the covers, was out of

the question. She would stay up all night if necessary, monitoring the TV and the Web site until she was sure the students were safe.

Twisting her hair into a knot that barely fit inside a plastic cap, she took a quick shower and slipped into a long, silky blue robe. Then she curled up on the couch with a glass of Pinot Grigio, her laptop and the remote control, determined to hunker down indefinitely.

She had just taken the first sip of her drink when someone knocked on the door to her condominium. It was an odd occurrence for multiple reasons. She rarely had visitors. It was nearly eleven o'clock at night. And her building had excellent security, which meant she should have gotten a phone call from the front desk announcing any guest who sought admittance.

Sliding to her feet, Sasha considered her options carefully. There was the pistol in the bottom drawer of her nightstand. Or a call to the front desk. Or…

Forget those screwups at the desk. Just call 9-1-1!

But that seemed imprudent, given the nagging sensation in the back of her tired brain that her visitor was probably Carmine Martino, determined to collect on his bet.

Which led her to her final option—one she didn't usually consider. She could simply kick the crap out of any assailant. Wasn't that the most practical part of her Athena Academy legacy?

Smiling at the thought, she walked over to the door and peeped through the peephole. Then she frowned in confused disbelief.

Jeff?

Without thinking, she threw open the door and demanded, "What's wrong?"

"Nothing. Can I come in?"

She was literally stunned. This guy never, *ever* came to her place. She always went to him, which made sense, since it wouldn't have been prudent for an FBI agent to be spotted entering the residence of a Mafia boss's daughter. Not prudent for Jeff, and certainly not for Sasha.

So why was he here?

Stepping aside, she allowed him to enter. Then she asked hesitantly, "Did you guys apprehend Vincenzo Martino?"

"We're still working on it." He gave a long, appreciative whistle as his gaze traveled around her sumptuously furnished living room. "Nice place."

"My design work pays all the bills. And, yes, the down payment came from my mother's trust fund, but every penny of that was completely legitimate. Not that it's any of your business." Sasha felt her temperature rise. "Even if every inch of this place was financed with mob money, I don't have to explain it to *you*."

Jeff turned and gave her a patient smile. "All I said was, it's a nice place. You look good, too, by the way."

Sasha sucked her breath in so quickly it made her chest ache. What the hell was he doing? Being *nice* to her? *Complimenting* her? Using his Summit voice on her in person, when he surely knew it was meant solely for electronic communications over safe distances?

But there he was, sounding strong and safe and sexy. Combined with his deep green eyes and admiring smile, the effect was lethal. Yet she knew it was false—this guy thought she was a crime waiting to happen!—so she steadied herself, then demanded, "Why are you here, Agent Crossman?"

"Sorry, I know it's late. I just wanted to apologize for the way I acted earlier."

Sasha moistened her lips. "Pardon?"

"You did a great job today. And I gave you a rough time. I'm sorry."

"You *always* give me a rough time," she reminded him. "What's so different about today?" Before he could respond, she insisted, "Don't give it another thought. I'm used to it."

"That's my point. I've been wrong. I admit it."

She would have been shaken by the sentiment had she not noticed his gaze slip, just for a moment, from her face to her body, which probably looked fairly good in this particular robe. "Oh. My. God. Don't even *think* about it. Just go home and sleep it off."

He flushed. "It's not that, either. Although like I said, you look great. You're amazing, actually. If we land Vincent the Butcher because of you—well—"

"So? You came here—at eleven o'clock at night— to apologize for calling me a spoiled Mafia princess? Fine. Apology accepted. Now go home."

Jeff frowned. "I never called you that. At least…"

"Not to my face? Yeah, you're a classy guy. No doubt about it." Stepping close to him, she raised her chin defiantly. "You know what really bugs me? All these months, you've been railing about my divided loyalties and crappy motivation because of my so-called vendetta against my father. But you know what? I think *you're* the one with a vendetta. Against *me*."

"That's not true," he assured her, using his Summit voice again.

"Isn't it?" She smiled grimly. "You've seen all my advantages—fancy houses, elite prep schools, zillion-dollar weddings and colorful relatives. And then there's you. So drenched in normalness you can't possibly relate to all that. So you denigrate it."

He arched a teasing eyebrow. "How am I drenched in normalness? If that's even a word, which I doubt."

Sasha bit her lip, regretting the display of temper. Wasn't she just feeding the stereotype? The hot-blooded Italian female? Plus, he was right about normalness. It wasn't a word per se, but it fit him sooo well.

Except for his body, which was anything but normal. And his face was superior, too. And his voice. And to be fair, winning the Heisman Trophy in his junior year at Princeton was nothing to sneeze at, especially since her father—Big Frankie—had reportedly made a bundle on a related bet.

Jeff touched her shoulder lightly. "Come on, Sasha. Let me apologize. I've been tough on you. For a lot of reasons. I see now I was wrong. You're invaluable to my operation. And the most amazing person I've ever worked with."

"But…?" She licked her lips. "You still don't trust me. Right?"

"I've always trusted you. It was your motives I questioned. Because of your relationship with your father." He exhaled sharply. "I'm sure I would have reacted the same way you did if I—well, if I suspected my father of—well, of doing what you think your father did."

"You can't even say it!" She backed away in embarrassed disgust. "That's the real reason you didn't trust me. You have so much contempt for the world I grew up in, you can't believe—not even for one minute—that something or someone decent could come out of it."

"Sasha—"

"Your father would never have anyone killed. Even if your mother had had sex with another man right in front of his eyes! They'd all just troop over to group counseling, right? But scum like my father and me—"

"Cut it out," he instructed firmly. "I never said that. And I never thought it, either. Not once."

She forced herself to settle down. Then she said with a sigh, "You figured I'd forgive Dad one day, right? And then my loyalty to you would shift back to him."

"Loyalty to me, loyalty to him." Jeff exhaled again, this time in clear frustration. "That's my point, Sasha. You're setting yourself up for a huge disappointment—or worse, if you look at it that way. Real loyalty has to be grounded in something unshakable. It's great that your culture respects family above all else, but that opens the door to factions, infighting, jealousy—"

"What's *your* loyalty grounded in?"

"I guess, justice. The rule of law. Our legislatures and courts. Not personal vengeance and passion."

"Judges and politicians are just as corrupt as anyone else who wields power," Sasha insisted. Then she turned away from him, folding her arms across her chest. "Maybe you should just go."

"Hey." He rested his hands on her waist and massaged it lightly. "Don't be mad, okay?"

She turned back to him, completely disoriented. "What are you doing?"

"Tell me to stop," he suggested hoarsely.

She wanted to say something—anything—but found herself moistening her lips instead.

Countless fantasies, some from earlier in Sasha's life, some from the day she first met this frustrating, judgmental hunk, flooded her mind and body with heat and excitement. Not that she needed it. He was supplying more than enough juice with his hot, appreciative stare.

Then he pulled her against himself, and she gasped at the hard-body feel of him. In an instant his tongue was sparring with hers, his hand roving under her robe, his breathing growing ragged and needy—

And then—as if to rescue them from themselves—there was another unexpected knock on the front door.

"Damn." Jeff realigned Sasha so that her cheek was nestled against his chest. "Are you expecting someone?"

She loved the erratic way his heart was pounding, mostly because it offered proof that he was as excited as she. Not that other proof hadn't been pressed against her, but that was just physical. Just a guy thing. This breathless lack of control was something else. Emotion. Confusion.

All the things Sasha was experiencing.

"I wasn't expecting anyone. Especially not you," she told him.

"Yeah. Me, either."

She pulled free and tried not to smile too widely. "It's probably Carmine Martino. Here to collect on his bet."

Jeff's amorous expression rearranged itself instantly. "He can collect on my fist, the asshole."

"Earth to Jeff. If he sees you here, my cover's blown, remember?" She stroked his tightened jaw. "I can handle him, believe me. Go hide in the bedroom."

Jeff shook his head. "I don't want him alone with you. Not ever."

"I won't be alone with him. You'll be in the next room. Plus," she added playfully, "I can kick his ass. *And* yours. Thanks to my fancy prep school."

He hesitated, then grinned. "Yeah. I know all about that from your file."

"Don't forget it," she said in mock warning. "Now shoo."

Still smiling, Sasha forced herself to recover from the lip-lock with Jeff, then took a few moments to re-belt her robe, which had been forced open during the kiss. She knew she should change into something less sexy, but her clothes were in the bedroom with Jeff and the bed, and that combination seemed just as dangerous as whatever was waiting for her in the hall.

Moving to the peephole, she was surprised to see that her second visitor for the evening wasn't Carmine, either. Instead, it was a bored-looking delivery boy with a long white box. And once again, security hadn't alerted her, which was baffling. Not to mention, annoying.

Your Christmas bonus is in jeopardy, boys, she warned the front-desk crew.

Then she took a moment to warn herself, as well. *Since when are flowers delivered in the middle of the night? Something screwy's going on.*

Her best guess was that Carmine had sent them. He would have ways of getting them past the guards, either covertly or otherwise. If that was the case, she needed to get this over with as quickly as possible, then get back to Jeff—hopefully for another round of X-rated kissing.

Wise up. You're still Franco Bracciali's daughter. This could be a completely different kind of package, so stop being such a sap. Girls who let strangers into their homes in the middle of the night make headlines the next morning, and not in a good way. So forget about sex and try to focus, will you?

Clearing her throat, she called out, "Who is it?"

"Flower delivery. Sorry for the late hour, but it's a rush."

Sasha scowled. "Just leave the box where I can see it through the peephole, then go. Sorry about your tip, but like you said, it's late."

"No problem, ma'am. Have a good night."

Jeff was beside her before she could open the door. "Flowers? What's that about?"

"I don't know," she admitted. "How did he get past security? In fact—" she arched an inquiring eyebrow "—how did *you* get past it?"

"The alarm system on the delivery door in the alley is prehistoric. Typical of these ritzy buildings—all the show is up front. But I reset it after I was inside, so…" His tone grew brisk. "Stand back. I'll handle it."

She laughed. "You're kidding, right? It's *my* condo,

so you stand back. Never let it be said that a Bracciali allowed an honored guest to get blown up on our turf."

"I knew you led an interesting life," he drawled, "but this just about beats it."

She liked the way his green eyes twinkled when he teased her, but reminded herself that he had mostly been an enemy—or at least a detractor—for the majority of their relationship, so she shouldn't let her guard down so easily.

Turning away from him, she leveled her eye with the peephole again, then had to admit, "It looks legit. Let's check it out."

Opening the door, she edged into the hall and knelt beside the long white box. "No ticking," she told Jeff, half jokingly.

"Allow me." He grabbed her by the elbow, pulling her to her feet. Then he pushed her behind himself before nudging the lid with his foot. The box opened easily, revealing a bouquet of long-stemmed red roses.

"Ooh, nice." Sasha knelt again, scooping the flowers into her arms. The she flashed Jeff a playful smile. "You didn't send them, did you?"

"Given how things are going, I kinda wish I had. But no. You've obviously got another secret admirer. Some sort of belated Valentine's Day gift."

Sasha could see a tiny envelope nestled between the dark red blossoms. Pulling the card free, she opened it and scanned the simple inscription.

Your cell and landlines both roll to voice mail. We need to talk. Check your e-mail. AA.

"What does it say?" Jeff demanded. "Are they from Martino?"

Sasha pursed her lips, buying time to decide how to respond. Given what was going on at Athena Academy, this mysterious message could only be about the kidnapped girls.

Which meant they had found a way to allow Sasha to help! And it also meant she had to get rid of her sexy guest. Fast.

"It's from my father," she lied finally. "He feels awful that we couldn't attend the wedding together. He thinks it's time to talk."

"Man, that's huge." Jeff rested a comforting hand on her shoulder. "Are you ready for that?"

"Honestly?" She gave an audible sigh. "It bothered me, too, avoiding him the way I did. Gianna and I— and her sister Vittoria—were inseparable when we were little. We played in that ballroom on bad-weather days while Dad and Uncle Antonio sat nearby talking. Obviously they were up to no good, but still…"

"Still, it was innocent in its own way," Jeff agreed. "I get that, you know. You think I'm constantly judging you, but the truth is, I get it. That's the only reason I've ever thought you'd crack under the strain. Because it *is* a strain. He's your father. You love him. I *get* that."

Sasha stood and looked him in the eye. "Thanks."

"What are you going to do?"

"I don't know. I could call him. Or I could blow it

off. I've done that before. But either way, I need to think it through. Alone. I'm sorry."

"No problem. I should be going anyway. This was sort of nuts from the start. Not that I planned it. At least, not from the start." His handsome face flushed. "Did I mention how good you look?"

Sasha felt her cheeks redden. "You look good, too. I guess we were set up by our own hormones."

"Yeah?" He chuckled. "I like that."

She couldn't help but smile. "You'd better go."

He nodded, but didn't move toward the elevator. "I know this sounds corny, but I'm gonna remember that kiss for a long, long time."

"Me, too." She gave him another, more wistful smile. "Too bad I wasn't wearing the bra-cam, or we'd have videos of it. For old times' sake."

"Actually…" He rested his hands on her hips as he'd done just before their kiss. "I'm kind of glad you *weren't* wearing a bra."

"Mmm." She brushed her lips across his, then pulled free quickly. "Definitely time for you to go, Agent Crossman."

"Yeah. I'll call you." He cleared his throat, then explained, "To let you know what happens with Vincent."

"Right." She bit her lip again. "Bye, Jeff. And thanks."

Her words brought a smile to his lips. "My pleasure. Get inside, Camper. And lock the door. The security in this dive sucks."

His expression—not to mention his tone—was so seductive, she felt herself beginning to melt again, so she gathered up the flowers and the box, then bustled past him, calling good-night over her shoulder. Then she followed his instructions by engaging the dead bolt as soon as she was inside the condo.

"Ohmigod," she told herself, leaning against the door and exhaling with exaggerated need. "What was *that* about?"

It was a question she could have dwelled on—and drooled over—for hours, if Athena Academy hadn't been waiting to hear from her.

When Sasha dialed the number supplied in the e-mail from AA.gov, Allison Gracelyn, an Athena board member who now worked for the NSA, answered on the first ring, saying only that a car would be arriving for Sasha in ten minutes. That gave her just enough time to don a pair of black jeans and a stretchy purple V-neck sweater. Then she grabbed her favorite butter-soft black leather boots and a cozy parka, along with her purse, and headed for the door.

Unfortunately, her *third* unexpected caller of the evening was waiting in the hallway. And this time, it really was the much-expected Carmine Martino, who asked pointedly, "Going somewhere?"

Oh, crap, Sasha complained to herself. But aloud, she kept her cool. "A delivery guy just dropped off some flowers. But he took off before I could give him a tip. So I wanted to catch him—"

"He'll live," Carmine assured her, his thick voice indicating he had had too much to drink. "The real question is, who the fuck is sending you flowers in the middle of the night?"

"A client, if you must know."

He grinned. "The fat one that got trapped in her zipper?"

"She isn't fat. Not at all. It was a defective zipper…." Sasha narrowed her eyes in warning. "Go away, Carmine. If you want to visit, come back at a decent hour."

"I don't want to visit. I want to collect on my bet." He pushed her into the living room, then closed the door behind them and warned, "No more tricks."

Sasha's training, both from Athena Academy and from her boutique-but-effective karate classes thereafter, would have allowed her to teach him a lesson, but she knew it would raise questions about her seemingly innocent lifestyle, so she decided on a different tactic. "We can sit on the sofa and talk. *After* I get these roses into water."

"Sitting on the sofa is a good start," he said with a leer. "Hurry up. I'll pour the booze. Where is it?"

"Check the sideboard. I have a little of everything. The glasses are on the top shelf."

With her purse still clutched under her elbow, she grabbed the flowers and headed for the kitchen. Once there, she fished out her cell phone and address book, thumbing until she found the number for Antonio Martino's *consiglieri.* Dialing rapidly, she listened to the ringing as she shoved the roses into a vase.

"Who is this?" a gruff male voice answered.

"This is Sasha Bracciali. Don't talk, just listen."

The man was apparently good at taking instructions, because his only reply was soft, steady breathing. Encouraged, Sasha hid the cell phone among the blossoms, then returned to the living room, where Carmine was waiting for her with two glasses of red wine.

Setting the vase on the sideboard, Sasha insisted in a firm voice, "I don't want any trouble, Carmine. You need to go home and sleep it off before you do something we'll all regret."

"You're so full of yourself," he retorted, slamming the glasses down, then stepping to within inches of her. "We can do this friendly, or we can just do it. It's you're choice. Either way, you're gonna thank me for it."

"My father would be furious if he knew you were doing this. Your father, too."

"Fuck 'em both. And you. Literally in your case," he added with a grin, reaching for her neck with one hand while his other began unbuckling his belt.

But the sound of a phone, ringing from inside his jacket, stopped him, at least momentarily. "Fuck! Who the fuck…?" He pulled out the phone and scowled at the display. Then he grimaced. "I gotta take this. Don't go away." Flipping it open, he asked carefully, "Pop? Is everything okay?"

Sasha watched as his eyes widened with obvious fear. "Sure, Pop. I was just—yeah, yeah, I got it. I'm going. *Fuck…* Yeah, yeah, I'm going."

Sasha backed away, trying not to let Carmine see how entertained she was by his transformation. Not that she blamed him. She had heard some fairly gruesome stories about Antonio Martino's temper, and she imagined Carmine had felt the sting of his displeasure more than once in his twenty-nine years.

"You bitch," Carmine whispered, his face purple with anger. "I can't believe you had the fucking nerve to call him."

"Shh…" She put her finger to her lips, then inclined her head toward the roses. "He's still listening. You'd better go, Carmine. We'll just chalk this up to all the excitement over the wedding, and a little too much Chianti. Okay?"

"Bitch," he repeated, but fear had returned to his voice. And while he clearly wanted to threaten her—or worse—he settled for flipping her off, Martino-style. Then he stormed out of the condo, slamming the door behind himself.

Sasha retrieved the phone and held it to her ear as she walked over to re-secure the dead bolt. "Zio Antonio? *Multo grazie.* I know he wouldn't have hurt me, but I was still scared."

"I'm very disappointed in my son," Antonio assured her solemnly. "First he ruins Gianna's wedding day, then he dares threaten an angel like you. And after I spoke with him this very evening about the need to treat you with respect. Can you forgive us?"

"I'm just so grateful for the rescue."

"Anytime. Any place. I hope you know that, Sasha." The don paused, then said bluntly, "Your father will be very angry about this. And with good reason."

"Except he won't ever know," Sasha promised. "It's not like I talk to him these days. And even if I did, you took care of everything. So why bother?"

"You're a good girl," Antonio told her in a husky voice. "And my son is a fool. Sleep well, *cara mia.* Don't worry about a thing."

"I won't," Sasha assured him softly, genuinely grateful for his solicitude. "Ciao, *zio*."

Aware of the fact that Allison Gracelyn worked in Washington D.C., Sasha half expected the Athena Academy limousine to take her to O'Hare Airport so that she could meet with the board member on the East Coast. And if not, then to Arizona, where the Gracelyn family lived, and where the school itself was located.

But to her surprise, the driver took her to the nearby Grand Union Hotel and instructed her to go directly to Room 2003. And so after a quick stop in the restroom to check her appearance—Allison was something of a heroine to her after all—Sasha made her way to the twentieth floor.

Allison answered the door right away, greeting Sasha with warm enthusiasm. "Come in. It's great seeing you again."

"I wasn't sure you'd remember."

"You make an indelible impression," Allison assured her. "We met at the welcoming reception when you first came to our school, and then again at your graduation. Correct?"

Sasha felt a surge of pride that this lovely, accomplished woman would remember such details. Of course, it was probably all in a file somewhere. And Allison undoubtedly attended *all* the initiations and graduations—

"At the initiation, you and I spoke about the portrayal of Italian-Americans in movies and on television. But at your graduation, all you wanted to talk about was your acceptance to the School of Design. Your enthusiasm was contagious. And I hear your success has been electric, as well. We're all very proud of you."

Sasha bit her lip. "I'm so flattered you remember all that. Especially considering everything that's going on." Daring to grab Allison's hands in her own, she demanded, "Is there any news?"

"Come and sit with me." Allison led her to a large table and motioned to one of the overstuffed chairs that surrounded it. Once they had settled in, she explained. "One girl has been rescued. That's the good news."

"Oh! That's such a relief. But…"

"The other girl is unharmed. Unfortunately we were unable to rescue her. Mostly because she didn't cooperate with us."

"Why not?"

Allison grimaced. "She wants to investigate from the inside. To learn who masterminded the kidnappings, and for what purpose."

"Cool kid."

"I suppose. But she's driving us crazy in the process."

"I can imagine." Sasha took a deep breath, then said in a rush, "I really appreciate getting all this information, especially firsthand like this. But I've got to ask. Why are you telling *me* of all people?"

Allison gave her a confident smile. "Because you—of all people—are the perfect person to help us recover the missing student. Assuming of course, that you're willing."

Chapter 3

Tossing his car keys onto his cluttered desk, Jeff Crossman strode to the only window in his sparsely furnished studio apartment, then shoved his hands into his jacket pockets and stared through the miniblinds at the neon lights that illuminated the freezing Chicago night.

"Un-*effing*-believable," he murmured to himself. "You kissed Big Frankie's daughter? You must be out of your effing mind."

He could just imagine what Winston Lowe and Chuck McBride—the younger, less-experienced agents on his Organized Crime team—would say if they heard about this. Those guys had been openly and obnoxiously wild about Sasha Bracciali from the start, to the point where the Special Agent in Charge—namely

Jeff—had had to pull rank on them more than once, warning them to cut it out when the compliments started flying too thick and fast.

"You're an effing hypocrite, Crossman," he assured himself now, although that characterization wasn't completely true. He had never denied that she was pretty— okay, *smoking* hot—but he had been determined his team would treat her with respect. She was, after all, a nice, decent girl trying her best to do what was right.

But he had also seen her as a liability, and now as he stared out into the night, with the haze of their kiss beginning to fade, he focused on other, less sexy parts of their incendiary encounter. In particular, he reminded himself of her accusation: that he had been conducting a vendetta against her.

Those words had shocked him, but didn't they hold a grain of truth? He *had* been uncomfortable with the idea of handling her, right from the start. Not because of her social and financial advantages, real or imagined, but because of her motivation. Because to Jeff, motive was everything when it came to evaluating an asset.

He could respect straight, uncomplicated revenge as a motivator. It actually made things simple. And he also appreciated the most common incentive of the garden-variety snitch—cold, hard cash.

In contrast, he didn't trust an asset whom the Bureau was manipulating into cooperation by threat of imprisonment. Nor was he comfortable with someone whose sole motive contained any other element of fear. It made them too emotional, which in turn led to surprises and complications.

Jeff Crossman didn't like complications.

Because of your normalness, he reminded himself, but his goofy smile faded quickly. He needed to stop fantasizing about how sexy and vulnerable she had been at her apartment, and start remembering the reason he had gone there in the first place.

To apologize, yes, but also to have a talk—the talk they should have had that first day, when she had walked into Jeff's downtown office, a tentative smile on her face, her hand outstretched to meet him. She had looked so pretty. So hopeful. So very, very dangerous.

Because as a professional, he had forced himself that day to look past the pretty face, the waist-long wavy hair and dynamite body—to see into her heart, her soul, her brain. And he had seen a needy daughter whose father had devastated her with betrayal and hurt so intense, she now needed to lash out at him—or more precisely, at the world that had created him. The world that had allowed Frankie Bracciali to order a hit on his own beloved wife, Sasha's mother, because of alleged marital infidelity.

Not that Sasha had been willing to work directly against her father. She had been clear about that from the start, insisting that Frankie Bracciali and his organization were off-limits. She would, however, use her contacts and background to help bring down anyone else.

It had seemed too good to be true. And then she had looked Jeff right in the eye and told him confidently that it wouldn't make sense to waste time on her father's dealings in any event, because "these days, ninety-nine percent of Dad's business is legitimate."

Those words, more than anything, had confirmed
Jeff's belief that Sasha was a deluded, emotional girl
who still loved her father as fiercely as ever. If it came
to a choice between Frankie Bracciali and an investi-
gation—and that day was bound to come—pretty little
Sasha would choose her father over law and order
without a moment's hesitation.

Jeff didn't blame her for that. Didn't judge her for it
as a daughter, or as a human being. But in her capacity
as an asset, he had believed it made her worthless.

Over the ensuing months she had done a good job.
A *great* job, in fact. But it wasn't until the Martino
wedding that she had conclusively proved Jeff wrong.
She had been nothing short of brilliant at that reception,
even before she got a shot of Vincent the Butcher's
renovated face with her crazy-ass bra-cam. Just the way
she had handled herself—so cool, so professional—
had impressed her reluctant handler beyond words.

Anyone else would have been distracted and sub-
verted by waves of nostalgia and confusion, but not
Sasha. Despite her clear affection for the bride and her
warm history with the Martino family in general, she
had been all business. Completely focused on the
ultimate goal—finding a way to track down and apprehend Vincent "the Butcher" Martino.

And man, had she delivered.

To Jeff's discredit, he hadn't been willing to accept the
truth right away. Instead he had struggled with it,
weighing her every word, every movement, intent on
finding proof that her emotional ties to Antonio Martino—
the man she affectionately called "zio Antonio"—

provided justification for not fully trusting her. It was only when she had walked out of the debriefing, her head held high, her long legs and pretty ass mocking him with every stride, that he had realized it was time to admit the truth.

He had been wrong. From the start. About everything.

She was an incredible find, an invaluable asset and one-*effing*-hell of a female.

And for reasons that had made perfect sense at the time, he had felt the need to tell her that. In person. Right away, even though the hour was late and she was probably in bed. He had convinced himself he *had* to go over there—to her personal residence—and apologize right away.

Now he knew better. Somewhere along the line, his body had taken over, conning his mind into thinking his purpose was to talk, when all the while, he had had a much more basic objective: to act on impulses that had been suppressed and denied for so many months, he hadn't even remembered they were there until it was too late. Until he was drowning in her eyes. In her silk-clad curves. In her kiss.

Un-effing-*believable, Crossman.*

"I guess you've heard I've been working with the FBI's Organized Crime Unit. But only as an asset, Allison, not an agent," Sasha explained with an apologetic smile. "I'm flattered—and trust me, I'll gladly do whatever you ask—but I'm a little confused. There are so many other alumni with more impressive qualifications and relevant experience. Really outstanding women in every sense of the word. So? Why me?"

Allison pursed her lips. "I should probably start at the beginning. But let me just say first, I disagree with your self-assessment. Your qualifications are as impressive as any Athena Academy student, past or present."

Sasha felt her cheeks redden, and she knew it wasn't just from embarrassment over the praise. It was also confusion, because what Allison had just said simply wasn't true. Athena alumni included daring pilots, skillful spies and computer geniuses. There was simply no way Sasha could compete with them, nor did she want to. She was a dress designer who moonlighted as an FBI informant, and she was perfectly content with that life.

Allison cleared her throat. "Okay, here's what we have so far in a nutshell. The two students are Teal Arnett, age seventeen, and fifteen-year-old Lena Poole. They each have amazing abilities. Superabilities, in fact. Strength, speed, and in Teal's case, some talent as a psychic. Coincidentally, both of the girls' mothers were treated at the same fertility clinic before they were born. Thanks to another Athena alumna we know now that their eggs—and those of many other girls—were genetically enhanced by unscrupulous scientists. Anyway—" she paused for a deep breath "—we weren't aware of the girls' superabilities when we invited them to attend Athena Academy. Believe me, they were more than qualified based on high IQs and athletic accomplishments."

Sasha knew her eyes were wide with childlike disbelief but she didn't care. "My God, it's so amazing. There was nothing on the news about any enhanced abilities. But that's why the kidnappers targeted these particular students, right? They want to study them. But to what end?"

Allison smiled. "That's the very reason Teal refused to be rescued, to find that out.

"She managed to get a psychic message to one of our contacts, and we were able to track them from Los Angeles to Colombia."

"Wow."

Allison sighed. "Before we could reach them in Colombia, they were moved again. Somehow the kidnappers knew we were going to make the rescue attempt."

"Because they intercepted Teal's psychic message?"

"No. Her talent doesn't work that way. We think they had someone on the inside, at the Academy or perhaps at the NSA."

"Oh no."

Allison nodded grimly. "In any case, we were able to get our hands on the other girl, Lena, thank God. But they took Teal to Prague. We had a nearly successful rescue there, and we found out about other girls with genetic enhancements. Unfortunately, they got away with Teal again, but we were able to apprehended a doctor named Jeremy Loschetter who was involved with the scheme. He provided some useful information about the person who organized the original abduction, a blackmailer named Arachne who has an interest in genetic research. We aren't sure how everything ties together, or whether Arachne is also involved with the group who has Teal now, but we're exploring all options."

"'We' being the NSA?"

Allison paused again, this time for a sip of water. Then she murmured, "I belong to another, smaller group. Once you're officially on board, I'll share all that with you."

"I'm on board," Sasha assured her. "I still don't quite get why you chose me, but it's too late now. You're stuck with me till Teal is safe."

"Good."

Seeing that Allison was uncomfortable with what had to be said next, Sasha prompted her cheerfully. "How does a Mafia princess with a vendetta against her own father fit into all this?"

Allison's perfectly shaped eyebrow arched in gentle disapproval. "That's an odd way to characterize yourself. But you're correct. Your connection to your father's organization makes you the perfect woman for this assignment." She hesitated, then asked, "How much do you know about what's happening in Kestonia these days?"

"Kestonia?" Sasha grimaced. "They just had a bloody coup, led by a ruthless autocrat named Vlad something-or-other. Oh no! You're not saying Teal is in that hellhole, are you?"

"I'm afraid so. The men who thwarted our last rescue attempt were Kestonian."

"Oh no."

"Access to the area isn't just restricted. It's virtually impenetrable. Vlados Zelasko has an iron grip on the borders. On everything, in fact."

"Why would *he* want Teal?" Sasha wondered aloud. "Isn't he busy solidifying his power base? The area has to be unstable and vulnerable. Doesn't he have enemies to contend with?"

"He killed them all, apparently. As a result, his regime is supremely secure, at least for the moment. His next step, according to his public statements, is to put Kestonia on the map. One way to do that is to involve his country in international trade. Black-market-style trading, mostly."

"That's where I come in?" Sasha guessed. "You think Dad might have some way of contacting this guy?"

"Almost certainly. There's a gathering of various crime lords in Kestonia this week. From all over Europe, and from the U.S., as well. Zelasko will meet with the underworld chieftains, then cap it off with an ostentatious ball to showcase his new regime."

"Right! I remember reading about that," Sasha agreed, thinking back to a colorful spread in one of her design magazines. "He wants to prove that Kestonia isn't drab and standoffish, so he's inviting dignitaries and royalty from around the world. It should be a fashion bonanza, especially because the guy is so totally photogenic."

"They say he's mesmerizing in person," Alison confirmed.

"Maybe so. But in my experience," Sasha told her carefully, "Mafia types don't like that kind of splash. They prefer to keep their lavish parties under the radar."

"I agree. It's likely that many of the crime lords won't attend the actual ball. But still, it's part of the conference, intended as a signal that Kestonia has become a major world player."

Sasha rubbed her eyes, suddenly weary. "And in the middle of all this, poor Teal sits in some hideous cell, scared to death?"

"According to her psychic messages, her kidnappers have been careful not to injure her. Still, we can't rely on that."

"I agree." Sasha felt a surge of renewed excitement. "Will Teal be able to send *me* messages?"

"I'm afraid not. One has to have psychic ability for it to work well. And she is apparently out of range, or perhaps drugged, because our contact hasn't heard from her since a few days after the last rescue attempt."

"So she won't be expecting me. But she'll be expecting someone to show up, because she knows we won't let a seventeen-year-old girl handle all this alone." Sasha grimaced. "In addition to me, how many rescuers are you sending?"

"We sent one already. She failed." Allison flashed a sheepish smile. "This time it will just be you."

Sasha drew back in surprise. "I'm pretty sure Dad can wrangle me some sort of entrée into Kestonia. But once I get there—"

"Once you get there, you will use your natural ingenuity and creativity—the things that make you so unique and amazing. You will also use your Athena training. I'm told you've kept up with your karate?"

Sasha nodded.

"Zelasko is so suspicious, it borders on paranoia. If he thought for one second that U.S. government agents had infiltrated his domain, he might do something extreme. Maybe even hurt Teal."

Sasha nodded her agreement quickly. "I just hope I don't let you down. For Teal's sake."

"We have enormous confidence in you, Sasha."

She took a deep breath. "I'll talk to Dad first thing in the morning. He'll be so happy to hear from me, he'll do whatever I ask. Let's just hope he has the right connections to make this happen without raising Zelasko's suspicions. Dad's business is mostly legitimate these days," she added pensively, "so the connection will have to be made through another family. The Martinos, maybe. They're our closest friends."

"Actually, the Martinos appear to be on the periphery for this particular syndicate. But your father's connection is very direct according to reliable intel."

Sasha winced. "I see."

Unbelievable, Dad. What are you doing? Backsliding? Just when our family was really getting out of the crime business at last?

"According to our reports, your father isn't attending the conference himself. But he's sending a representative."

"Probably my cousin Mark. He's more or less the heir apparent, since Dad's only child doesn't want anything to do with the family business."

Allison pursed her lips. "Would your father be willing to send you, too? Or would he worry about your safety in a strange country?"

"He'll worry. But if I want to go, he'll send me. That's for sure."

"It would be even better if you went alone—"

"No problem. Dad won't come, because he can't leave Illinois, thanks to a court order in a case where he's a reluctant witness. And my cousin—well, I can handle him. I agree," she added briskly, "it's best if I go alone. And soon. Right?"

"Thank you, Sasha. I know you'll do well." Allison smiled. "I assume your father will make the transportation arrangements. We can supply you with information and a few toys that might come in handy. Unfortunately, that won't include communication equipment. You'll be out of contact with the rest of the world while you're in Kestonia. And we can't supply weapons, either—Zelasko's men will search your luggage and purse, and frisk you, as well. You'll have to arm yourself with whatever you can find once you get inside Kestonia."

"The toys you mentioned aren't weapons?"

Allison laughed. "No. They're much, *much* better."

Sasha bit her lip, wondering how she would get through so complex an operation without Summit's voice whispering advice and encouragement in her ear. "I'll need to tell my handler something. Otherwise, he'll wonder what's going on if he can't contact me."

"Tell him you're going to spend some time with your father. A week or two. We understand that you just performed well for the Bureau under very stressful conditions. They won't object to your taking a little time for yourself."

Sasha frowned. "You're saying I can't tell Jeff the truth?"

"Is that a problem?" Allison was clearly surprised. "I had the impression you and he didn't get along."

"It's been tense, but we've been making progress, trustwise. I don't want to jeopardize that."

"To be frank, we're controlling access to this information and being even more discreet than usual. We might have a leak."

"You don't have to worry about Jeff. He's the most trustworthy person I've ever met. Like a rock, really."

"Oh?"

"Check out his background. He was a star quarterback until he got a really bad concussion and the doctors warned him not to play anymore. Then the FBI recruited him and he's been a star there, too. Completely obsessed with honor and justice—" She stopped herself, noting the flicker of concern in Allison's brown eyes. "I don't know why I'm making such a big deal about this. I guess because I'm used to having Jeff plan strategy with me. But you're right— this has nothing to do with him. I'll handle it the way you suggested."

Allison eyed her for a long moment, then nodded. "I'm glad that's settled. Luckily, I've planned an op or two myself along the way, so maybe I can be of assistance."

"That sounds great."

"Excellent." Her new mentor's tone turned brisk. "Let's get down to details, shall we?"

It was almost 3:00 a.m. before Sasha returned home and crawled into bed for a few hours' rest. She was sure that despite her exhaustion, she wouldn't be able to fall asleep. Not after the multiple stimuli that had assaulted her body and her brain that evening. The wedding and all the memories it had elicited; the encounter with Vincent the Butcher Martino; the kiss; the upcoming reunion with her father, to be followed by a daring rescue of a genetically enhanced child…

But to her surprise, she drifted into a deep sleep almost right away. As a result, when her alarm rang promptly at eight o'clock, she was more than ready to jump out of bed and take on the world.

Starting with Jeff Crossman.

She liked the idea of talking to her handler early in the morning. The air was crisp, almost biting, but clear of snow or rain. People were heading to church. There was a pure, homespun feel to the day. Nothing romantic about it, and definitely nothing sexy or obscene.

Still, it bothered her that he had sounded so good—downright rumbly, in fact—when she'd called him. And there was the complication that he had asked her to come to his private apartment, rather than the office he shared with his team members. Both locations were downtown, but Jeff had reminded her that the office building was closed, and any meeting there would seem suspicious. She had agreed, only questioning the arrangement after he had already broken off the connection.

Now she stood outside the door to his apartment and reviewed the cold hard facts, beginning with their first meeting.

She remembered *that* encounter vividly. She had been nervous, but also excited to embark on her lofty new project. It had meant so much to her that the FBI's Organized Crime Unit might be able to make use of her, so that no one else had to suffer the fate of her mother and be killed by "the mob." It was time for *that* brand of violence to end, once and for all.

Then she had braced herself and stepped into the office of Special Agent Jeff Crossman—the man who would be "handling" her. One look at him, and she had had only one thought: she had died and gone to informant heaven.

That's how amazing he had looked to her that autumn afternoon. Like a god. Not one of the Roman deities, of course, but maybe one of the Celtic ones? She had no idea about them—her whole universe, until now, had revolved around Roman mythology, thanks to her father—but one look at Jeff Crossman's broad shoulders, emerald eyes and lean muscles had made a Celt out of Sasha, at least for the moment.

A very short moment, as it turned out. Because once he opened his mouth, he had proven himself to be a first-class jerk.

Give the guy a break, she chided herself now. *He apologized, didn't he?*

She gave a nervous laugh, remembering how hot that apology had been, and imagining what might have happened next had Allison's roses not intervened.

Focus, Sasha! Don't think about the kiss. Or those shoulders. Or his Summit voice. This meeting is just a formality. Your mission is to save Teal Arnett, not to get laid. Puh-leeze try to remember that. I'm begging you!

Laughing at herself again—who knew she was so weak for football players?—she raised her fist and rapped sharply on his door with her knuckles.

Chapter 4

"Hey, Sasha. Nice to see you again," Jeff said with a warm smile.

Ignoring how adorable he looked in gray warm-up pants and an untucked white tee, his wavy blond hair still damp from his shower, Sasha handed him the box of doughnuts she had purchased from a nearby bakery. Then she strode into the middle of what appeared to be a one-room apartment. "I'm sorry for calling so early, and for barging in on your day off. But I've got a lot on my plate today, so thanks for seeing me right away."

Jeff peeked into the cardboard carton. "These look good. I guess I should have brought something to your place last night."

"You brought plenty," she assured him drily. Then she surveyed his living quarters with exaggerated thoroughness. "I see now why you were so impressed with *my* apartment."

He laughed. "Yeah, this joint's pretty grim. But I'm making payments on a beach house in San Diego, and I spend most of my time at the office anyway, so…"

Leaving the doughnuts on the counter, he walked over to her. "You said you've got a lot on your plate. Starting with me, right? I agree. We need to talk about last night. So have a seat." He gestured toward the bed. "Want some coffee?"

"No, thanks. I had some earlier." Sasha hesitated, then opted for a nearby desk chair rather than the comforter that had been spread over his otherwise unmade and still-warm-looking bed.

"Right. Let's get to it then." He sat across from her. "Obviously, I screwed up. But I swear, I didn't come over there last night to hit on you. At least not consciously. I just felt like my apology was way overdue. You've been a tremendous asset. I don't want to blow that, assuming I haven't already."

"We're fine." She grimaced sheepishly. "When I said I had a lot on my plate, I was talking about my father."

"Oh, right." He flushed as he jumped to his feet. "I'm such an idiot! Did you talk to him? How'd it go?"

"I didn't talk to him yet. I'm headed there next. But…" She didn't have to feign the confusion in her voice. "I think this is it, Jeff. The big moment for him and me. I can't just keep ignoring him. Or ignoring the problem. So I'm going to force myself to hear him out. Talk it through. It won't be easy. And I don't want to rush it. So…" She took a deep breath, then blurted out,

"I need some time off. From our stuff. Our *business* stuff, not the personal involvement. Not that we're involved. But you know what I mean."

"Yeah." He sat on the bed again, then studied her intently. "Take all the time you need. And just for the record, I think you're doing the right thing."

"Thanks."

"As for our personal involvement…" He gave the seat beside him an inviting pat. "Come here for a minute."

She winced.

"I won't bite you. *Or* kiss you. I just want to talk."

She steadied her racing heart, then scooted over, sitting a safe distance from him and smiling warily. "Any chance we can postpone this till I see how it goes with Dad?"

His green eyes warmed. "It's gonna go fine with your old man. He loves you. And you love him. Right?"

Sasha nodded.

"It'll make you an even more valuable asset for us. Not because we expect you to inform on Big Frankie or anything, but because it'll remove a giant unknown from the equation where you're concerned. I'll be relying on you even more than I have been. And hopefully I'll be treating you better. More like an equal partner." He edged closer. "It's gonna be tough, because you're so sexy. But if I want to be your handler, I can't—well, handle you, so to speak. And I definitely want to be your handler, because I think we're gonna do great things together."

She could see that he had rehearsed those words— most of them, at least—and she was touched by how difficult it still seemed for him to deliver them. "I know.

Don't worry about it, Jeff. I want to keep working with you, too. Plus," she said with a wistful smile, "we've got less chance than Romeo and Juliet, romantically speaking. Two different worlds and all that."

"Don't kid yourself," he murmured. "We'd be amazing together. That's the worst part of it, for me at least. I'll definitely have to be on my guard against it. Because that kiss," he added reverently, "is gonna stick with me for a long, long time."

Sasha licked her lips, enjoying the forbidden thrill his words were sending through her. If it weren't for her new mission—the need to save Teal—she might actually have argued with him. Or maybe even kissed him again.

"I know what you're thinking," he warned, his green eyes darkening. "I've been telling myself the same thing. We're both adults. We can handle it. But that's nuts. Right?"

"Probably."

"I already worry every time I send you into a dangerous situation. If you were my girlfriend, I'd really go nuts."

"Me, too."

"You, too?" He winced. "You mean you'd worry more?"

"No. I'd be so distracted. Your voice already gets to me when you whisper instructions. Or try to boss me around."

"Yeah?" He gave a sheepish grin. "Right in the middle of the op?"

Sasha licked her lips, then nodded. "I *love* it when that happens."

"Man…" He exhaled sharply, then leaned into her, covering her mouth with his own while urging her with gentle hands to lie back onto the bed.

Sasha's mind reeled with delight. "Jeff…"

"One kiss, then cold turkey," he promised, his voice descending into a sexy growl. "Man, you feel good."

One kiss.

Apparently he planned to make the most of it, because his hand journeyed almost immediately under her blouse, caressing her breasts, then expertly unhooking her bra to gain more complete access. Sasha wanted to protest, but her own curiosity was strong, and her willpower was weak, so she followed his lead, allowing herself to explore his tightly muscled chest under his T-shirt as his rough fingers sent wave after wave of pleasure through her.

This is our one chance, she reminded herself, giddy with arousal. *So he's right to make it count. Plus, you could get killed in Kestonia! Give him something to remember you by. We'll be good after this. And meanwhile, yowza.*

Inspired by his commitment to her pleasure, not to mention the hedonistic urgency as he ground himself against her, she slid her hand under the elastic of his sweatpants, then ran her fingers along the length of him, enjoying the fullness.

He gave a long, low groan, then told her ruefully, "We should stop."

"One time, then cold turkey," she reminded him breathlessly. "Why not make it count?"

"You're sure?"

"Mmm, more than sure."

She began stroking him again, and he flashed a sexy smile, then reached under her skirt and up along the inside of her thigh until his fingers reached their target.

"Wait, Jeff. Let me just—" She struggled to sit up, stripped off her boots and skirt, then wriggled out of her blouse and bra. At the same time, Jeff tore off his own clothes, revealing the hunkiest physique Sasha had ever seen at such close range.

They greedily appraised one another for a few seconds, then Jeff got down to business, pulling her panties off her so that she was wearing only her pink-and-blue argyle knee socks. Then he was on her again, nuzzling her neck while reaching over to open the top drawer of his nightstand.

"Rubber," he explained.

Sasha almost laughed out loud to see her sophisticated handler reduced to one-word grunts. Then he was kissing her again, this time between her thighs, and her laughter turned to a decadent moan as he coaxed throbbing waves of heat and energy to that spot.

She was so close—and frantic to continue—but he interrupted himself and transferred his mouth to her neck.

"Jeff…"

"Don't worry, I've got it," he promised. And it was true. His first thrust made her gasp with renewed anticipation, then he satisfied her with lovemaking so intense, it was as though they were *both* about to leave for Eastern Europe on a suicide mission.

As they recovered in one another's arms, Jeff gave her a sheepish smile. "That was some kiss. Thanks."

She bit back an embarrassed laugh. "There's a handler joke in this somewhere, but I hope we never find it."

"Yeah, I'm scum," he admitted with a chuckle. "But in my defense, I've thought about you a *lot* these last few months."

"*That's* your defense?" She laughed lightly, then hopped out of bed, grabbed her clothes and darted into the bathroom. "I'll just be a sec!"

Slamming the door behind herself, she looked into the mirror over the sink and arched a disapproving eyebrow. "Nice job, Bracciali. When you go into denial, you don't go halfway, do you?"

It was true. She had always been so careful before taking any relationship, no matter how hot, to this level. Sure Jeff was gorgeous, and sweet, and sexy, but under any other circumstances, that wouldn't have been enough. Not this quickly, at least.

"But you could die in Kestonia," she reminded herself, only half joking. "The question now is, if you survive, can you go back to being *just* his asset? Did you mean what you said about cold turkey?"

She honestly didn't know.

Dressing quickly, she returned to find him standing right outside the bathroom door, his green eyes warm with concern. "Are you okay? I can't believe we did that. I kept expecting you to stop me."

"I would have, but you're pretty good at it."

He grimaced. "I'd love to take credit, but the truth is, you were just in denial over the prospect of talking to your dad. Maybe looking for an excuse to postpone it. And like a jerk, I took advantage of that."

Sasha touched his tightened jaw. "You're overanalyzing it, Jeff. Like you said, we've obviously been thinking about each other that way for a long time. It was bound to surface eventually. I'm glad it did, so we can deal with it, one way or the other. After I talk to Dad, of course."

"About your mom? Are you sure you're ready for that?"

"I'll never be ready. But it has to be done. He'll probably lie anyway, so…"

Jeff eyed her hopefully. "Maybe that's better, right? The truth might hurt too much. So don't push it. The less you know about his business, the better it is for you, actually."

"His business is legitimate," she retorted instinctively, even though Allison's words were echoing in her head, reminding her that her father might be making an exception for the lucrative Kestonian market.

For a moment she thought Jeff was going to argue with her, but instead he just shrugged his shoulders again. "Whatever you say."

Sasha studied his guarded expression. "Are you worried about my reconciling with him? In terms of my usefulness to you, I mean?"

"No. Not at all." He flashed an encouraging smile. "I trust you, Sasha. Without reservation."

"Why? Because I got you a picture of Vincent Martino's new face?"

"Because of the *way* you got it for me. Not from a desire to get revenge for your mom's murder. Just because you want their brand of ruthlessness to end once and for all. You took no pleasure in what you did last night. In fact, it hurt you to do it. I respect that," he added softly. "But I don't want to see you get hurt where your father is concerned. It's not necessary. So be careful."

"Thanks." She smiled gratefully. "Did they arrest Vincenzo yet?"

"We're still working on it. By the time you check in with me next, it should be done." He cleared his throat. "How long are you thinking? A week? Two?"

She nodded. "At the most. If I need longer than that, I'll call you."

"Call anyway, day or night, if you need to talk. If it gets rough…" He hesitated, then pulled her into a bear hug. "Don't let my sex-maniac routine scare you off. I can be a good friend. I hope you don't need one, but if you do, call me."

"I will." She wrapped her arms around his chest and squeezed gratefully. He felt so big and strong and safe, and once again she wondered how she could possibly pull off the rescue in Kestonia without him whispering encouragement and advice into her ear.

"Hey." He tilted her chin upward with his fingertip. "Is something else bothering you? Other than the man-handling and the date with your dad?"

"No," she murmured. "But I'd better get going or I'll lose my nerve. And as for the manhandling, well…" She stepped back, then admitted, "I may have lied about that cold turkey business."

"Huh?"

"You're a brilliant strategist, right? So while I'm visiting Dad, try to strategize a way you can be my handler *and* my manhandler. Okay?"

"Sasha—"

"I've got to go." She grabbed her coat and purse off the chair and strode to the door, afraid to turn back toward him, even to say goodbye. Something inside told her that if they made eye contact now, she'd be back in his arms for the rest of the morning, and there wasn't time for that.

Not now, because she needed to rescue Teal.

And maybe not ever.

But she wasn't ready to concede that yet.

Spoiled Mafia brat, she accused herself with a rueful laugh as she dashed down the three flights of stairs to the street, then hailed a cab to take her to her childhood home for the first time in almost eight years.

She would have loved to surprise Big Frankie, but security at his two-story brick house was too tight to allow a strange vehicle to approach without someone noticing, so she instructed the cab driver to pull right up to the front curb, then took a moment to compose herself.

To her amazement, the emotion that was causing her hands to tremble was pure excitement untainted by dread. Was it possible she was really ready to face him? Or more likely, had Gianna's wedding gotten to her so much that the little girl in her needed to touch base with her daddy—to pretend that nothing had come between them?

The house was set back a good fifty feet from the street, and Sasha knew she was being watched. She could be intercepted easily before she reached the porch despite the lack of fencing around the property. There were always men in the apartment over the garage, visiting, plotting or just catching a few winks. And her father was almost certainly sitting at his desk, which was positioned in front of a huge bay window that looked out on the street. In warmer months, he could usually be found in the backyard, tending his fruit trees and garden. But in winter, he practically lived at his desk in the den.

Pulling out a compact, she checked her makeup, and was amused at the flush that lingered on her cheeks from her encounter with Jeff. Not exactly the first look she wanted her father to see after so many years. He was a pretty good judge of human nature, and he'd want to know who the man was, the same way he had demanded to know about every boy she had ever spoken to in Chicago and Arizona during her teenage years.

Probably not the right time to tell him that you're hot for an FBI agent, she teased herself as she applied a light dusting of powder to her otherwise radiant glow. Then she winced, remembering that that wasn't half the story. She was an FBI snitch in her own right. What would her father say about *that?* Subdued, she paid the driver and sent him away, then turned back to the house just as the front door opened and Big Frankie Bracciali stepped into view.

At fifty-five, his hair was the same vibrant shade of blue-black as Sasha's, without a hint of gray. Still he looked a little older, she realized in surprise. Strong as a bull, yes, and commanding as ever, but there was something a little different behind his deep brown eyes.

It wasn't age that had changed him, it was sadness.

She knew that because as soon as she lifted her hand in a halfhearted, vulnerable wave, the years dropped away, and his expression became almost celestial with love and relief.

"Dad…" She bit her lip, then raced toward him, throwing herself into his arms, shocking herself even more than him with the intensity of her display.

"Mio Dio," he whispered into her hair as he crushed her to his chest. "Is this true? Are you here?"

"I'm here," she assured him, laughing and sobbing all at one time.

He grabbed her by the shoulders and pushed her a few inches away, enough to stare down into her face as he demanded frantically, "You're not dying, are you?"

Laughing again, Sasha sandwiched his cheeks between her palms. "Of course not, silly. Do I look that bad?"

"You're a vision," he corrected as he hugged her again. "As beautiful as—well, just as beautiful as ever."

As beautiful as your mother…

Wasn't that what he had almost said? The same wonderful refrain he had uttered thousands of times. But he didn't dare say it anymore.

And she didn't dare hear it. Not yet, at least. So she brushed a flood of tears from her eyes and suggested gently, "Shall we go inside?"

He seemed speechless at the thought, then he nodded. "Yes, yes. Of course. Come in, come in. Are you hungry? Wait until Rocco sees you! He'll prepare a feast."

"He still cooks for everyone on Sundays?"

"Today he cooks for you, and you alone. My God, Sasha." Frankie shook his head, then took her warily by the hand. "Come inside and tell me what's wrong. Whatever it is, I can fix it. I promise you. Whatever it is, you made the right decision coming home."

"I keep telling you, it was just the wedding," Sasha assured her father as he fussed over her, serving her mimosas and reminding her that he had money, power and influence, all of which were at her disposal, if she would only tell him what she needed.

He was so radiant—and so wary—that it made her ache with guilt. Of course, she could banish that guilt easily by thinking about her mother's murder, but to her surprise, she wasn't tempted in the least to do so. The truth was, she had missed him, too—much more than she had dared admit to herself until now.

"There was a little girl dancing on the tops of her father's shoes, like you and I used to do," she told him with a hug. "Remember?"

"How could I forget?" His brown eyes sparkled with tears. "You should have been there earlier. When Antonio danced with his daughter the bride. And I wondered to myself whether I would ever know such happiness—the love of a daughter—again."

"Oh, Dad! I never stopped loving you. Didn't you know that?"

He smiled wistfully. "I used to plan your wedding in my mind. I even knew what song I would have them play when I danced with you."

"*'Volare?'*" she guessed.

Frankie nodded. "Do you remember how you would sing it when you were so small? Even then, I knew you'd grow up to be a beautiful woman one day, and some man would take you from me. But instead, I pushed you away, all by myself." Touching her hand, he added in a soft whisper, "I'm so grateful to have you here again. Tell me why."

Sasha bit her lip, regretting the need to deceive him, when the need for them to speak the truth to each other was so intense. So long overdue. But this was a necessary lie if she hoped to rescue Teal, so she forced herself to tell him, "I almost came home last month, Dad. To ask you a favor. But at the last minute, I couldn't. Then yesterday, at the wedding—well, it's like you said. Seeing Gianna with zio Antonio made me so jealous, and that ballroom brought back so many memories, so… Here I am."

"And now? Will you allow me to do the favor you mentioned? The one you almost asked me for last month? It would be my honor, Sasha. Ask me anything."

"It's probably too late. And it doesn't really matter—"

"Ask it. I'll move heaven and earth to do it for you."

"Dad." She smiled shyly. "It's not that big a deal. Just a party I wanted to go to. I was hoping you could wrangle me an invitation. But it's less than a week away now—"

"A week can be an eternity," he reminded her. "What party is it? Something in Miami? New York? My connections are as strong as ever, sweetheart. You're as good as invited already."

"Well…" She reached into her pocket and pulled out a folded article from one of the designer magazines she kept stacked neatly beside her sofa. Fortunately for her, she had fallen behind in her reading, and had been able to retrieve several stories about Vlados Zelasko's upcoming ball from the January issues. "Look at this, Dad. A real old-fashioned gala, complete with princes and kings and who knows who else? It's a million miles away, in the middle of nowhere, but it's going to be so unique. Such a fashion extravaganza. And according to this article, there will be a quote-unquote underworld contingent attending from all across Europe, so I was just hoping somehow you might know some of the people involved."

When her father hesitated, she assured him quickly, "I know your business is legitimate these days. I'm not implying otherwise. It was a long shot anyway. Forget it. It's too late, and it doesn't really matter. Not at all. I'm sorry I asked such an impossible favor. It wasn't fair of me."

"It's not impossible," Frankie murmured. "Just dangerous, Sasha. These people are ruthless in ways we can't even imagine. For me to send my own daughter among them? *That's* the part that is impossible."

Sasha laughed. "Aren't you forgetting something? They taught me all kinds of karate at that fancy school you sent me to. I can take care of myself."

Big Frankie grinned. "I remember how you'd come home and practice those fancy kicks on Rocco and the other men. We were all so proud of you. Sore, but proud." He cleared his throat, visibly weighing his next words. "If you were to attend this party, would you be taking a young man along?"

"I wish. Unfortunately, there's no one in my life at the moment."

He seemed surprised, then shrugged. "In any other situation, I'd escort you myself, but I'm involved in some court proceedings. Your cousin Mark was scheduled to attend, but he's in the hospital—"

"Oh no! What's wrong?"

"Lead poisoning," her father admitted with a sheepish smile, using the family euphemism for a gunshot wound. "He'll be fine, but can't travel for a while."

Sasha pursed her lips, sobered by her father's confirmation of Allison's information. "He was planning to attend? In other words, you're backsliding? After all your hard work to make the family business legitimate? What went wrong?"

"My domestic business is ninety-five percent legitimate," he assured her. "A little high-class money laundering from time to time is our only vice here at home. But Asia and Eastern Europe have been a gold mine for us for years, Sasha. We'd never survive if we didn't dip our buckets in that well from time to time."

Hoping her disappointment didn't show on her face, she asked lightly, "Are you dipping your bucket in the Kestonian well?"

Frankie nodded. "I was going to send Rocco in Mark's place, since he's my most trusted man. But quite frankly…"

Sasha smiled. "He's a talented cook and great at scaring guys to death, but seriously, Dad. You can't expect him to represent you in delicate negotiations." Lowering her voice, she suggested slyly, "Why not send me? I could advance my own business at the gala, and represent you in your dealings with Mr. Zelasko."

When Frankie stared at her, she wondered if she had gone too far. Then a grin spread across his face. "It was enough of a miracle that you came home at all. But is it possible you're considering—"

"No, no, Dad!" She shook her head frantically. "That's Mark's destiny, not mine. I'm all about the glitz and glamour, remember?"

When his face fell, she laughed and hugged him. "The good news is, I've been running a successful business for almost five years. Half talent, half saleswomanship. Give me a few juicy details that will make you indispensable to Kestonia, and I'll do the rest."

"And Rocco will go with you for protection."

"I hope you're kidding," she drawled. "I want to make a splash in the fashion world, not a belly flop. You know how much I love him, but seriously. Rocco as my date? I don't think so." She flashed a confident smile. "I'm going alone. Just do what you do best, okay? Tell that Zelasko fellow that you'll string him up by his balls if anything happens to me in his godforsaken country."

Frankie roared with laughter. "You may have gotten your looks from your mother, but you got your guts from your old man. You know that, don't you?"

"You'll make the arrangements, then?"

He shrugged. "Let me give it some thought. And in the meantime, let's go try some of Rocco's calamari."

"So *that's* what that heavenly smell is! Yum, you've got yourself a date, Big Frankie."

Over the next few hours—and a six-course meal— Sasha received an education, Bracciali-style, about her father's business. True to his word, his domestic holdings were almost completely legitimate. But internationally, he was so deep into money laundering and "protection," it made her head spin.

And the thought of what Jeff Crossman would do with this information made that swimming head even dizzier.

Except Jeff already knows, she assured herself more than once during dinner. *That's why he felt so sorry for you, and saw you as such a dupe. But try not to think about that, because this works for Teal. Right?*

After dinner, Big Frankie supplied the last piece of the puzzle when he rejoined Sasha in the living room to announce, "Our people are in touch with Zelasko's people. There was some grumbling about the late notice, but it sounds like it will work out. The only question is, do you know what you're doing?"

"I can't miss this ball, Dad. It's the fashion event of the millennium. Maybe even the last of its kind. I'm so grateful to you for helping me get there."

Frankie's brown eyes glazed over with tears. "You're my little girl. I'd do anything for you. Anything but endanger you. And somehow—"

"I'm a twenty-seven-year-old woman going to a party," she reminded him playfully. "Time to let go, Dad."

When he winced, she added quickly, "I'll be careful."

"I still think Rocco should go. For protection."

"Puh-leeze don't do that. I'm trying to make a fashion statement."

Frankie hesitated, then said firmly, "I've already set

the terms. If Zelasko lets you in, he also guarantees your safety. He knows better than to cross me."

"So it's all set." She rested her hands on his shoulders. "You can't imagine how grateful I am, Dad. I wasn't sure about coming here today, but it's been so…well, so right."

"Except we never talked about what happened to your mother."

Sasha drew back, truly stunned that he had taken this bold step. Was he willing to risk their lovely reunion? To bring up the subject himself? It didn't make sense!

Without thinking, she whispered, "Not now."

"I know." His eyes pleaded with her for trust. "It's too soon. It's a miracle that you're willing to come here at all. And I'd never jeopardize that. Not for one instant. But someday…"

Sasha winced, then nodded. "Yes, Dad. Someday we need to have that talk."

"And when that day arrives…" He reached into the pocket of his black blazer and pulled out a mini tape recorder. "It's all here."

Sasha shook her head instinctively. "I don't want it."

"My stubborn little angel." Frankie patted her arm. "Take it."

"But, Dad—" she scanned his eyes anxiously "—what *is* it?"

"It's the truth. When you're ready, you'll listen. And then we'll talk. For hours. We'll talk and cry and talk. I've hoped for a chance to give this to you. So please take it."

"Dad—"

"If you're never ready, so be it. I'll be selfishly grateful. But if you decide you need to hear it, I'll be grateful, too, because the lies will be gone, and the truth will be the only thing between us."

Tears blurred her vision as she tried to imagine what that could mean. The truth would be the only thing between them? Didn't that confirm that her father had in fact killed her mother? Not that she had ever doubted it, but there had been some comfort in the fact that he had denied it.

Did he honestly intend to stop lying to her? Now of all times?

"I don't want it, Dad."

"Then throw it away," he advised sadly. "I won't try to stop you."

A slow, painful panic seeped into her soul. "Just tell me to my face, then. Right here, right now. I can take it."

"No," he murmured. "I thought when you first arrived that you were ready, but you're not. I see that now. Go to your fancy ball, sweetheart. Have the time of your life, dancing with all the handsome men. And then when you're ready, listen to the tape. After that, if you're willing to take your rightful place by my side, I'll be the happiest man on earth. And if you never speak to me again, I'll still cherish this day we had together. It's more than I thought you'd ever give me."

Sasha stared at him, alarmed by the finality in his tone, and chilled by the hope in his offer. Did he really think she'd take over the family's criminal enterprises one day? Was she *that* good an actress?

That good a liar?

What kind of daughter was she, to put this man through so much?

He killed Mom, she reminded herself frantically, but somehow, that wasn't enough. Not for this.

Stuffing the tape recorder into her purse, she grabbed his hands into her own and insisted, "Whatever else happens from here on out, it doesn't change the fact that we had this nice day together. Right?"

He cocked his head to the side. "Is there something else, Sasha? Something you're not telling me?"

"Did I tell you I love you?" she asked with a teary-eyed smile. "Because I do. I always will." Brushing a kiss across his cheek, she added firmly, "I'll listen to the tape on the plane. And when I get back, we'll talk. Take care, okay? And give Mark my love." Noting his pained expression she hugged him and insisted, "Don't worry. I got my guts from my old man, remember? I have a feeling they're going to serve me well in Kestonia."

Rocco insisted on driving her home, which was a godsend because his nonstop chatter distracted her from other, more sobering thoughts.

Rocco Andretti was the Mafia version of a jack-of-all-trades—a former hit man turned bodyguard who could have been a chef. His loyalty to her father was beyond question, and while that meant he was also fiercely loyal to Sasha, she had no doubt what he'd do to her if he ever found out she was an FBI snitch.

Still, he was entertaining, especially when he told her about her father's new girlfriend, whom Big Frankie

hadn't thought to mention over dinner. The woman—
Annette Jarrett—was an old friend of Sasha's mother,
and since she was also the sister of Rocco's wife, the
bodyguard was delighted with the match.

Sasha liked the idea, too, since she didn't want her
father to be lonely. But still, it would be strange to have
another woman in her father's house.

This new piece of information was a lot like her
lovemaking session with Jeff or the tape in her purse,
she decided finally. She simply couldn't afford to think
too deeply about it until Teal was safe. She needed to
refocus her energies on her upcoming trip, and so, as
soon as Rocco had delivered her to her apartment safely,
she sent him away, then pulled two medium-size suitcases and a garment bag from her closet and placed
them on the bed.

Her father had told her not to pack until they got
official confirmation from Vlados Zelasko that Sasha
would be allowed to enter Kestonia, but she wanted to
be ready the moment permission arrived. Given the
tight timeline ahead of her, the trip would be a nonstop,
derriere-numbing combination of plane, train and limousine rides, which would give her plenty of time to
catch up on her sleep and to read all about the toys the
NSA had supplied to her via Allison.

They weren't exactly James Bond-level gadgets, but
still they were intriguing. The first was a bottle of pills that
looked like aspirin but actually interfered with alcohol absorption, so that Sasha could keep her wits about her
when plied with liquor, which apparently happened to
guests with great regularity at official Kestonian functions.

It was also possible that the pills could help Teal, assuming the girl was being drugged, and assuming further that the Kestonians were using an intoxicant that was susceptible to the anti-absorption process.

A second bottle, this one labeled as airsickness medication, contained capsules filled with knockout powder she could slip into someone else's drink. Fast dissolving, and even faster acting, they could hopefully get her out of a rough situation or two, especially since the subject would have a peaceful sleep and no direct memory of the events leading up to his or her nap.

The final items were more complicated, at least for Sasha. A pair of silver earrings studded with crystals doubled as tiny feed recyclers that could be used on the cameras in Zelasko's surveillance system. The image shown on the monitors wouldn't reflect what was actually going on in the area being surveilled. The NSA had intel about the system used in Kestonia, and Allison had explained that the video quality was quite poor, but still enabled the security staff to distinguish an intruder. Disabling the feed entirely in a particular sector of the fortress would be the only surefire way Sasha could explore without risk of being discovered.

Then there were packaged plastic bandages in various sizes, the type any traveler might carry in case of blisters or paper cuts, although some of the pieces were big enough to cover an enormous wound. The clear strips that peeled away from the adhesive bands were made of a sophisticated latex compound and could be used to copy fingerprints from a hand or a surface. The copy could then be used to trigger a print-activated security device. Similarly, the NSA had supplied silicon powder in a silver compact in case indirect prints were the only ones available.

Finally, there was a pen that could memorize a magnetic code from a key card and transfer it to the security strip on a phony credit card the NSA had supplied to Sasha. It was hoped that between this and the latex prints, she could gain access to Teal. According to reliable sources, Zelasko didn't use retinal scans, which would have been much harder for a novice like Sasha to duplicate, nor did he rely upon memorized entry codes. Assuming that intel was correct, she had everything she needed to deal with his digital security system.

Because I can drink him under the table, knock him out, get his prints and codes and be halfway to Chicago before he wakes up? she asked the absent Allison. *I think you're being just a tad optimistic, considering that science has always been my weak point. And technology? Fuggedaboutit.*

The manuals for the pen, the latex and the earrings had been cleverly disguised as pages in a bestselling espionage novel Sasha could take on the plane with her and read in full view of curious onlookers. The NSA had also supplied her with a Kestonian-English dictionary and a travel book on Eastern Europe.

And if you run out of things to do, you could always listen to the tape about Mom's murder....

It was the first thing she stuffed into her carry-on bag, but did she dare listen to it before successfully rescuing Teal? She honestly didn't know which would be worse:

knowing the tape was there but not listening to it, or subjecting herself to the details—or more likely, another set of lies—which were sure to undermine her poise and confidence.

When the phone on her nightstand rang, it provided a welcome distraction, and Sasha dived for it without bothering to check the incoming number, hoping it was Allison with an update on Teal. Or her father with the green light for the trip.

Or Jeff…

Or with your luck, it'll be Carmine, she teased herself before answering with a breathless, "Hello?"

"Sasha Bracciali?" asked a clipped, heavily accented female voice.

"This is she," Sasha murmured, remembering that Allison had mentioned an intermediary named Delphi who might be contacting her by e-mail with more instructions for the rescue. No messages had arrived in Sasha's in-box yet.

Maybe *this* was the mysterious Delphi?

Her pulse quickened as she said, "May I ask who's calling?"

"Certainly," the voice assured her coolly. "You are having the great honor of speaking to Major Svetlina Zelasko, beloved sister of the supreme commander of Kestonia."

Chapter 5

Wishing she had more impressive titles than *Mafia Princess* and *Unpaid FBI Snitch*, Sasha murmured, "This is a lovely surprise, Major Zelasko. I assume you're calling about my request to visit your beautiful country?"

"I am told you wish to attend our gala."

"Yes, very much."

"I am also told you are the designer of gowns in America."

"Well, I'm one of them," Sasha agreed.

"It is my wish that you will design a gown for me."

"Oh! Of course. I'd love to," Sasha told her, amused that *her* career, rather than Big Frankie's, might be her ticket into Kestonia. Then she realized what the major was really saying, and she corrected herself quickly.

"Do you mean, for the ball? I'd love to create something for you, but there's not enough time. It's this Saturday night, correct? I can't possibly get to Kestonia before Thursday, and that's only if I leave right away."

"Then you will leave right away."

Sasha winced at the imperious tone. "Do you mind if I ask you a few questions? About your dress size for example? I'm not a miracle worker, but—"

"I am one-point-seven meters tall and my proportions are perfect."

"Lucky you," Sasha said, grabbing a pen for some quick arithmetic. "So you're about five feet seven inches, more or less? That's just about my height. Assuming you're not too busty, I might just have something you could wear. Something really gorgeous."

"You are asking if my breasts are large? They are not large. They are not small. They are perfect."

"Once again, lucky you. Especially because I have two sensational gowns, and I'd be happy to bring them both to Kestonia. You can choose one—or both—as my gift to you."

"These have been worn by you?"

Sasha grinned in frustration. "I'm afraid so. But only once each, and I had them dry-cleaned the very next day."

"Ah." The major hesitated, then explained. "If you were seeing the atrocity that my servant has devised for me to wear, you would understand that this is a serious matter."

"I take fashion very seriously, believe me."

"Good. You will come here with no delaying."

Sasha cleared her throat. "The arrangements have been made, but we're awaiting official confirmation—"

"I *am* official. Did you not listen? I am a major in the Kestonian army. And the only sister of Vlados Alexander Zelasko, the Supreme—"

"Grazie, grazie," Sasha interrupted. "I'm on the next plane. Thanks for everything, Miss... What shall I call you? Major? Svetlina?"

"You may call me Major. And I will call you Sasha. It is a Polish name, is it not? Yet I approve of it."

Unbelievable!

Aloud all Sasha said was, "Is Svetlina really Kestonian? It sounds Russian."

There was a long, offended silence, then the caller muttered, "You will arrive without delaying? And bring with you my gowns?"

"I'm on my way," Sasha confirmed. Then she forced herself to add an obsequious, "Thank you for the phone call. I'll be forever in your debt."

"You are welcome. And you may attend the gala yourself if you wish. As long as my dress is completed to my satisfaction in time for the grand entrance."

Sasha laughed. "Why do I see mice and a pumpkin in my future?"

"Pardon?"

"Never mind. It suffers in the translation. I'll see you in a couple of days, Major Zelasko. Thanks again."

Ordinarily Sasha would have allowed the flight attendants to ply her with rich food and champagne on the transatlantic journey, but she needed a clear head, so she snuggled into her sumptuous first-class seat, sipping carbonated water and nibbling on fruit and cheese as she studied the manual and dictionary. She had brought the tape recorder on board, too, but kept finding excuses not to listen to it, the latest of which being that she should wait until they landed in Rome.

The Eternal City was the perfect place to hear her father's confession for many reasons, all of them stemming from her childhood. He had taken her there so often, teaching her the history of Italy through mythology and proud readings from the journals of Caesar and Cicero. While other tourists flocked to Venezia or Firenze, the Braccialis treasured their Roman roots second only to their Sicilian ones, so much so that even when they were in Rome, they rarely spent time at the Vatican, choosing instead to linger for hours at the Colosseum and Pantheon.

Big Frankie and Rome—it was a combination seared into Sasha's imagination. She had visited the city a few times since her mother's murder, but it hadn't been the same without him. She even wished he could have come with her for this part of the trip, but she knew that it was better this way. For all that their reunion had been a lovely one, the wounds were still there, not fresh, but not gone.

Would the tape recording change that? Or make it worse? She couldn't begin to guess. But she suspected that her father had planned her itinerary with a stop in Rome in hopes that she would listen to the tape there, in the city that meant so much to both of them. Of course, he had had more practical reasons, too, because even though Italy was a bit out of the way, Kestonia-wise, Big Frankie's most dependable contacts were there, and could ensure that the remainder of Sasha's trip went smoothly, delivering her safely to the infamous Kestonian border.

After that, it would be Vlados Zelasko—a murderous, backstabbing dictator—who would guarantee her safety. Not the most comforting thought in the world, but Sasha was used to dealing with dangerous, powerful men. Assuming that her twin skills of flirting and lying translated well across cultural lines, she might just have him eating out of her hand.

The winter air in Rome was balmy by Chicago standards, even though the Italians were bundled up in parkas and furs. Sasha yearned to take a stroll, perhaps picking up a gelato while window-shopping and drooling over the latest fashions. But there was no time, so she asked the driver to take her directly from the airport to the Colosseum, which she had chosen as the perfect spot for listening to the tape.

Stepping out of the limousine, she paused to admire the 160-foot-tall structure, imagining as she always did what it must have been like to attend an actual event in such a magnificent venue. A little violent, maybe, but so rousing. So romantic. So Roman.

The driver had arranged for someone to meet them with a ticket, allowing her to bypass the long line of tourists. Jeff would probably call her a spoiled princess if he could see this, but she didn't care. This was her world—or at least, an important part of it. This, along with parties and shopping and clothes. If he wanted to be her boyfriend—and she had almost decided that she was going to *make* him want that—he had better learn to live with her faults.

Making her way inside, she could hear bits and pieces of information from surrounding tour guides. *First century* A.D.... *Three rows of eighty arches... 70,000 spectators... A fortress in the Middle Ages ... Periodically plundered for raw materials...*

Dates and numbers and names—none of it meant a thing. No one really needed a tour of this place. One had simply to look around to feel the majesty of the towering walls, imagine the cheering crowd, visualize emperors in purple and gold, and hunky gladiators steeling themselves for battle as lions and tigers bounded into sight, roaring and ravenous.

Despite the crowds, Sasha imagined herself alone, suspended in time and space, experiencing the arena on her own terms. Standing where her ancient countrymen had stood. Allowing the majesty of the place to humble her, yet also to fill her with pride.

Remembering why she was really there, she moved to an empty alcove and leaned her cheek against the cool concrete. The gods would protect her here no matter what she heard on the tape. She would draw strength from these massive walls and spirit-filled aisles to deal with the confession, as well as whatever lay in store for her in Kestonia. Without further hesitation, she pulled out the recorder and held it to her ear as she pressed the play button.

Franco Bracciali's voice was rich with emotion. "I have protected you from the truth for so long, my darling daughter, the lie has become an old friend. Almost a member of the family. By choice *and* by blood, one might say. I've told myself I was lying for your sake, but it has hurt you as much as the truth ever could. So I've decided to confess—"

Sasha stabbed frantically at the off button, realizing too late that she wasn't ready after all.

"Sasha Bracciali?"

Startled, she looked up to see two men in exquisitely tailored suits. "Yes?"

"Your train leaves in one hour. We need to collect your baggage and take you to the station." Motioning to his companion, the speaker added, "Tony will travel with you at your father's request. But we need to move quickly."

"I'm ready," she assured them. "But Tony? You don't really need to go with me—"

"It's my pleasure. And Big Frankie insists. So…" Tony gestured toward the exit. "Shall we?"

She persuaded them to stop by the Bracciali penthouse so she could use the bathroom and check for messages on her laptop, which she was leaving behind for security reasons. To her dismay, an unnerving e-mail from Delphi awaited her.

According to the message, someone had attempted to hack into alumni files through AA.gov, the Athena Academy Web site. The breach had been detected before anything could be stolen, but Sasha was one of the intended targets, along with six other former students, all of whose names Sasha recognized as government agents, either with the FBI, CIA or NSA.

Delphi concluded by stating that Allison and the NSA were concerned and were considering aborting

Sasha's mission. If she wanted to cancel it herself, they would more than understand.

Sasha stared at the names of the other alumni, trying to imagine what was in the hacker's mind. Obviously he or she had heard about Sasha's trip. They knew the official reason or reasons—representing her father's interests and indulging her own love of dress design by attending what might just be the last grand ball ever held on the continent.

But what if this hacker also knew Teal was in Kestonia? And wondered about the fact that Sasha was an Athena Academy alumna? The question in the intruder's mind—and the reason for the attempt to access the records—was then obvious. Was this a coincidence, or was Sasha working for the government?

They're just double-checking, she decided in relief. *You're a dress designer with no intelligence training whatsoever. You travel for fashion-related purposes all the time. They only need to search your name on the Internet to know that. Fancy parties, wild international celebrations—if one of your clients is there, so are you.*

But you've never once been involved in anything with the government, at least as far as the outside world knows. And if any insiders knew about your snitching— which is hardly intelligence work!—you'd be dead by now. So the hacker is just double-checking.

It made sense, especially given the illustrious list of graduates they were also investigating. These were the women Athena Academy would tap for assistance. These were the women the NSA would turn to. Women of substance, training and spotless integrity.

Not Sasha. Her Mafia ties aside, she had attended

college at a design school! Not that her education hadn't been sound, but it was a far cry from the others, who had graduated from Harvard, Yale and the like.

So she responded to Delphi with a simple, confident:

I'm not worried. It's just a fishing expedition. Let's proceed as planned. Wish me luck!

Then she locked her laptop in a cabinet in the guest bedroom, grabbed her purse and headed for the door.

Tony was a man of few words, but his demeanor—not to mention his double-wide physique—told onlookers all they needed to know. He was there to protect Big Frankie's daughter, and doubtless had a pistol under his suit jacket. Perhaps a knife, as well. His steady brown gaze told the world he wouldn't hesitate to use either.

Sasha had to admit, he made her feel safe. He also made her feel smothered, and she realized that if it hadn't been for the rift with her father, she would have had many other such experiences over the last seven years. Big Frankie would have insisted on making arrangements, providing drivers, posting guards at doors, all in the name of keeping Sasha safe.

Instead, she had learned to feel safe on her own. She hadn't really appreciated until now how much her karate classes, running her own business and traveling alone all over the world had done for her. And once she had learned to feel self-sufficient, she had met Jeff, aka Summit. He made her feel safe, too, not by stifling her, but by encouraging and empowering her. By telling her she could do it. She could walk through a crowd of criminals with a receiver in her ear and a camera in her bra, accomplishing something that no one else had been able to do.

So what's your bottom line on Jeff? she asked herself as the snow-covered German landscape rushed past her window. *Do you want him as your boyfriend or your handler?*

She was pretty sure Jeff would never agree to be both. And maybe he was right. The closer they grew romantically, the less likely he'd be to send her into dangerous situations. He'd become more like her father, wouldn't he? Overprotective? Not willing to take chances no matter how valuable the prize?

But as your boyfriend, wouldn't he be that way anyway? So even if you got another handler, Jeff might interfere with your assignments. Or at least, worry whenever you were on one.

Discouraged, she wrapped a blanket around her shoulders and decided to get some sleep. There wasn't anything she could do about the situation with Jeff at the moment, and if things didn't go well in Kestonia, her love life was definitely going to become the least of her problems.

The four-hundred-mile boundary line surrounding Vlados Zelasko's empire was for the most part impenetrable, consisting of craggy cliffs on three sides, marshy terrain on the fourth. Where stretches of crossable land occurred, a twelve-foot electrified fence had been erected to deter entry, with only one heavily guarded crossing station left on a single main road for ingress and egress.

As Sasha's limousine approached that point, she tried to imagine who would even *want* to gain access to this place. It seemed like all the traffic should be in the other direction, with Kestonians dying—sometimes literally—to get out. Instead, according to recent newspaper accounts, the citizenry supported Zelasko and were proud of his efforts to turn their country into an international player.

But from Sasha's viewpoint as they neared the heavily manned guard station, Kestonia was almost laughably unattractive, like something out of a poorly shot vampire movie. All she could see was desolate, snow-covered terrain culminating in a mountain, at the top of which stood a village dominated by a Gothic-style castle.

"I should have brought my pitchfork and a torch," she told Tony.

"If Big Frankie could see this, he wouldn't let you go one step farther."

"Luckily, Big Frankie and Big Vlados have a gentleman's understanding. I'll be perfectly safe. But it *is* creepy, isn't it?"

A guard carrying a machine gun approached them, ordering all occupants to vacate the limousine. Sasha and the men complied right away, but while the driver seemed nervous, Tony eyed the soldier with cool composure. "I'm escorting Sasha Bracciali to the castle at Zelasko's invitation. So step aside."

"She is invited. You are not," the guard told him in simple but effective English. "We will drive her to the castle. You will drive away. Quickly."

"*Bastardo,*" Tony began, but Sasha grabbed his arm and instructed tersely, "You need to go. They won't hurt me unless you provoke them, so please, get back into the car."

When he winced, she kissed his cheek with genuine gratitude. "You got me here safely. And if I'm lucky, you'll be the one who picks me up next week. That way I'll know my trip back to Roma will be a safe one." Resting one hand on his arm, she reached with the other one to pat the driver's shoulder. "Go on now. Both of you. I'll be fine."

The driver didn't need any more encouragement before diving back into his seat, but Tony didn't budge. Instead, he informed the guard, "It's a free country, buddy, on this side of the line at least. So I think I'll just stay for a while and watch."

Touched, Sasha kissed his cheek again, then turned to the guard, who led her across the metal-paved border to a waiting jeep, where her suitcases were already being loaded. For some reason, that sight caused a tinge of panic to invade her confident mood. Or perhaps it was just foreboding. In any case, she found herself seriously wondering for the first time whether she and Teal would make it out of Kestonia alive.

Not that she wanted or needed Tony's help. He'd probably just get in the way, so she was glad he was standing on the other side of the gate.

But she could certainly use a little assistance from a guy named Summit right about now, if only to hear his sexy, reassuring voice whispering in her ear as she left the safety of her father's world and began the last leg of her journey to Vlados Alexander Zelasko's ancient fortress.

* * *

"Hey, Jeff. Look what I bought for Sasha." Special Agent Winston Lowe opened a bakery box and revealed an oversize cannoli. "Get it? She said Vincent use to slip her a cannoli…."

"Grow the fuck up," Jeff advised his subordinate, although he silently agreed that Sasha would enjoy the stupid joke. "Just get rid of that thing and concentrate on your job, will you?"

Winston arched an eyebrow. "What's wrong?"

"Nothing." Jeff shook his head, admitting to himself that it was true. Nothing was wrong, and everything was right. They were just about to nail Vincenzo the Butcher Martino. And Jeff was professionally and romantically entangled with the world's sexiest female. He had no complaints, but still, something was nagging at the back of his mind. Some detail he had neglected, despite the fact that he was a detail man at heart.

"Sasha will laugh, Jeff. She loves this kind of thing."

"Except she's not going to be around this week. Or next. She took some time off. To take care of some personal business."

"That explains a lot," Winston replied, flashing a pain-in-the-ass grin. "You're grouchy when she's here. But worse when she's not."

"Funny." Jeff scowled, wondering if his associate was half as perceptive as he seemed. Probably not, but that didn't change the truth. Jeff's mood—not to mention his hormones—*had* been on a roller-coaster ride lately because of Sasha Bracciali. And now that he had kissed her—okay, *more* than kissed her—he was more confused than ever, to the point where he was actually considering a full-blown affair with her despite the obvious perils and conflicts.

"Where is she?" Winston persisted.

"Off the record? She's with her father."

Winston's eyes widened. "Yeah?"

"It was bound to happen eventually. She's his daughter. They couldn't stay strangers forever."

The younger agent pursed his lips. "I guess that proves you were right after all? She won't be useful anymore?"

"Actually, I think I was wrong about that. This is a healthy step. For her and for us," Jeff insisted. "It won't interfere with her work, because it was never about the feud with Frankie in the first place."

"You're admitting you were wrong?" Winston whistled. "Man, this really *is* a day for surprises."

Jeff scowled again, but inside, he had to admit it was true. After all his worrying, it was a relief to know that Sasha was just what she seemed to be—an amazing asset. Smart, dedicated, gorgeous, resourceful—and so sweet it made his teeth hurt.

He might have confessed as much to Winston, but at that moment, the door opened, and Chuck McBride came into the office, looking like he'd lost his last friend, and saying, "Hey guys" in a tone that suggested they were all doomed to a life of loneliness and despair.

Winston didn't seem to sense his friend's mood. Instead, he said brightly, "Look what I got for Sasha. The cannoli of her dreams. She'll love it, right?"

Chuck didn't even crack a smile. In fact, the huge

dessert didn't seem to register at all. Instead, he flopped into a chair and muttered, "We may have a problem, boss. A big one."

"Go on."

Opening his briefcase, Chuck spilled its contents onto the conference table. "These are routine surveillance shots from O'Hare."

Jeff walked over to take a look. "Did some new honcho hit town?"

"Nope. Someone left." He held up a picture of Sasha. "She boarded a flight for Rome Sunday night."

Winston joined them instantly. "Rome? I thought you said she was with Frankie."

Jeff cleared his throat. Then he said with a shrug that he hoped covered his shocked reaction, "Frankie has a town house in Rome. Maybe they decided to have their reunion there."

"Except Frankie can't leave the state. Remember?"

"Oh, yeah." Jeff scowled. "That's right."

"That's not all." Chuck proffered a sheet of paper. "I checked her phone records, and she got a weird international call on Sunday. From Kestonia. That's just wrong. Right?"

"Kestonia?" Jeff rubbed his eyes, trying not to listen to the alarm bells in his head. "I'm sure there's a perfectly innocent explanation for all this. Frankie sent her to Rome for a treat. And she's got clients all over the world. Who told you to check her phone records anyway? She's on *our* side, Chuck. Since when do we treat her like a suspect?"

"Sorry, Jeff. I just figured you'd want to know what's

going on. She left the country, right? That's significant."

"It's Sasha," Winston interrupted loyally. "I agree with Jeff. There's got to be a reasonable explanation for all of this. She fingered the Butcher, for Christ's sake. If she didn't prove herself with that, then what the hell will it take?"

"I'm sure there's a logical explanation," Jeff agreed. "And I'll find out what it is. But meanwhile, nice work."

Chuck rolled his eyes. "Finally! I thought you'd be glad to get some dirt on her. Even though I feel like crap for being the one to supply it. So let's just figure it out once and for all, okay? I mean…" He eyed Jeff warily. "She's in Italy. And Vincent the Butcher is there, too. That means something, right? Like maybe she isn't on the level after all?"

"She's in Rome. Vincent's in Palermo," Jeff muttered. "For Italians, that's as different as Alaska from Hawaii, so let's not crucify her yet, okay? I still think her father was so glad to see her, he gave her a trip. But I'll check it out, because that's our job."

Chuck nodded. "When does your flight leave? For Rome, I mean. Wouldn't it be weird if you ran into her there?"

"I'm rendezvousing with the international team in Rome, but we leave immediately for Palermo to take down Vincent. So I doubt I'll be seeing Sasha."

"Still—"

"I'll take care of it," Jeff repeated, adding more diplomatically, "Like I said, nice work. Why don't you guys just take the rest of the week off?"

Winston arched a skeptical eyebrow. "Really?"

"I won't be here. Neither will Sasha. So what is there to do? Just enjoy yourselves at the Bureau's expense. You've earned it. But first—" he gave the younger agent a final, authoritative glare "—get rid of that goddammed cannoli."

Chapter 6

There were soldiers everywhere. Blank-faced, robotic men wearing black parkas over dark green uniforms and carrying rifles, machine guns and pistols. They were in the jeep that transported Sasha up the mountain. They stood at attention along the narrow paved road leading to Zelasko's stone fortress. When she finally alighted from the vehicle and approached the entrance, they surrounded her, their expressions still vacant. No trace of humanity, or sexual attraction, or chauvinistic sympathy.

Nothing.

Sasha had met more than her share of bad guys: sociopathic hit men, bloodthirsty sadists, calculating opportunists. But these Kestonians were different. Not necessarily scarier per se, but scarier to *her* because of their unfamiliar attitude.

As she walked toward the ten-foot-high double doors that had been opened to admit her, she craved the sound of Jeff Crossman's voice in her ear. This was the first time in her life she had walked knowingly into danger without Summit to guide her. And at that moment she knew for sure that no matter how sexy he was, or how much fun he might be, she needed him more as a handler than as a boyfriend. She only hoped she'd have the chance to tell him that face-to-face before she died a lingering, painful death.

What did you expect? she asked herself as panic welled up inside her. *Did you really think you'd be safe here? Remember Mom? The gentlest woman on earth, with the quote-unquote body of a goddess. Everyone said so! But someone riddled that body with bullets without a second thought. Because killing for Big Frankie wasn't just that thug's job. It was his privilege. His honor. His destiny.*

And these men feel the same way about Vlados Zelasko!

Too late, she realized that Delphi had been right. Even if the hacker hadn't managed to access Sasha's records, he or she had been suspicious enough to try. What if they had shared their suspicions with Zelasko?

If these soldiers suspect you're working for the NSA, they'll torture you for information about Teal! Then they'll toss your beaten body into some hideous mass grave. Why didn't you abort this crazy mission when you had the chance?

"Miss Bracciali?"

She managed to focus on the speaker, a thin man with a disturbingly nasty smirk.

At least he's showing some emotion, she observed wryly. *You know what Summit would say: Just smile and pretend to cooperate. Watch for an opportunity, and then get the hell out!*

So she nodded and said sweetly, "Yes, I'm she. My father is Big Frankie Bracciali, a vital figure in Kestonia's future. I'm here on his behalf. And I believe General Zelasko's sister is expecting me."

The man was visibly unimpressed. "Surrender your handbag and coat to my soldiers so that they may be searched with the rest of your belongings."

"Okay." She handed her purse to one of the guards, then took off her black cashmere coat and proffered it, as well.

The contemptuous man eyed what was left, namely Sasha's boots, black skirt and gray silk blouse. She was pretty sure he intended to frisk her. The question was, would she allow it? He didn't seem interested in her sexually, but still, the thought of his hands on her bare legs was downright creepy. Why couldn't she have worn jeans or slacks?

"Surrender your boots."

She moistened her lips, then nodded, trying not to show how relieved she was that he hadn't tried to remove them himself. Moving to one of the ornate wooden benches that lined the arched hallway, she sat down, unzipped each boot, and handed them over. Then she stood and said coolly, "That's as far as I go, sir. You can pat me down in a civilized manner if you must, but don't even *think* about anything else."

"Nothing else will be necessary," a new voice assured her, and she turned to stare into a pair of confident black eyes belonging to a tall, well-built man in a dark green uniform. His broad chest was covered with glittering medals, but he didn't need them to tell her he was a born leader.

Vlados Zelasko—she recognized his chiseled features from his photos. President. Dictator. Supreme Commander of the Realm.

Generalissimo.

"You did not expect to be searched?" he asked coolly.

She wanted to give a witty reply—something about having left her Uzi in her other boots—but her mouth was too dry, so she just locked gazes with him and said nothing.

"You are angry?"

Try terrified, she suggested silently, wondering where he was headed with this line of questioning. Did he think it mollified her? Or maybe he was mocking her. It didn't really matter. She had no response for either.

"Speak," he commanded.

"What is there to say? You gave your word to my father that I would be protected. Not manhandled and insulted."

"What man has handled you? What insult has been made?"

"What protection has been offered?" she retorted. "Your sister invited me. If you don't want me here—"

"You will come with me," he interrupted, turning away from her and striding down the long, stone hallway.

He didn't glance backward, and she knew exactly why not. He was sure that she would follow. That she wouldn't dare disobey.

And he was absolutely right.

* * *

Zelasko led her to a small sitting room with no windows, then he motioned to a red velvet settee. "Be comfortable."

"Thanks." She sat, crossing her legs at the ankles, conscious of her stocking feet.

"So." He appraised her openly. "You are here."

Sasha nodded.

"But before here, you were in Rome. Why is that?"

She cleared her throat, then reminded him, "I'm Italian."

"You are American."

"Italian-American. And my father has a network of colleagues in Rome. He's passionate about my safety. So am I," she added with a wry smile.

Zelasko seemed unamused. "Why are you here?"

"Like I said, your sister invited me. But I'm also representing my father, Franco Bracciali, at the conference."

"No other reason?"

She hesitated, then flashed a warmer smile. "The truth? I want to go to the ball. It's the last of its kind. Dignitaries from four continents. Gowns. Jewels. Flash. It's what I live for."

"And yet you had no interest in it until this week."

Sasha winced. "That's not true. I had plenty of interest. It's just—" she spread her hands in front of herself expressively "—I didn't want to ask my father for a favor. I don't expect you to understand why, but—"

"You were estranged from him?" Zelasko arched an eyebrow. "That is the correct word?"

"Yes. That's the perfect word. We were estranged."

"And now you are not? That is convenient," he drawled. "Tell me why you are so nervous." Before Sasha could respond he added bluntly, "Tell me about this Athena Academy that you attended."

Oh no.

Rising slowly to her feet, she forced herself to glare into his dark eyes. "I'm nervous because of the way your men treated me. And now you! A famous dictator who can have me thrown into a dungeon any time he wants. I'm at your mercy, General Zelasko. That's not something I'm used to. Where I come from, no one would dare interrogate me this way."

She took a deep breath, then continued. "My relationship with my father is none of your business. And why do you care what schools I attended? If you're worried I can't design a dress for your sister, think again. It's my profession and I'm very good at it."

A slender man stepped from the shadows and asked quietly, *"Prezydente?"*

Zelasko waved him away, then turned back to Sasha. "Sit down, Miss Bracciali. You are making my men as nervous as they made you."

She hesitated, then returned to her seat.

"It is a school for girls, is it not? I am told it is many hundred miles from your home. Why did you choose it?"

"I didn't choose Athena Academy, it chose me," Sasha said with a weary sigh. "It's by invitation only. They contacted my mother and she thought it would be a good experience for me. She was right."

"They choose their students based on special abilities, do they not? What is your special ability?"

"I had high test scores, but I think it was my artistic ability that caught their eye." She cleared her throat again. "Could I get a drink of water? I did a lot of traveling today, and my throat is parched."

"I am told you enjoy champagne," he replied, then he turned to the man in the shadows. "Nikko? *Szampam, zyb!*"

Nikko clicked his heels and exited the room.

"Thanks." Sasha smiled. "My most relevant education is from the School of Design, you know. I graduated at the top of my class—"

"I am interested in the Athena Academy only. Tell me about your training there. Martial arts and firearms, yes?"

"It wasn't a *military* academy, if that's what you think. It was a classical blend. A sound mind in a sound body. That sort of thing. I took the regular subjects, plus some additional foreign languages and lots of art classes."

"I am told that the students form groups named after gods and goddesses. What was the name of your group?"

Sasha arched an eyebrow. "You're very well-informed, General. My group was the Muses. Because three of us were artists of one type or another. A dancer, a singer—"

"You enjoyed it?"

"The school? I adored it," she admitted wistfully. "It was so different from the world I knew, and even though I felt like an outsider sometimes, I was still grateful for the opportunity. They widened my worldview—made me believe I could be anything I wanted to be. And then they encouraged me to apply to design school, which *really* changed my life forever." She paused to accept a tall crystal goblet of champagne from a tray Nikko had brought to the room. "Thanks. This looks yummy."

Zelasko took a glass, too, and offered a quick toast in Kestonian, adding quietly, "Continue."

"Okay, where was I? Oh right, design school. *Those* were the most important years of my life. If only my mother hadn't died while I was there, it would have been perfect."

"She was murdered, was she not?"

Sasha took a sip of champagne, then nodded.

"And you suspected your father? So you became estranged? But suddenly, you have forgiven him. That is convenient."

"So you said before." She set her glass on a nearby table, then gave him a stern look. "I'll admit it. I wanted to attend this ball so much, it made my heart ache. I even had a picture of you in your uniform tacked to the wall of my bedroom because the articles in my fashion magazines captured my imagination so completely. But my pride wouldn't let me ask Dad for help. Not until this weekend when we attended the wedding of an old family friend. It brought back so many memories...."

She paused to accentuate the catch in her voice. "I saw the bride dancing with her father—my uncle—and I realized that I couldn't bear it if Dad and I didn't find a way to patch things up before *my* wedding day arrived. I knew Dad had to be feeling the same way, too. And suddenly it seemed like the perfect time. Not just because of the ball. But I'll admit, that was a factor. Because, like I said, this may be my one chance to ever attend such a regal extravaganza."

Zelasko stared for a moment, and she was sure he was about to hit her with another accusation. But instead, he murmured, "My photograph was on the wall of your bedroom?"

Sasha bit back a smile. "Do you want to see it? It's in my purse. The one your men took—"

"Nikko!" Zelasko issued a quick order, then assured Sasha, "It will be only a minute."

"Thanks, General." She licked her lips. "The picture's pretty wrinkled. I've had it for almost two months, and carried it across the ocean with me. So don't expect much."

He hesitated, then suggested, "You may call me by my given name. It is Vlados. Or Vlad, if you prefer."

"Okay, but…" She bit her lip. "I've never known a general before. It's kind of fun calling you that, if you don't mind."

She loved the glow of pride and vanity in his eyes, signaling that the interrogation had finally taken a turn for the better. If only she had thought to pull out that crumpled picture right away! Thank God she was enough of a pack rat to have kept the January issue of her design magazine an extra month.

Nikko returned with the purse, and Zelasko took it from him, digging unceremoniously until he found the picture. Then he smiled with satisfaction. "It is a good likeness."

"You're just what American girls dream about. A handsome prince in a faraway land holding a fancy dress ball. I'm sure I'm not the only one who saved that picture. Of course for me," she added teasingly, "it was purely for professional reasons."

Zelasko grinned. "I see you are no longer nervous."

"The champagne helped," she quipped. "And it helps to see that my purse is still in one piece."

He handed it to her, his expression now solemn. "We searched only for weapons. Your privacy was not disturbed. You will find the rest of your luggage in your room. A servant will unpack the cases for you if you wish."

"Thanks. And my boots?"

Zelasko glanced at her feet. "My men consider the boots a security risk. They will be returned to you at the termination of your visit." He paused to give Nikko a quick order, then explained, "Colonel Kerenski will find something else for your feet. I am aware that the stone floor is cold."

"Thanks."

He stepped closer, staring down into her eyes with warm interest. "You will rest for a while. Then you will dine with me. That is acceptable?"

"It's an honor," she murmured despite the warning bells clanging in her brain. She recognized Zelasko's aroused look all too well. It was the same one Carmine had had when he'd asked her to dance at the wedding. It was never good news, especially for a woman alone in a foreign dictatorship. With the dictator himself, no less!

She was grateful to Nikko for returning quickly with three pairs of sturdy, oxford-esque shoes in varying sizes.

"Oh, good!" She eyed them critically, wondering if even the largest of them would fit her. "Kestonian women must have small feet," she murmured, reaching for the most promising candidates.

"Our women are known for that," Zelasko confirmed.

Unwilling to ask for an even larger pair—wouldn't that put the reputation of American women into question?—Sasha forced her feet into the biggest shoes, then gave a pained smile.

Luckily, Zelasko had been distracted by the ringing of a cell phone in his jacket pocket. Answering in Kestonian, he frowned, then barked something unintelligible.

"Maybe I should just go," Sasha whispered to Nikko, but Zelasko motioned for her to stay.

Then he said, "You may be of assistance with this matter. Be seated again. Please."

"Okay." She sank back onto the settee. "How can I help?"

"You recognize the name Shannon Conner?"

Silently imploring her weary brain to keep up with the day's events, Sasha nodded. "She's a reporter for ABS news. And she was a student at Athena Academy for a short while. But she left before I got there, so I never met her. Why do you ask?"

"She and her associates with cameras are standing at our border requesting admission. She wishes to give news coverage of the ball."

Sasha winced. She didn't know much about Shannon, other than the fact that the reporter had been a consistent thorn in the paw of Athena Academy because of her insistence on trying to ruin the school's reputation. Still, Shannon had rocketed to fame on the basis of sensationalistic stories and an amazing ability to be in the right place at the right time, newswise.

"My question to you," Zelasko said, his tone imperious, "is whether I should allow this? She will put my country into the eye of America. I desire such publicity. But can I rely on her to be discreet?"

Shannon Conner in Kestonia? Sasha had no doubt *that* was a bad idea. But she wasn't about to trade on Zelasko's fledgling trust in her opinion, so she told him, "I'm a big fan of Shannon Conner, General. I mean, Vlados." She flashed a flirtatious smile. "Her stories are the best. Full of drama and intrigue and innuendo. Plus, she and I have something in common, because I've heard she felt like an outsider at Athena Academy, too. Poor thing. I actually admire the fact that she left the school rather than just kowtow to them. She's been sort of an antihero to me for years."

Zelasko pursed his lips. "You said you loved that school. But now I am told you did not."

"I did. I always will. But I didn't fit in. I wasn't what they wanted. Don't ask me to explain," she pleaded. "I thought we were talking about Shannon."

He pursed his lips, then nodded. "You are certain I should allow her to enter my country?"

"Selfishly? I'd love it. If publicity is what you want, Shannon's your girl. From what I've heard," Sasha added slyly, "even if there's no controversy, she'll make one up. She's determined to find a scandal behind every rock, even if it means creating her own. You'll be on the front page of every newspaper in America."

"Scandal?" Zelasko's handsome features twisted into a scowl. "There can be no scandal. Not if Kestonia is to enter the upper echelon of political society."

He barked a series of orders into his phone, then closed

it and smiled grimly. "She is a spirited woman. She has threatened to remain at the border until I meet with her."

"Have you seen her? She's very pretty. Very blond. You might want to reconsider."

Zelasko reached out to touch Sasha's hair, which was hanging in a loose braid down her back. "I prefer this."

Her cheeks burned, but she didn't pull away, reminding herself that lust was less dangerous than suspicion when ruthless dictators were involved.

But apparently some suspicion lingered in Zelasko's mind, because he suddenly demanded, "It is a coincidence, is it not? That two females from the Athena Academy have appeared at my border in less than twenty-four hours?"

"I'd be shocked if only two of us showed up," Sasha told him with a shrug. "This is the geopolitical social event of the decade, isn't it? Athena produces more than its share of politicians and society women, not to mention intelligence officers. They'll be attracted to this event just like Shannon was. Just like I was."

She bit her lip and pretended to be embarrassed. "I must seem frivolous to you, for taking up so much of your time when you have a million things to do. Plus, I don't want to keep your sister waiting. I brought some gowns for her to try on. They were in the black garment bag your guards confiscated. Sorry, Nikko," she added, sending a smile in the underling's direction.

Zelasko burst into laughter, then explained to Nikko, "She knows I will send you to fetch those gowns."

The young colonel smiled at Sasha and assured her, "It will be my honor to do for you."

She smiled gratefully. "You're sweet. I'll show you which bag it is. Vlados?" She boldly extended her hand for the general's kiss. "I'll see you at dinner."

She was in Kestonia. She had evaded the dungeon and the rack, at least for the moment. She had even managed to catch the Generalissimo's eye. A quick survey of her luggage had demonstrated that nothing had been taken. In fact, everything but her carry-on bag had been neatly unpacked, with the items either placed in the drawers of a hand-carved maple dresser or pressed and hung in a matching armoire in her guest room.

So far, so good, she decided as she snuggled under an eiderdown quilt atop the king-size bed. *I could get used to this if it weren't for Vlad the Lascivious. Or the fact that I'm supposed to be rescuing a helpless teenager.*

She was feeling more confident about that, at least. Making it through Zelasko's security measures seemed like a coup. Then there was the appearance of Shannon Conner at the border, which Sasha hoped was a sign that the newswoman was the hacker who had tried to access Sasha's files. It made a certain amount of sense. Any good reporter would want to know as much as possible about the players in her story, so if she heard Sasha was attending the ball, she would have wanted to know why. And given Shannon's brief experience at Athena Academy—not to mention her feud with them—she would have known about the Web site and would have been more than happy to try and exploit it.

And lucky for you, you were able to neutralize that particular problem, she congratulated herself. *Jeff would be so proud of you.*

Do you know what this really means? she asked herself suddenly. *Maybe you don't need him more as a handler than a boyfriend after all! Not that a little backup wouldn't be fun, but a boyfriend… Well, let's face it. You need one of those, too. To keep you company in fabulous beds like this one.*

She glanced longingly at the phone on the bedside table and wondered if she dared call Jeff in his capacity as her lover. She could pretend to be calling from her father's house.

He'd be so sweet. So supportive. So irresistible.

And you'd be lying to him again. Nice way to kick off a romance, Bracciali. Plus, that line is surely tapped. Or traced. Or whatever. If El Prezydente knew you were in touch with the FBI, he'd have you shot at sunrise. So forget about Jeff, and try to get some rest.

She was truly exhausted, yet the thought that Teal was being held against her will somewhere inside Zelasko's stronghold haunted her. She needed to formulate a plan, or at least, the beginnings of one. Meanwhile, Nikko had promised to return in one hour to escort her to the suite of Major Svetlina Zelasko, aka the Generalissimo's sister.

After that, you've got your dinner date, she reminded herself wryly as she buried her face in a fluffy pillow. *If he really does like dark-haired girls with big feet, you're in for a world of trouble.*

* * *

"Hey, Alex. Got a minute?"

"Jeff!" Alex Sutter, Jeff's Washington D.C. supervisor, half rose from his chair and extended his hand across the top of his desk "I thought you'd be headed for Italy by now."

Jeff accepted the handshake, then settled into the only guest chair in the modest-size office. "I was scheduled to fly straight from Chicago to Rome, but I decided it would be better to arrive with the team. So I'm leaving with them from National in about an hour. Meanwhile—" he lowered his voice, conscious of the still-open door "—I've got something to tell you. Off the record for now, if that's okay. This is just a heads-up."

"Sounds mysterious. What's going on?"

Jeff exhaled sharply. This was the moment he had been dreading. As much as he liked and respected his supervisor, he had no idea how the guy would react to something like this. "My asset, Sasha Bracciali, told me she was planning to spend a few weeks reconciling with her father. You know who he is, right? Big Frankie Bracciali." When Alex didn't react, Jeff forged ahead. "We have intel that she's actually in Rome. With*out* Big Frankie. I'm sure there's a logical explanation. He probably sent her there for a vacation in honor of their new relationship. Still, she's out of the country. In Rome of all places. Given this business with Vincent Martino, I figured someone here at headquarters should be in the loop."

Alex's expression still hadn't changed. Instead, he said quietly, "Close the door, Jeff."

Surprised, the agent did as instructed. Then he assured his boss, "It's no big deal. I trust Sasha implicitly. More so than ever these days."

Alex cleared his throat. "The thing is, we know exactly where Sasha Bracciali is. And it isn't Rome."

"Huh?"

The supervisor leaned forward, his face now filled with concern. "I apologize for springing it on you like this. I wanted to tell you from the beginning, but it's top secret. She's on an NSA op, Jeff. Ultra hush-hush. You know how those guys are."

Jeff stared in disbelief. "NSA?"

"Right. She's working with them—"

"Since when? She's *my* asset, goddammit. They can't just appropriate her—*steal* her!—without telling me. For *what?* What the hell are they up to?"

Alex winced. "They didn't exactly twist her arm, buddy. Word is she was hot for the assignment. Apparently she's got connections over there. High up."

"Connections?"

"It's complicated, or so they tell me. And it goes way back. To her high school days at least."

Jeff sat back in his chair, stunned by the suggestion. "Are you saying she's *their* asset, too? Or…their operative?"

"All I know for sure is, she's got a helluva lot more juice—and training—than we ever knew."

Jeff forced himself to remain calm. "I know some of those NSA guys. Whose team is she on?"

"She went alone."

His fists clenched. "What are you talking about? *Alone?* She's not ready for anything like that."

His supervisor leaned forward again, all compassion gone from his expression. "I'm sure they know what they're doing. Like I said, she was hot to do it."

"That's nuts." Jeff shook his head. "Why all the secrecy? Why cut *me* out? If they're using her for her Mafia connections—"

"I never said that," Alex retorted. "All I know is, she's got NSA connections that made her perfect for this op. Let it go, Jeff. For both our sakes."

"Let it go?" He shook his head again, almost dazed by the concept. "She's in Europe, right? But not Italy?"

Alex shrugged.

"Damn… At least in Rome she'd know her way around. I don't care how much goddammed training or how many goddammed connections she has, she's not ready to go solo in a foreign country. I'm her handler. I *know.*" He glared at his supervisor, assuring him bluntly, "No way can I let this go."

"I can see that. Unfortunately, you have your orders. And your own mission. To bring the Butcher to justice once and for all. I thought that was your highest priority. Your Holy Grail."

"It was. It still is. But—"

"She's Big Frankie Bracciali's daughter, Jeff," Alex reminded him with an unexpected grin. "No way would the NSA send her into danger. If they did, there would be no safe place on earth for them to hide. You know that, right?"

Jeff squirmed, unconvinced.

"They're professionals, buddy. Sure we razz them, but for this sort of thing they're the best. She'll be back in one piece in no time, and you can rake her over the coals for holding out on you. Dump her if you want. I wouldn't blame you. But for now, let her do her job while you do yours. Right?"

Jeff scowled.

"Didn't you just say your team leaves for Palermo in an hour? Be with them, or you'll have bigger problems than a missing asset. Your whole career will be missing." Alex's tone softened. "She'll be fine. And even if she's not, what of it? You've always said she's a pain in the ass. But the good news is, she's a pain in *their* asses now. Right?"

Jeff hesitated, then nodded.

"And meanwhile, we've got our own job to do."

"True."

Alex smiled. "I'll let you know the minute I hear any more about her status. How's that?"

"Works for me." Jeff stood and extended his hand across the desk again. "Thanks for trusting me with this, buddy. I won't forget it."

"Good luck in Palermo. Bring back the Butcher and we'll both be heroes."

"The Holy Grail," Jeff drawled. "Believe me, I won't come back empty-handed."

Chapter 7

"Major Zelasko?" Holding Sasha's garment bag and satchel in one hand, Nikko Kerenski stood in the hallway with Sasha and knocked gently on Svetlina's door. Then he called out something in Kestonian. To Sasha, he explained, "She expects you."

"Thanks." Sasha gave him a reassuring smile, pleased with the respectful way the colonel had treated her from the moment he arrived at her guest room to escort her to Svetlina's suite. On the way, he had carefully explained that he was the second-highest ranked officer in the Kestonian army, an army in which there was only *one* general—Vlados Zelasko.

"What's his sister like anyway? On the phone, she seemed awfully bossy."

"Bossy?" Nikko shrugged. "I do not know that word."

"She gives lots of orders."

"She is a major in the Kestonian army. To give orders is her duty."

"Good point."

"But also her pleasure," Nikko added slyly.

Sasha laughed, and was about to solicit more dirt when the door was flung open by a dark-haired woman wearing a ball gown of gold brocade so sumptuous Sasha could barely resist reaching out and touching it.

"You are late. Come in," the woman insisted. Turning to Nikko, she fired off commands in Kestonian, and he hurried to a coatrack where he hung the garment bag while dropping the satchel on the floor. Then with an apologetic glance at Sasha, he rushed out of the room.

"Close the door, Miss Bracciali. There is no time to waste. One look at this monstrosity tells you so, does it not?"

Sasha took a deep breath, then shut the door behind herself and walked to the center of the room, studying her hostess in wary silence. Even in an evening gown, this woman was a soldier, which appeared to be part of the problem. The dress was so feminine—so absolutely magical—that the contrast with lean shoulders, muscled arms and ramrod-straight posture was downright jarring.

It wasn't that Major Svetlina Zelasko was unattractive. Or at least, not exactly. But she was no beauty, either, and appeared to lack any semblance of grace.

Svetlina had been studying Sasha in return, and now remarked, "I see it is true. We have the same size. And you have brought the gowns just as you promised. I now pray for a miracle, if only to save this worthless servant from a beating."

"Huh?" Sasha followed the major's annoyed glare toward a corner of the room where a tiny young woman was literally cowering. "Oh, I'm sorry! I didn't even see you there. Hi. I'm Sasha Bracciali."

"Yes, from America," the servant agreed, taking a few shaky steps forward. "Thank you for coming. I am Niski."

"Nice to meet you, Niski."

"Enough!" Svetlina's black eyes flashed with impatience. "She is the maker of this monstrosity. Do you see how I look? This miserable girl would make me a fool."

"Actually…" Sasha stepped right up to the major and touched the extravagant fabric of the off-the-shoulder creation. "It's exquisite work. So delicate. Almost angelic. The problem isn't the dress, Major Zelasko. It's just not the right dress for someone of your stature. You're so…well, regal. So commanding. You need something bolder. I think I have just the gown for that."

"I am regal and I am bold," Svetlina agreed.

"Look." Sasha unzipped the garment bag and pulled out a waltz-length gown. The skirt was navy-blue taffeta, the bodice in the same color, but of rich velvet. It was strapless, but the scalloped cut to the neckline—one of Sasha's signature designs—would almost certainly draw the eye away from Svetlina's shoulders, softening the effect of her overtoned physique.

Niski squealed with delight and seemed to forget that she was afraid. Instead, she rushed over to Sasha and gathered the dress into her arms. "It is beautiful!"

"Bring it to me," Svetlina ordered her. "I must wear it to be certain."

Niski quickly helped her mistress out of the golden gown, which Svetlina allowed to crumple to the floor. Stepping out of the pile of brocade, she stood seminaked for a moment, as though flaunting her body at Sasha. Then she allowed her servant to help her into the blue dress.

"Perfect fit," Sasha murmured, reaching down to scoop up the brocade gown, then shaking it to remove any speck of dust.

"Yes, I am perfect for this," Svetlina agreed, striding to a full-length mirror and nodding with approval. "It is your gift to me?"

"Yes. Absolutely."

"Good. And…" The major looked down at Sasha's feet. "Also those shoes?"

Sasha winced. She had thrown the Kestonian oxfords into the back of the armoire in her room in favor of something a little more stylish—her favorite tango shoes. Fashioned from soft copper-tone leather, they were strappy and sexy, and she'd kill before she'd part with them.

Not even for Teal? she challenged herself, but the thought of her precious shoes on this unpleasant woman's feet made her sick. She had to believe Teal wouldn't want that, either.

"I'm sure they're way too big for you," she assured Svetlina. "When I met your brother, the General, he told me that Kestonian women are known for their tiny feet. Unfortunately, I can't say the same for myself. I mean, just *look* at these giant things!"

Svetlina nodded as though acknowledging that they were in fact enormous.

Meanwhile, from the corner of her eye, Sasha noted that Niski was stifling a laugh, and she reminded herself to thank the servant later for not pointing out the obvious—the tango shoes would be far too small for Svetlina.

A phone on the dressing table began to ring, and Major Zelasko crossed to it and picked up the receiver, then began speaking rapidly in Kestonian. After a few moments, she hung up and announced, "It is necessary for me to leave. You will stay. When I return, we will have our contest."

"Contest?"

Svetlina wriggled out the blue dress, then abandoned it on the floor as she stalked over to a large closet and pulled out a uniform. "Niski!"

The servant ran to assist her, and in less than a minute, the major was fully dressed in a starched white blouse and a dark olive skirt with a matching jacket. Sasha had to stop herself from admitting out loud that of all three outfits—the gold dress, the blue one and the uniform—this was the one that suited the woman best.

"Do not leave," Svetlina reminded her, then she disappeared without another word.

"Wow. She's quite a gal," Sasha said with a teasing smile. "It must be an adventure every day, working for her."

Niski smiled. "I am so happy that your shoes are still your shoes."

"Me, too. And I'm glad she left us alone, because I've been dying to tell you how much I adore this dress. And this fabric! I'd kill for a bolt of it." Stroking the golden gown, Sasha asked hopefully, "Do you think Major Zelasko would let me wear it to the ball?"

"That would honor me," Niski told her softly. "You will be a beautiful Kestonian princess."

"Like the ones in the portraits out in the hall?" Sasha asked, referring to the paintings of regal men in uniforms and exquisite females with elaborately braided hair and stunning gowns that lined every walkway in the fortress. "They inspired your design, right? You're talented, Niski. You should come to the States and work with me."

"Leave Kestonia? My family? My home?" The girl shook her head. "That would not be. But again you honor me."

"Are you married?"

"One day soon. We wait for permission. Major Zelasko has promised to assist, but she is so angry to me. Because of the dress. I am grateful to you," Niski added fervently. "She will be happy now because of you."

Sasha glanced toward the door. "What did she mean when she said she and I would have a contest?"

"She will fight you. It is my prayer that you will not be injured."

"Fight me?" Sasha winced. "You mean, with her fists?"

"And a knife."

"What?"

"She is champion. When she hears from her brother you are fighter, too, she decides she must fight you."

"With a *knife?*"

Niski nodded. "She will kick you, too. With her very big feet."

Sasha laughed in spite of herself. "You're hilarious. Anyway, thanks for the warning. We'd better hang these dresses up before they get wrinkled." She carried both gowns to the closet, which was dominated by a row of uniforms, all cleaned, pressed and ready for the major.

Inspired, Sasha murmured, "Niski, I haven't eaten in hours. Could you possibly—"

"Yes, yes. Of course. Please sit and wait."

As soon as the servant had left, Sasha transferred one of the uniforms to the garment bag along with the gold gown, then zipped it securely. She was barely finished before the door opened again, and Svetlina stepped back into view.

"You are still here," the major noted.

"You ordered me to stay."

"True. Where is Niski?"

"She's getting me something to eat. While she's gone, I was hoping you'd let me give you a manicure." Sasha stooped and picked up her satchel. "I've got all my supplies right here."

"It is not necessary. Niski will do that."

"I have some special paraffin that will soften your hands. Your dance partners will be impressed, I promise you." Sasha hoped her smile seemed innocent, so that the woman wouldn't suspect she was about to have her finger and palm prints lifted. "It's a special technique, Major Zelasko, and it would be my honor to try it on you."

Svetlina shrugged. "First we will have our contest. Perhaps I will break a fingernail. And you will repair it for me. If you are still able."

Because you're gonna beat me senseless?

Sasha managed a confident laugh. "I don't know where you got this idea from, Major, but I don't engage in fights with anyone, much less someone in great shape like you."

"You are trained. My brother the *prezydente* told me the details."

"That again? It was high school! Not boot camp. We didn't actually fight each other, anyway. We just did shadow sparring."

"Excuse me?"

"You know, like dance movements. It's a form of exercise in America. That's why I kept it up even after I graduated. I found a friendly class that meets three mornings a week and gives me a great workout. That way, I can eat and drink anything I want and still not gain weight."

"It is for vanity? Not for fighting?"

"Right," Sasha confirmed, silently apologizing to sensei Robert Hakira, who not only trained his students to fight like champions on weekday mornings, but also held a special Saturday class for six of his best pupils, Sasha among them, where he taught the art of defeating an armed opponent, specifically, those armed with knife, sword or firearm. Because of him, Sasha was confident she could take Svetlina. But she might get cut or bruised in the process, which could interfere with her ability to rescue Teal. And on a more superficial level, if she ended up going to the ball, she didn't want the effect ruined by cuts and bruises.

"So it is true?" Svetlina was demanding. "Americans are soft?"

"Don't judge us all by me. I never took self-defense seriously because there's no one in America who would dare lay a hand on me, Big Frankie Bracciali's baby girl.

"But believe me," Sasha continued, her voice hushed, "if I'd known about the treatment I was going to receive in Kestonia, I would have studied *real* martial arts before I came here."

"You have been treated poorly?"

"Well, let's see. Your brother's guards bullied me. Then *he* interrogated and threatened me. And now *you* want to fight me with a knife. So, yes, I think it's safe to say I've been treated poorly."

Svetlina smiled. "You are frightened?"

"No," she said quickly. "Not exactly. I'm just not used to this."

"Yes, I see." The major licked her lips. "My brother is very impressed with you. If he could see you now, he would be surprised."

"Don't say anything, please? I'm trying so hard to make a good impression."

"I am told you succeeded. Did he not invite you to dine with him tonight? Alone? In his suite?"

Sasha flinched inwardly. This was the first she'd heard that they were eating in his room. *Ick.*

"It was such an honor that he asked me. I don't want him to think I'm a wimp."

"Wimp?"

"You know. Scared. Helpless."

"Do not worry," Svetlina reassured her with a grin. "It will be the quality he most prefers of you."

"You are a vision of beauty, Sasha Bracciali." Zelasko kissed his guest's fingertips. "Thank you for honoring me with your presence."

Sasha moistened her lips, impressed in spite of herself. This man who had seemed like such a monster was suddenly a nobleman. And sexy in ways few men could even try to be. Yet with him, it was clearly natural. The same raw, animalistic power that had frightened her now acted as a magnet, drawing her close, and because it benefited Teal, she allowed herself to embrace the confusing rush of attraction.

In place of his uniform, he wore black slacks and a black silk dress shirt unbuttoned at the collar. He was freshly shaven and smelled of expensive musk. But it was his black eyes and smooth voice that demanded Sasha's full attention, hypnotizing her with the promise of seduction.

She had debated how to dress for this command performance, choosing between a blue silk suit and a ruffled black cocktail dress. Now she was sure she had chosen correctly. The dress had a halter-top and a semi-plunging neckline. She could see from the way Zelasko's eyes darted over her that he planned to explore every bare inch of her before the night was over. This outfit would make his job quite a bit easier.

"Sit here." He took her by the hand and led her to an upholstered dining chair, one of a pair that had been pulled up to a cozy round table. Candles blazed in the center of a rose-laden display, abetted by the gleaming silverware and light-splitting crystal of the place settings.

"It's so pretty, General. I mean, Vlad."

"I have decided you are correct. You must always call me General. Even though in truth it is you who is in command."

Whoa, nice line… She gave him a flirtatious smile and settled into her chair.

He stood back and studied her openly, his gaze coming to rest on her feet. "The infamous copper shoes. It is a shame they were too large for my sister's feet."

"She told you about that?"

"She tells me everything." He licked his lips, then surprised Sasha by pulling the other chair over so that he could sit directly in front of her without the table between them.

He took her hands in his own. "She told me something else. That you are afraid for your safety in Kestonia. Is that true?"

Sasha grimaced. "She wanted to fight me. With a knife."

He chuckled. "Yes, that sounds like Svetlina. But there is more, is there not? She said you wished your father's bodyguards were here to protect you. Is that true?"

Sasha sighed, trying to appear docile. "I hope I didn't offend your sister. Or you. It's just that I've been so pampered my whole life. So sheltered. You and Major Zelasko are soldiers. You have no idea what it's like to feel this helpless."

He cupped her chin in his hand. "There is no one here

who would dare harm you. You have always been under your father's protection, and that was good. But now you are under *my* protection, and that is invincible."

"Oh, Vlad…"

He pulled her to her feet, then into a long, passionate embrace that left no doubt over his state of excitement.

So it's true? You do like your girls helpless? I think I can accommodate you.

Knowing her voice would be thick with arousal—she was only human after all!—she pulled free and murmured, "You're going a little fast for me, General. I don't mean to seem ungrateful—"

"What have I just told you?" he demanded gently. "There is no need to be frightened of me. Even if you wished to leave now—to return to your room and lock the door—I would not be angry. You may do or say whatever you wish. In fact, I insist upon it."

"Really? That's so classy. No wonder your subjects worship you. And—" she paused to smile impishly "—I wish I'd known about this before I wore the quote-unquote infamous shoes. I've been dying for a tour of your castle, but I didn't want to anger you by asking for it."

"A tour?" He pursed his lips. "But in these shoes, you cannot walk?"

"Right. I should have worn the sturdy ones you gave me, but let's face it. These are prettier."

"Yes, we must face that," he agreed. "The Kestonian shoes are in your room?" Before she could answer, he shouted, "Nikko!" and the door burst open.

Vlad quickly instructed his subordinate, who was gone in an instant.

"Wow, I hope you pay him a lot. He's always doing something for you."

"It is his honor to serve me." The dictator offered her his arm. "Shall we have our tour?"

She smiled and accepted the gesture, hoping to appear shy.

Vlad frowned, then stroked her face with his free hand. "You are still frightened?"

"No, General. I trust you."

His smile was dazzling. "To a Kestonian, that is the ultimate compliment. And now, let me show you my home. After that, we will eat together, and then we will see what else the night has planned for us."

She had already acquired finger and palm imprints from a ranking Kestonian officer, as well as a full uniform. Now, as she walked the halls with her seductive escort, Sasha gathered more and more intel that she prayed would help with Teal's rescue.

As predicted by the NSA, the fortress had excellent security, even in the section that housed the private living quarters of the Kestonian elite. There were video cameras in virtually every corner of the hall ceilings, reminding Sasha that she still needed to master the equipment Allison had supplied to her. Unfortunately, Sasha had been directed to dispose of the "instruction manual" at the Rome airport, so the final details would have to be learned by trial and error. Luckily, Vlad had assured her the video cameras in the residential areas were only there to protect the royal family while they slept, not to invade anyone's privacy. For that reason, they were only operational from nine at night until six in the morning, in contrast to their twenty-four-hour use in the rest of the castle.

According to the dictator, the fortress was more than eight centuries old and had been built atop the ruins of an even older structure. Within the walls were all of the important offices of state as well as housing for the *prezydente's* family and most of the highly placed staff. A well-lit tunnel connected the living quarters to the offices and other assorted work areas.

"We have cottages, too," Vlad explained. "Had you visited in summer, you would have been allowed to stay in one for more privacy. But in winter, it is more pleasant to be in the main house. The snow here grows quite deep."

"It does in Chicago, too," Sasha assured him. "But I'm happy with my room. It's very warm and cozy."

They turned a corner and were confronted by a second tunnel that was not as well lit. "What's this?" she asked.

"It leads to an older section that is no longer in use. You would not be interested in it."

Sasha's pulse quickened, and she said teasingly, "Let me guess. That's where all the political prisoners are?"

"I do not keep prisoners," he replied with a hint of a smile. "It is much more economical to execute them immediately."

"I don't believe that. You're not at all barbaric. I see that now. The publicity you've gotten has been awfully unfair."

"Yes." He scowled. "It is my hope that the opulence and sophistication of the grand ball will soften those opinions. In time, our economic and scientific advancements will convince the world once and for all that we are the first in a new breed of nation—small but progressive."

"But in the old days?" Sasha persisted. "Prisoners were tortured in the old section?"

He exhaled sharply, as though frustrated. Then he took her arm again. "You will not be satisfied until you see for yourself. The curiosity of a woman, yes?"

She gave a light laugh. "I thought you liked the fact that I'm a woman."

"I like it very well," he agreed. "Shall we go?"

She had expected to find some sign of life—specifically some sign of Teal—but Vlad had spoken the truth. The dungeons were empty, and while spotless, they seemed dank from lack of use.

What were you planning to do if you saw her? she asked herself glumly. *Grab the poor kid and make a run for the border?*

But if Teal wasn't here, where was she? In the cottages? That didn't seem prudent. Or perhaps she was in a completely separate location. The logistics of finding her in that case were daunting, given the harshness of the Kestonian winter.

"There are stories in these walls," Vlad told her softly. "The history of my country. Sometimes violent. Always passionate. At times, even romantic." Backing her unexpectedly against a stone wall, he lowered his mouth to hers, kissing her roughly while pinning her tightly in place with his hips. His mouth became a weapon, violating her with such cruel disregard that bile actually rose in her throat.

In her heart, she thanked him for the harsh behavior. Until now, she had been confused by her half-fascinated reaction to him. To his power. His commanding manner and confident mastery. But this kiss wasn't masterful, it was selfish—the kiss of a man to whom all others were just pawns to be used for his own enjoyment and advancement.

Because of Teal, she allowed him to maul her for a few extra moments. But it was clear that if she didn't do something soon, she was going to be the mother of his children, so she pushed her hands against his chest and gasped, "Please, General. I need to say something."

His black eyes were smoldering with desire and frustration, but he pulled back a little and demanded, "What is it?"

"This is too fast for me. I just met you today. There's something between us—that's obvious. Something amazing. But still, this is too fast."

He grinned. "You are frightened of your feelings? I am complimented. In America, men do not kiss you this way?"

"No. Not ever."

"As you said, you have not known a general until now." Pressing his mouth against her ear, he murmured, "There is something you do not know. Something that will change your mind. I have chosen you."

"Really?" She tried to wriggle discreetly out of his grasp. "For what?"

"As a candidate. For my bride."

"*Bride?*" she demanded frantically. "That's crazy, Vlad. You just met me."

His expression grew cold, and she realized she had made a serious tactical mistake. This man's ego was so inflated, even the slightest hint of resistance constituted a monumental insult.

She sandwiched his face between her palms. "I'm so flattered, but—"

"Enough! We will speak of it no more."

"At least, not for now." She tried to smile. "You just surprised me, General Zelasko. I wasn't ready for anything like this. I liked it—I mean, what girl wouldn't? You're rich and powerful and gorgeous! I just wasn't ready. Can't we start over?"

"You will return to your room and I will return to mine. Nikko!"

Sasha grimaced as the ever-present young colonel darted into view.

"Escort Miss Bracciali to her room. Then report to me," Vlad commanded, then he stalked away before either Nikko or Sasha could utter a word.

"Wow." Sasha winced in Nikko's direction. "I guess I made a huge mistake."

The young man's expression seemed shell-shocked. "He paid you great honor. And you…you rejected him."

"Did I? I didn't mean it that way." She shook her head. "Do you think he's going to deport me now?"

"Deport you?"

"Send me back to America?"

Nikko shrugged. "I cannot know. But you have other uses, do you not? You will represent your father tomorrow. For Prezydente Zelasko, that has great significance."

"I hope so," she murmured, wondering how she could have managed to offend the dictator so cavalierly. It wasn't as if he'd actually proposed. He'd just elevated her to "candidate." Why couldn't she play along with that?

Trudging after Nikko through the dingy tunnel, she tried to imagine what to do next. She could send a note of apology, something subservient that also offered un-limited sex. But Zelasko probably *had* unlimited sex at his disposal already. She could claim that he had scared her—wasn't that what he loved in a woman? Or she could just avoid him like the Kestonian plague for the rest of her visit.

Except, she needed him because she still didn't know where Teal was.

They were passing a row of offices, heading for the second tunnel, when Sasha saw someone approaching. It was a female soldier carrying a tray from the living quarters toward the offices. While it was impossible to be sure, it looked like a tray of food.

At almost nine o'clock in the evening, when all the offices seemed to be vacant.

She's bringing it to Teal, Sasha's instincts told her. *Maybe they're keeping her in an office! But which one?*

She needed to see where that tray was going, so she slumped onto the floor, leaning her back against the wall and covered her face with her hands. "I'm so stupid! I offended General Zelasko. What if he never forgives me? What if he throws me out of Kestonia? My father will *kill* me if I mess this up."

"Miss Bracciali!" Nikko knelt beside her, clearly

aghast. "Sasha! Do not do this. It will be worse for you if you do. You must compose yourself before the general sees you."

She peeked between her fingers in time to see Nikko wave the other officer away. The woman seemed perplexed, but finally shrugged and headed down the hall, away from the tunnel, pausing in front of the third door on the right, then pressing her hand against a security panel.

Sasha's heart almost stopped, but she knew she couldn't let Nikko see her reaction, so she grabbed his sleeve and insisted, "You'll tell him, won't you? Tell him I didn't mean to offend him. I'll go to bed with him right now—*right this minute*—if he'll just promise not to tell my father how I insulted him."

Nikko's eyes clouded. "I will not take you to his bed. Only to your room. To sleep. In the morning, you will behave. You will not try to speak to the general. You will attend the conference, then return to your room. After that, you will attend the ball. Then you will go home to America and marry an American."

She gave him a grateful smile, even though it wasn't clear whether he was concerned about her, the general or himself. In any case, he was right. She needed to lay low for a while.

"The gate will descend in five minutes," Nikko warned. "My card will not open it. We must hurry."

"Gate?"

"For the tunnel. It will close at twenty-one hundred hours for the night."

Sasha filed the information away, pleased to think

that she could avoid the key card issue completely if she just got to Teal early enough in the dark winter evening.

Offering Nikko her hand, she allowed him to pull her to her feet. But she *didn't* allow him to see how fascinated she was with the fact that the uniformed woman with the tray had disappeared into the third office on the right.

Chapter 8

Nikko brought Sasha's breakfast to her bedroom on a tray, a sign that she was still persona non grata in the eyes of the generalissimo. It was actually a relief, since she had managed to design a rescue plan, thanks to long hours of sleeplessness, and she was intent on putting it into action right away. Even if she hadn't been so ready for action, the idea of meeting a bunch of underworld chieftains over breakfast just didn't appeal to her. Better to wait for the conference in the afternoon, assuming she and Teal were still in Kestonia by then.

When she mentioned to Nikko that she might go outside for a taste of fresh air, he cautioned her to bundle up well and to follow any and all orders given to her by military personnel. He even offered to escort her, but she insisted that she needed to do something on her own so that her confidence would be strong when she addressed the conference attendees that afternoon. He seemed to understand, and after a few minutes of polite visiting, he left her alone.

Wolfing down a sweet roll and some coffee, she quickly changed from her jeans and sweater into the stolen uniform, which fit amazingly well. Before she finished buttoning the white blouse, she used an adhesive bandage to tape four of the anti-intoxicant pills to her midriff. Then she carefully placed a set of Svetlina's handprints in the inside pocket of the jacket.

She didn't have a cap, but she'd noticed Svetlina didn't wear one anyway, at least not consistently. The woman with the tray had worn one, but perhaps she had been of a lower rank, or had come from the outdoors. The important thing was that Svetlina wasn't just a major. She was Vlados Zelasko's sister, and could do whatever she wanted. All Sasha had to do was conduct herself with confidence and she'd do well, too, assuming she got the final touches just right.

The first was easy—styling her hair like Svetlina's. The color was very close to Sasha's, but Sasha's was so long, she took a few extra minutes to ensure that the prim knot she formed at the nape of her neck didn't look too bulky.

If she came face-to-face with anyone, she knew this disguise would fail her. But considering that the office was so close by, she was hoping she could avoid direct contact with others. This disguise was really for the video camera, and seemed authentic enough for a grainy black-and-white image. She would keep her head down on some pretext to avoid a front view, and from behind—well, she was hoping that if the monitors were staffed by men, and she swayed her hips a little, she could help them forget why they were watching her in the first place.

All because you're too inept to use the video feed recyclers, she complained to herself, but she knew it wasn't entirely her fault. The NSA's printed instructions had been subtle by necessity, and had assumed some basic knowledge of electronics that she simply didn't have. Even if she had mastered the theory, she would need to find the central feed box to attach them, so she'd still need to impersonate an officer as she roamed that section of the castle.

Now for the final step in the charade, she told herself, slipping into her long black wool coat, then pulling a bright blue stocking cap over her head, hiding her unusual hairstyle. She had told Nikko she was going outside, so it would make sense to him, or to Vlad, if they saw her dressed for the outdoors. She might even take a quick look around out there first, just to check out other exits. If by some miracle Teal was able to leave right away, they'd be much better off getting to the outside quickly.

Of course, what they'd do then was anyone's guess. Still, if the opportunity presented itself, Sasha was ready to go for it.

Especially if Teal's superpowers are in high gear, she encouraged herself as she left the safety of her room and walked down the long hall leading toward the castle entry. Rather than use the grand receiving hall through which she had entered the day before, she planned on taking a side door that Vlad had pointed out to her on the tour. He claimed that in summer it led to a beautiful garden, but in winter, the small yard was bleak, serving mostly as a quick route to the guest cottages and the parking area.

As was her habit in winter, she pulled her leather gloves out of her pockets and slipped them onto her hands just as she approached the door. Then she buttoned the top button of her coat, braced herself and stepped outside.

But nothing could have prepared her for the blast of icy wind that hit her full in the face, causing her to gasp as her throat closed in self-protection. It took a few seconds to realize that it was really just a breeze that had greeted her. The shock had actually come from the stinging, subzero air itself.

"You're right, Vlad. Chicago didn't prepare me for this," she croaked, pulling her collar higher on her neck, and wondering if her nose was as red as it felt. Or maybe it was blue like her hat!

She was light-headed, and reminded herself that altitude could be a factor, as well. But if that was going to be a problem, she needed to know about it now, so she resisted the urge to dash back inside. Instead, she followed a narrow path that had been dug through the snow, leading out toward the cottages, which seemed deserted, just as Vlad had claimed. The parking lot was empty, too, except for a smattering of jeeps and snowmobiles.

She was about to take a new path along the side of the castle, hoping to find an alternate entrance to the office area, when she realized that a black Hummer was approaching from the direction of the border. Instead of driving toward the castle, it turned onto a narrow lane that led to one of the cottages.

So? Someone's staying there after all? she asked herself, changing directions to catch a better glimpse. Her eyes were beginning to adjust to the stinging air, and she could see that Vlad and Nikko were standing in a courtyard between two of the guesthouses. The Hummer pulled up and a driver alighted, hurrying to open the rear door of the vehicle. A tall man in a dark coat, dark hat and sunglasses got out and strode right up to Vlad, shaking his hand heartily.

This guy must be mega important—or need extra privacy—to merit a cottage in winter, she told herself, edging even closer. But it wasn't really the man who interested her.

It was his car.

And to think you were actually considering those stupid snowmobiles as escape vehicles! she teased herself. *This is more like it.*

Allison Gracelyn had warned her that the NSA didn't dare wait for her and Teal at the border. For one thing, they didn't know exactly when Sasha would make her move, and for another, they would attract attention, putting Vlad on alert even more than he already was. So the NSA had provided the locations of three safe houses in the area surrounding Kestonia. Assuming Sasha and Teal made a clean escape, they needed to keep moving for another hour or so at least before they actually reached safety.

So why not in a Hummer?

After the three men had conversed in front of the cottage for a few more moments, Vlad shook the stranger's hand again and strode back with Nikko toward the parking lot, where they climbed into a jeep and took off.

The new arrival, however, didn't go inside just yet. Instead, he watched as his driver and another civilian unloaded his luggage, which they carried into the house while their boss wandered around, appearing to study his environment closely.

Either he's worried about his safety, or this is all new to him. Or both, Sasha reasoned. *But he must be here for the conference, right? Or the ball? Which means, you'll meet him eventually. And since you need to get your hands on his keys if you want to escape in the Hummer, why not introduce yourself now?*

Hoping that he was a crime boss familiar with her father's work, she took a deep breath and quickly crossed the remainder of the parking lot until she was on the edge of the courtyard, where the Hummer driver appeared out of nowhere, stepping between her and his boss, his expression menacing.

"Hi," she said with a smile. "I just came by to meet the new neighbors. I love your car, by the way."

When the man just stared at her, she murmured, "Do you speak English?"

"Sasha?" a voice from behind the driver asked softly. "Is that you?"

The driver stepped aside, his hand still tucked inside his coat in a gesture that warned Sasha he had a gun.

As he did so, his boss removed his sunglasses, and she gasped at the shockingly familiar face.

"Zio Dante? *Dio mio!* Are you really here?"

Part of her wanted to ask a million questions. Part wanted to run away.

But instincts inherited from Franco Bracciali sent her in the opposite direction, right into Vincenzo the Butcher's arms. "Oh my God! You'll never know how happy I am to see you."

"È giusto," Dante murmured to his driver, waving him away as he hugged Sasha warmly. "I am surprised to see you, too."

"My father didn't tell me you were attending the conference. It's such a relief. I feel like such a fool for coming here alone."

Dante pushed her to arm's length, then nodded. "I was told your cousin Mark would be representing Big Frankie's interest."

"Change of plans. I wanted to go to the ball, so I conned Dad into sending me instead. I must have been out of my mind. Have you ever felt such cold weather? Or seen such a desolate landscape? And General Zelasko—well, don't even get me started on *him*."

Dante beamed. "Come inside. We'll have an espresso and talk."

Inside? Too late she remembered that she was wearing a Kestonian uniform! So she told him quickly, "I definitely want to visit. But I just stepped out for a minute to get some air. If you can call it that! I'm supposed to be practicing for my speech this afternoon. Daddy brought me up to speed on most of his business, but I want to do it just right. And I want to *look* good, too, which means I've got to do my hair and nails." She grinned and added, "I already feel more confident, just knowing there'll be a friendly face in the audience."

"Regrettably, I won't be there, Sasha."

"Pardon?"

He sighed. "I'm not here for the conference. I needed someplace to hide that was completely out of reach of the authorities. I'm a hunted man. And—" his gaze penetrated hers "—I have been betrayed."

"Oh, no. How awful."

He nodded, still watching her closely. "No one must know I'm here."

"I won't tell a soul, I promise." She bit her lip. "At the wedding, you said you live in Rome. If it's not safe there anymore, why not go back to Chicago where my father and my uncle Antonio can help you?"

He hesitated, then asked her, "Do you remember a man named Vincenzo Martino?"

"Of course. I adored him. He used to bring me cannolis and tell me wonderful stories about the Roman gods and goddesses. He disappeared a long time ago and—oh!" She took a step backward, knowing that her expression showed shock and fear. After all, she *was* afraid. In fact, she was terrified of what this man might have guessed about her role in his unmasking.

When his gaze softened, just a little, she dared move closer again. "Is it really you? Oh my God, you look so different. But I knew your voice sounded familiar." Smiling shyly, she added, "I guess I really did win that bet with Carmine."

He gave a pained smile. "The feds were after me, so I had surgery. Then I lived in Palermo for years, perfectly safe. Now I'm stuck in this godforsaken place until we discover who ratted me out."

"Could it have been your surgeon? That's what always happens in mystery stories."

"It was someone at the wedding," Dante corrected her firmly. "I'm almost sure of that."

Sasha pursed her lips, then nodded. "I think so, too."

"Really?"

She nodded again, this time as if the very thought made her angry. "I had a bad feeling that day. Didn't Carmine tell you? I *knew* something was wrong."

Dante's eyes narrowed. "Tell me why."

"It's like I told him that day. I'd been to his house hundreds of times. But I never once saw muscle outside the door to my uncle's study. Not even during the drug war. Not until that afternoon. It sent the worst shiver down my spine." She sandwiched Dante's face between her hands. "You're safe here, uncle. Vlados is so powerful, he's practically omnipotent. No one would dare harm you. You have to stay inside the cottage, though. Especially for the next few days. You know why, right? This place will be teeming with strangers by this afternoon, and it'll be even worse when they start arriving for the ball. Promise me you'll stay inside."

"You're scolding me?" He smiled proudly. "Your mother used to do that, too. Warn us not to take chances."

"She was right," Sasha retorted. Then she sighed wistfully. "I'd better get back to the castle. I ticked off the generalissimo last night, romantically speaking, so I'm sort of in the doghouse. I'm hoping I'll redeem myself if I do a good job this afternoon. I wish you could be there for moral support. Maybe when it's over, we can have that visit."

"The barbarian is interested in you?" Dante frowned. "I don't blame him, but he'd better be careful. He may be a powerful ruler, but you're still Big Frankie Bracciali's daughter."

"That's what I told him last night. He backed off pretty quickly. It was kind of flattering, actually. Just a little too much, too fast if you get my drift."

Dante's scowl deepened. "Do you want me to talk to him?"

"No, no!" She gave a light laugh. "What good is it to attend a fancy ball if the handsome prince is afraid to dance with me?"

Dante laughed, too. "Typical woman. You want his attention, but on *your* terms. As your uncle, I approve."

She kissed his cheek. "I'd better go. Promise me you'll stay inside. And call Carmine right away. Ask him about those two thugs who were guarding zio Antonio's study, especially the one with the scar. I didn't like his attitude."

Dante grinned. "We'll follow that up. Come for a visit soon."

"I will. I promise." She waved, then turned and trudged back to the parking lot, where she chose the path that led to the part of the castle dedicated to official Kestonian business.

Her heart had been pumping so wildly during the

entire exchange with the Butcher, the cold weather had stopped bothering her. Even now, her senses were on full alert.

He didn't seem to suspect her of having betrayed him. Instead, he seemed to honestly believe that she hadn't recognized him as Vincenzo until today. Still, the possibility that he would begin to wonder about her...

That's crazy, she scolded herself. *The fact that you're here doesn't make you any more of a suspect than you ever were. No one knew Dante was coming here. Of course, once you tell Jeff, and the authorities raid this place, Vincenzo will know for sure who did it. And this time, you won't be able to charm your way out of it.*

It was a sobering development, one that could send her into a witness protection program for the rest of her life. Ratting out Vincenzo Martino once could get you killed. Ratting him out twice? That would require his men to send the world a message worthy of the Butcher himself.

As she neared the door to the office section, she saw that a guard was posted there, although he didn't seem very alert. He was staring off into the distance, and Sasha decided to follow his example and study her surroundings for a moment.

The area on which the fortress was located was actually an enormous ledge on the side of the mountain, making it virtually impenetrable. On the slopes below, Sasha could see signs of villages and farms. Above her, one hundred yards or so up the mountain, was a dilapidated church. Past that point there was nothing but rock and snow.

Nothing except a flat black door built right into the

mountain itself about three hundred yards above her. She had read about it in the guide books and knew it led to an armory, which reminded her of Allison's comment that Sasha would need to "arm herself" after she got to the fortress.

So far, she hadn't even managed to score a butter knife! Not that it mattered. Without the requisite training, a firearm—other than a pistol—wouldn't do her much good.

Returning her attention to the guard, she noticed that there was a panel beside him, imbedded in the stone wall, just like the one she had seen next to the gate in the tunnel.

The kind operated by a key card.

Inconvenient, but probably irrelevant, since she really only needed this door to get out, not in. She and the superteen could certainly take down one lazy guard between the two of them, weapon or no weapon.

"And speaking of the superteen," she told herself softly as she crossed to the path leading back to the garden area of the castle, "don't you think it's about time you met her face-to-face?"

A couple of soldiers glanced at her as she walked by them on her way down the hall that led to her room— *and* to the office tunnel. Sasha imagined it was mostly because she looked half-frozen. There was really no reason to dispel that image, since it helped explain why she hadn't yet taken off her coat and hat.

Bypassing her room, she continued her stroll until she had almost reached the tunnel. There was no one in sight, so she took a deep breath, then darted into one of several maintenance closets she had noticed on her tour. Her intent was simply to stash her coat and hat, but a control panel on the wall caught her eye and she studied it closely, realizing it was identical to the type used for video feed as described in the NSA literature. An old-fashioned padlock secured the panel's door.

Perfect! You can pick that lock, then use the earrings without anyone seeing you. Assuming you can figure out how to attach them. And assuming this is the correct control panel for the office hallway. The manual predicted more than one, remember?

Filing the information away for later, she smoothed her bun into place, reminding herself who she was. A high-ranking Kestonian officer. Sister to Vlados Zelasko. An imperious woman who berated underlings and challenged guests to knife fights.

Inspired, she stepped back into the hall and strode into the tunnel, now almost hoping someone *would* walk by her so that she could sneer at them. But there was no one around, and while she knew she was being watched from the video room, she simply didn't care. Even though she was fiddling with a loose button on her uniform jacket—her excuse for keeping her head down—she was projecting confidence along with a healthy dose of annoyance. She had a feeling the Kestonians knew better than to mess with Svetlina when she was in this particular mood.

Bravado aside, she was slightly giddy when she actually reached the third door on the right without being seen, stopped or shot. She dug into her jacket pocket, ostensibly for a tissue, but actually to affix the artificial palm print to her own hand. Then she wiped the panel with the tissue as if disgusted by some trace of dirt there.

Exhaling sharply, she finally dared to place her hand on the screen. A loud click greeted her, and she knew before she grabbed the handle and twisted it that she had succeeded.

Her heart was pounding again, so she took another deep breath before she pushed open the door, anxious for her first sight of Teal. Praying that the captive would be uninjured, she grimaced when she saw a girl-size lump in the bed, covered with a single layer of thin blanket.

Don't be hurt, she pleaded, dropping to her knees at the side of the bed as soon as the door had closed completely. Then she whispered Teal's name, surprising herself with her gentle, shaky voice. "Teal, honey? Can you hear me?"

"Mmm…sleepy," the girl replied hoarsely. "Not hungry."

"Good, because I didn't bring food. I brought reinforcements. Namely, me."

"Hmm?" Teal rolled toward her and opened one bloodshot blue eye.

"Hey, sleepyhead." Sasha touched her cheek. "Have you ever heard of Athena force? It's a good thing to have on your side at times like this."

"Athena?"

"Try to sit up, okay? You're not hurt, are you?" Sasha smiled encouragingly. "My name's Sasha Bracciali. I'm one of the Muses. We graduated nine years ago.

Allison Gracelyn sent me, honey. Try to focus, okay? I'm going to get you out of this place."

But not today, she added in apologetic silence. *They've really drugged you, haven't they? You poor kid.*

Teal finally seemed to be catching on, and struggled into a sitting position, her legs dangling off the narrow cot. "Sorry…medicine…"

"And lots of it," Sasha agreed, sitting beside her and wrapping her arm around her shoulders. "That's okay, we'll deal with it. I've got some pills for you to try."

"Pills?"

Sasha laughed at the complaining tone, taking it as a good sign. "They're more like anti-pills. If they work, they'll keep you from absorbing whatever's in the medicine the Kestonians have been feeding you."

"I like your laugh," Teal told her.

But a single tear that ran down the girl's cheek at the same time told the real story, and Sasha grabbed her into a full embrace, her own eyes beginning to brim over. "Oh, honey! I know it's been awful. But you're not alone. Not anymore. You've got me now."

"Just you?"

Sasha laughed again. "My father's a Mafia kingpin and I'm semiengaged to Vlad the Terrible. Plus, I'm an officer in the Kestonian army. See?" She indicated her uniform, then pulled up the blouse enough to reveal the bandage. Ripping it off, she showed Teal the pills. "I'm going to tape these under your bunk, okay? So that the Kestonians don't see them. I want you to take one the instant you hear someone at the door. You need to try to stay awake, okay?"

Teal bit her lip. "Can't I take one now?"

"You said you're not hungry. Did they give you a pill recently?"

"I think so."

"Then it's too late. Wait a while. We need it to be in your stomach the next time they drug you. Do you understand why?"

"So it interferes with absorption."

"Good." Sasha smiled with relief. "You seem a little more lucid. That's good."

Teal nodded. "Allison sent you?"

"That's right." Sasha patted her arm, then repeated everything she had said, just to be sure Teal was internalizing it. When she was done, she explained, "As soon as the drug is out of your system, we'll make our move. I'll impersonate an officer again, and bring you something to wear. Once we get in the hall, there's a door to the outside about forty-five feet away. We can get there easily, before the guys manning the video system can alert the soldiers. Once we do that, we'll grab a vehicle and head down the hill. Simple as pie. I wish we could do it now, but you're just too wobbly. You know that, don't you?"

"We can't just leave. There's something else we need to do first."

Sasha smiled. "I know you want to catch the bad guys, but we can do that just as easily in the States, where we've got computers and intelligence files to work with."

"What about my eggs?"

"Hmm?"

Teal grasped Sasha's hand. "They took my eggs. We need to rescue them, too."

"Oh, no." Sasha stroked the girl's cheek. "I'm so sorry, honey. They took them surgically? Is that what you mean?"

"I don't know. I heard them talking." Her tone grew panicked. "They're going to mutate them on purpose. To make freaks out of them. And they're using Dracula's sperm as the father!"

"Dracula?"

"Oh." Teal shivered. "I call him that because… well, because—"

"Because his name is Vlad and his eyes are hypnotic?" Sasha bit back a smile. "I take it you've met him?"

"He visits me sometimes. He's sexy. But scary."

"That's him all right." Sasha touched Teal's cheek again, her heart aching for the girl. Allison had briefed Sasha on this possibility, although they had hoped Sasha would be able to rescue Teal in time to prevent it. Much depended on where Teal had been in her menstrual cycle when abducted, and what sorts of injections had been used thereafter.

"Have they been giving you shots, Teal?"

She nodded. "In my stomach. And my thigh."

Sasha glanced at the door. "They might get suspicious if I'm here too long, Teal. For now, the only thing you have to think about is counteracting the sedative. If it's an intoxicant, the pills I gave you will work. If not, then you'll have to do it on your own. Pretend to take each pill, then spit it out after they leave. Or something like that."

"They watch me take them."

"Just do the sleepyhead routine. Like you're still kind of dopey. They won't suspect any intrigue if you can barely keep your eyes open."

"Okay." Teal snuggled against her. "Thanks, Sasha."

Some superteen you turned out to be, Sasha complained silently as she stroked the girl's soft blond hair. "I've got to go now, Teal. But I'll be back tomorrow night. There's a fancy ball that starts at seven o'clock. I'm going to sneak out while everyone's distracted. We'll leave while they're partying. Okay?"

"And get my eggs?"

"Teal…" Sasha grimaced. "We don't even know where they are."

"They're in the mountain."

"How can they be in the—oh… Do you remember going in there? Through a big black door in the side of the mountain?"

"It's where they study me," she confirmed. "It's a laboratory, Sasha. Disguised as a mountain."

Sasha didn't have the heart to tell the girl that there was no way the two of them could penetrate a mountain. A fortress had been tough enough! And they still had the border crossing to deal with, assuming they even made it down the mountain alive.

Once she's not so dopey, she'll realize it's impossible, she told herself firmly. *Just play along with her for now.*

"I'll try to figure out a way into the mountain, Teal. That's *my* job. Your job is to listen for the doorknob. When you hear it click, take one of the pills, then hide the rest quickly."

She cuddled against Sasha. "Okay."

"You need to keep pretending to be drugged, even after you sober up. Slur your words. Don't open your eyes all the way. Act like all you want to do is sleep."

"Like this?" Teal asked, tumbling onto her pillow and snuggling into it.

"Yeah, you're a natural. I think we've finally found your superpower. You're supersleepyhead."

Out of nowhere, Teal erupted into a fit of laughter. "Super*sleepy*head!"

"Hey, hey!" Sasha pressed her palm to the girl's mouth. "Sheesh, do you want the whole Kestonian army in here?" She laughed in spite of herself. "The good news is, that drug's definitely an intoxicant. Remind me never to go drinking with you."

Teal started giggling again, and Sasha shook her head in warning, then stood and straightened her uniform. "How do I look?"

"Beautiful."

"Not the look I was going for, but I'll take it." Dropping to one knee, she touched the teen's cheek one last time. "Hang in there, okay? It's almost noon right now. You've got to make it through another night, then be patient all day tomorrow. Before tomorrow night is over, I'll be back to get you once and for all."

"And my eggs?"

"We'll see."

"I'm not going without them. I don't want him to have them." Teal's lower lip quavered. "I wish we could just go get them *now*. And then go home. What if they decide to take me to the mountain again and study me?

They do that all the time! I won't even *be* here when you get back. What if they dissect me this time? To study my insides! What if—"

"Hey, Teal?" Sasha hugged her firmly. "Vlad's got a mega-meeting this afternoon. And a fancy ball tomorrow. You're the last thing on his mind right now. Plus, the place is crawling with outsiders. You've never been safer, relatively speaking, than you are today and tomorrow. Okay?"

Teal drooped back down on the cot in a fetal position, barely murmuring her assent.

Sasha patted the girl's hair, then stood and moved to the door. When she looked back, and saw that Teal was already dozing off, she wondered how she could dare walk out of the room and leave her all alone again. What if they *did* come for her? To run tests on her? Maybe even do surgery!

Even if all they did was scare the poor kid, Sasha couldn't bear it. She hated them now—Vlad, and the hacker and the crazy geneticist who had started this madness in the first place. She didn't just want to get Teal away from them, she wanted to crush them. To keep them from ever, ever hurting anyone again.

Forget about Vlad and the others. Once Teal is safe, the NSA will find a way to bring them down. You've got to focus on your assignment, just the way Summit would tell you to do. Make it through today and tomorrow without getting caught, then sneak out of that ball and rescue Teal.

And her eggs.

By the time Sasha made her way down the office hallway and through the tunnel to the residential section of the fortress, she was disgusted with herself for having lost focus so easily. Things were going well. Why? Because of careful, Summit-like planning. Why confuse the issue with dangerous ideas like breaking into a mountain? To rescue *eggs* of all things! Teal would just have to understand. Once sober, maybe she would.

Retrieving her coat from the maintenance closet, she carefully buttoned it over her uniform. Then she stuffed her blue wool hat in her pocket and loosened her hair from the bun, allowing it to flow freely down her back. That alone was a relief.

It was time to stop being an arrogant army major. Or a softhearted nursemaid. She had a speech to give in less than three hours, and she needed to be convincing if she wanted to protect herself. She was Franco Bracciali's daughter. That counted for something with the men in this fortress. It was time she gave them a little reminder of just who her father was. What he could do for them as his friends. What he would do *to* them as his enemies.

Enjoying her new role, she was smiling as she turned the last corner before her guestroom. Then she saw Vlad Zelasko striding toward her in full uniform and her cocky confidence vanished.

Not now.

With any luck he was still angry with her, and would ignore her completely. But from the smile that twitched his lips, she knew she wasn't going to be that lucky.

"Hello, Sasha," he greeted her.

"Ciao," she replied, not slowing her pace even a bit. But he grabbed her forearm before she could successfully pass. Then he grinned and demanded, "What is this mood?"

She gave him a haughty glare. "You're furious with me, remember? I'm saving you the trouble of having to play host."

"I've decided to forgive you for the insult."

"Lucky me," she drawled. "Unfortunately, I've decided that *I'm* the one who was insulted. You may be the leader of Kestonia, but I'm an American. In America, men don't hand out ultimatums on the first date."

"I apologize."

"Wow." She didn't have to pretend to be impressed. "Thanks, Vlad."

He chuckled and stepped closer. "I've decided not to marry you. Instead, you will be my hot date for the ball. That is the correct expression, is it not? Hot date?"

"More or less."

"And after the ball—" he cupped her face in his hand "—I will make love to you with the passion of a thousand stallions."

"Ouch." She gave an embarrassed smile. "Let's start with one stallion, then work our way up, okay?"

Vlad gave a hearty laugh. "Come and eat with me now. The cook has made *svatna.* Do you know it? It is noodles that are filled with duck."

Novelty aside, Sasha had to admit that *svatna* sounded pretty good—and she was hungrier than she had realized—but she wasn't about to go off with him right now, not while still wearing her uniform. "Nikko promised to bring a sandwich to my room so I could work on my speech. All kidding aside, Vlad, I *have* to do a good job representing my father. I owe him that."

"Interesting. Your loyalty to him is strong. Even though he murdered your mother."

Sasha drew back as though the dictator had slapped her. "He claims he didn't do it."

"Yet we know for a fact that he did," Vlad retorted. Then his tone softened. "Forgive me, Sasha. Have I gone too far?"

"There's no proof, so we can never know for sure," she murmured, but she knew that wasn't true. There *was* proof. Her father had given it to her. She had just been too busy—or too preoccupied, or perhaps just too cowardly—to listen to it yet.

"A sandwich sounds very delicious," Vlad told her gently. "I will join you in your room and I will help you with your speech, so that you do great honor to your father. How does that sound to you?"

It sounded dangerous. Not that she didn't appreciate the offer. Under ideal circumstances, having Vlad's help with her speech would be invaluable, even if she did have to fend off some romantic advances in the process.

Unfortunately, in these *actual* circumstances, she was dressed like a Kestonian officer. So all in all, it felt like a very *bad* idea.

Chapter 9

Sasha gave the dictator her brightest smile. "That's such a sweet offer, General. But let's face it. You and I in a room with a bed? Even if *you're* able to keep your hands to yourself, I don't think I could." She draped her arms around his neck. "I've got a confession to make."

"What is it?"

"Remember how I told you I had your picture on my bedroom wall? There's a fantasy that goes along with it. I walk into the ball and there you are, the handsome prince. We dance until we can't restrain ourselves any longer, then you carry me off to your room to make love to me. I know it's silly—"

"I am flattered. You see me as a prince?"

"Of course." She pulled her arms away and asked

teasingly, "What are you planning to wear? Your uniform or a tux? I'm sure you're amazing either way."

"But a tuxedo will help to better fulfill your fantasy?" His smile was surprisingly warm. "I have been having that debate with myself and Svetlina for weeks. The uniform shows strength. But I want to show the world more than that."

"Sophistication," she agreed. "Refinement. Enlightenment. If you were a less imposing man, I'd say you should wear the uniform to remind them that you're the supreme ruler of this domain. But anyone who looks at you will know that, no matter how you're dressed."

"Thank you."

She sighed. "Really, Vlad, I can't believe you're worried about this, poor baby. Maybe you *should* come in so we can talk about it—"

"There! That is why men must never show doubt or weakness to a woman. I do not want your pity, Sasha," he added, taking her hand and kissing it lightly. "I want your passion."

"Till tomorrow night, then?" she asked, trying to sound as throaty as possible.

He smiled. "I will see you in three hours. For the conference."

"Oh, right." She rolled her eyes. "See how easily you can make me forget my duty to my father? You'd better just shoo."

When he cocked his head to the side, she explained with hand waves as she repeated, "Shoo, shoo!"

Vlad laughed again, then bowed and turned away.

Sasha hurried into her room and shut the door

quickly before he could change his mind. "Whew, that was a close one," she told herself in a whisper. "You'd better hope Allison's knockout drug works tomorrow night or you're gonna be one ravaged damsel."

Still, she couldn't be too hard on herself. Not when things had gone so smoothly, relatively speaking.

So don't blow it now, she chided herself. *We both know why you want to go to his room tomorrow night. To get that key card, right? So you can rescue eggs? You're as loopy as Teal.*

Even without the eggs, the idea of seducing him in his own room made sense. His men would assume he and Sasha were in the throes of passion and no one— not even Nikko—would dare interrupt. It would give her a chance to quickly access his computer files and get the name of the mastermind behind the kidnapping. And even if she and Teal didn't go near the lab, they might run into some other obstacle during the escape that needed Vlad's key card.

To her dismay, she could feel her plan unraveling. For one thing, she had completely forgotten about the ever-present Nikko. What if he was standing watch outside Vlad's door when she left the bedroom? And what if Vlad locked the key card away because he was wearing a tuxedo not a uniform and didn't want to mar the look?

"This is one of the times when Jeff's help would come in handy," she muttered. Then she laughed and admitted that she could use one of his ex-rated kisses right about now.

As she hid Svetlina's uniform in her garment bag,

Sasha's thoughts drifted back to the day she had first met her handsome handler. Specifically, she reexperienced that moment of absolute attraction at first sight, followed by a thud—the thud of realizing he didn't trust her. *Couldn't* trust her.

He had made his objections clear. She had divided loyalties. Her motives weren't grounded in principle. These ops were dangerous.

Blah, blah, blah.

Then he had turned into Summit, right before her eyes. His voice had grown deeper. Softer. More patient. Totally trusting. He had shown her how to use the earbud. How to communicate without being detected. How to stick to a plan instead of second guessing herself into a premature burial.

We always keep it simple, he had told her. *If a plan gets too complicated when we're designing it, it's a sign we need a new one. If it starts getting complicated on site, just abort. I know they improvise in the movies, but this is real life.*

Then he had won her respect, if not her heart, by telling her, *You may feel like you're all alone, but I'll never be more than a hundred yards away. One hint of trouble and I'll be there in an instant. You have my word on that.*

It had meant so much at the time, but now she really understood what sort of safety net he had provided. No wonder she could strut through a Mafia wedding, recklessly disobeying his direct orders, deviating from the plan at her whim. Now that it was too late, she could finally appreciate how much his mere presence had done for her.

"So follow his advice," she told herself now. "Keep this plan simple, too. No eggs. No visits to Vlad's boudoir. In fact, skip the ball entirely! If Teal's not sober by tomorrow afternoon, she'll never be. So why not grab her then? Meanwhile, get your hands on Dante's keys to the Hummer. That's it. That's all you can do."

It didn't feel right. It needed work. But so did her speech, so she forced her mind away from Teal and Jeff, and turned her full attention to the family business.

The meeting was held in a wood-paneled conference room. There were no windows, not even the narrow, unopenable, unreachable ones that graced the walls of Sasha's room. Even the artificial lighting over the long oval conference table was minimal, with no attempt at all to illuminate the fringes of the room.

The main participants filed in and sat in preassigned leather armchairs at the table. A second group, also all-male, chose to stand along the walls, even farther in the shadows than the participants.

The underlings, the relatives and the muscle, Sasha guessed.

She knew that drill. Still, she would have thought in the fifteen years since she last peeked into such a room, they would have added more than one token female.

Some things never change.

She had entered with Vlad, who instructed her to sit at his right hand, while Nikko sat to his left. She wanted to believe it would impress the others, but they'd probably think he was just indulging his new mistress. If so, they would judge him harshly for such perceived weakness.

Nikko was Vlad's only visible bodyguard, although Sasha assumed he had some trusted officers among the standing-room-only crowd, disguised in dapper suits. Everyone's identity was being verified at the door. And everyone was patted down except Vlad and Nikko. The soldier who had checked Sasha was all business, and he had finished with her so quickly, she guessed Vlad had warned him in advance.

Aside from her two companions, she recognized only three faces: Salvatore Giambi from Las Vegas, Roberto Aguilar from Miami and Jerry King from New York. She assumed that a few other major cities in the U.S. were represented, but perhaps not. According to her father's briefing, Vlad had handpicked the attendees from all over the world. He had also ordained that the conference would be held strictly in English, so if anyone needed help, they should bring their own translator and have the communication equipment checked out in advance.

"Hey, angel face," Roberto Aguilar said cheerfully to Sasha as soon as he had taken his seat.

Noting Vlad's scowl, Sasha immediately insisted, "You've called me that since I was three years old! How's the family, tio Roberto?"

"They are well. Your family is fine, too, because you have made peace with your father. Good for you." He shrugged then added, "What's done is done. Look to the future I always say."

She forced herself not to react, but inside she was seething. *What's done is done? What if it had been* your *mother? Would you be so philosophical then?*

"There will be time for visiting at the gala," Vlad reminded the room, and everyone quieted down. She knew it didn't mean much—just a sign of generic respect for the host—but she imagined some of them were honestly impressed by the dictator's dress uniform, his chest covered with medals, and his imposing physique and self-confidence.

She could only imagine how they'd react once they saw him in action—so decisive, so imperial.

Vlad stood and inclined his head in a minimalistic bow. "I suggest we begin. Each of you was invited for a reason. A particular talent or resource that provides usefulness to my enterprise. Today you will prove to me, and to your future associates, why you are worthy of this great honor."

The men said nothing in reply, but Sasha noticed how they shifted in their seats, and she gave Vlad's shin a gentle kick. He didn't react, but he did add calmly, "And of course, I intend to prove to *you* why I am worthy."

Token applause rounded the table, and Sasha paid close attention to those who smiled and clapped too vigorously. Kiss-ups, or maybe just insecure about their quote-unquote worthiness. Either way, Sasha would think twice before she'd advise her father to accept such weak men as coconspirators.

At Vlad's direction, a gentleman from Poland spoke first. His English was choppy, so she assumed he was working with an interpreter. Given the handicap, he did a remarkable job of communicating energy and experience. Plus, he claimed to be flush with cash—in the two-digit billions—so Sasha assumed Vlad was impressed. She knew *she* was.

It hadn't occurred to her that Vlad would save her for last, and as the afternoon wore on, she began to panic. Each man was more articulate—harder to follow—than the last. What if she finished the speeches with a thud?

Get over yourself! Advancing Dad's career isn't your primary mission, remember? Just do a passable job. If they blame your poor performance on the fact that you're a woman, don't fight it.

If things really started going south, she'd just burst into tears or otherwise play into the stereotype. It would kill her, and perhaps damage her father's reputation, but it would save Teal—definitely an acceptable trade-off.

The new strategy relaxed her, allowing her confidence to return. She even realized that being the last speaker could work out perfectly. If it did, she'd have to remember to thank Vlad.

Nikko had assumed the duty of master of ceremonies after the first speaker was introduced, and he performed that job smoothly, barely glancing at his notes.

But for Sasha's introduction, he put the notes aside completely. "When Prezydente Zelasko invited the Bracciali family to attend our meeting, he assumed that their leader, Franco, would arrive in person. We were disappointed when legal matters prevented his leaving America. Then we learned that his only child and heir had graciously agreed to travel here. For many reasons, the *prezydente*—and I—ask you to treat her with the utmost of courtesy and respect."

Polite applause ensued, then Sasha stood and

nodded. "I'm honored to be part of this impressive assemblage, especially now that I've heard of your amazing careers and accomplishments. You probably haven't noticed, but I'm the only female here." She paused for some nervous laughter, then she explained. "As Colonel Kerenski mentioned, I am my father's sole heir. You may also have heard that he and I have had our differences these last few years. Let me assure you, gentlemen, while I may not have shown up for many Christmas dinners, I was kept informed, discreetly, about the family business."

She sent a warm smile in Roberto Aguilar's direction. "A few minutes ago, my tio Roberto referred to me as angel face—a nickname from my childhood. And it was a fitting one. I was a very happy child, and I'll tell you why. It was because I had a powerful, loving protector of my very own. His name was Franco Bracciali."

An unexpected sob hit her throat and she swallowed it. "I lived in a great city, but a very dangerous one. Plus, I had ears, so I knew that my father's business was complicated, and that he had made enemies who might wish to harm me. Yet I slept like an angel. Do you know why? Because there was no doubt in my heart that Big Frankie Bracciali would protect me. He was a legend in those days, gentlemen, and I suspect you've heard some of the old stories. Believe me, they're all true. Each and every one. Even the bloodiest and most ruthless of them. If you crossed the Bracciali family, you were dead. Maybe you didn't know it yet. Maybe you hid on the other side of the planet. But trust me, you were dead.

Of all my father's great qualities, that's the one that made *everyone* want to be his friend. It's the reason everyone wanted him to provide security for their enterprises. And it's the reason I slept like an angel."

Sasha paused, allowing the passionate blend of hero worship and cold, hard facts to sink in. Then she shrugged and said offhandedly, "But times have changed, haven't they? The best security now is the invisible kind. Discretion and tech training have replaced brute force as the primary means of enforcement in this modern world. If you have impenetrable, invisible security, you can own the world. Or at least, as much of it as it takes to satisfy your women."

They all laughed. Then she leaned forward, her palms pressed to the tabletop, and said with ringing authority, "The Bracciali family can provide that new breed of security to any project, no matter how large. But don't be misled. Behind the scenes, our muscle is still the best. The biggest, the strongest, and I promise you, the most ruthless when crossed. My father's tech experts are the best, too, but you'll sleep better at night—like angels, in fact—knowing Big Frankie Bracciali can and will *annihilate* anyone who tries to stand in your way. Let me give you a few recent examples— ones of which my father and I are particularly proud."

After that, Sasha was on a roll that ended in thunderous applause, even from the men who had looked crooked at her earlier. She took it as a compliment, either to her rhetoric or to her final anecdote—the one about the snitch who had been buried in London. *And* Amsterdam. *And* Orlando. That snitch's remains would *never* be reunited, thanks to the fine work of Bracciali security.

Her only worry now was that Vlad might ruin the effect of her speech by remarking on it, but he said only, "Thank you."

Then he cleared his throat and announced that three participants and their entourages were being asked to leave the room. There was no explanation, no offer that they could still attend the ball, just the promise that their bags were being packed, and that transportation out of Kestonia awaited them.

"Good riddance," Aguilar announced cheerfully as soon as the doors were closed again.

"We should probably inform Big Frankie right away, General Zelasko," Sasha murmured. "He'll want to keep a close eye on those three."

"I will inform him myself. Thank you for the suggestion. And now—" Vlad paused to straighten to his full, imposing stature, before assuring the remaining participants, "It's time for me to tell you exactly what I need from each of you, and how you will be compensated if you fulfill that commitment."

It took only fifteen minutes for Vlad to outline his needs. Then he spent another full hour speaking with each of his new associates in turn. In the interim, he instructed Sasha to accompany Nikko to a private bar adjoining the conference room to wait for him and to enjoy the private dinner that awaited her there, and she was glad for the opportunity.

Vlad had been masterful. She had watched as—one

by one—the hard-nosed gangsters had sat up and taken notice. She understood now why the Kestonian people worshipped him despite the brutality of his takeover. It had been swift, and on some level, they had been proud—and relieved—to be on his side.

Oratory, veiled threats and the promise of billions—quite a heady combination for men like Roberto Aguilar.

And for men like Franco Bracciali, she told herself with a sigh. *No way will Dad pass on this deal. I just wish he could have seen Zelasko in action. He would have eaten it up!*

"You did well. Better than the men," Nikko told Sasha as they dined together.

"With the exception of your boss," she reminded him. "He was amazing. And what about *you?* Cool, calm and collected. That's a great compliment in America."

"I was very nervous."

"Me, too. I thought— Oh!" She jumped to her feet the same way Nikko did when Vlad burst through the door.

There was no need to guess the dictator's mood. The meeting had been a complete success and he knew it. Still he asked Sasha playfully, "You were impressed?"

She thought about giving a sexy reply, but caught herself and murmured, "I thought I had seen everything. So many meetings like this at our house. But honestly, Vlad, I'm speechless."

"Good. You spoke for too long already."

"Excuse me?"

He grinned. "Shall I call you angel face now?"

She rolled her eyes. "If I was such a problem, why didn't you send me home with the other rejects?"

His eyes warmed. "You were magnificent. Not only for a woman, but even compared to grown men. Your father would have been proud."

"Thanks."

"I am convinced now that your reconciliation with him will survive. You love him—*worship* him—and that is good. All is forgiven. He found it necessary to kill an unfaithful wife, not because he wanted to, but because his reputation—his entire future, and perhaps even his survival—depended on how he reacted at that moment in time."

To her surprise, it was almost true. In the process of reliving those days, she had been forced to remember that any sign of weakness was a death sentence for someone in her father's position.

It also forced her to remember why she had walked out the door and refused to speak to him ever again.

"I have caused you depression?"

"Well, you killed the buzz, but that's okay. I'm glad you could sense how I felt about Dad, either in my words or in my attitude, because I don't want the other gentlemen to have any doubts about me."

"They will not. Not now," Nikko insisted heartily.

Vlad chuckled. "You are aware that Nikko is in love with you, are you not?"

The colonel flushed but said nothing.

"Don't tease him, General. Please? His introduction gave me an extra shot of confidence right when I needed it."

"Did it?" Vlad smiled. "You are pleased with us then? That is good."

Nikko smiled, too. "Are you looking forward to the ball, Sasha? And to the display of fire that will follow it?"

She felt her cheeks warm. "Well…"

Vlad chuckled and explained to his assistant, "She believes you mean the lovemaking that she will have with me. She does not know about the church."

"The church?"

"On the morning following the gala, I will blow up our old cathedral in a great explosion. To signal to Kestonia that the time for rebuilding has arrived, as I promised during my rise to power. It will be an impressive display." Leaning his mouth against her ear, he added provocatively, "Almost as impressive as our private display will be."

"Why do you have to blow up the old one? Doesn't it have historical value? I saw it from a distance and it looked so charming. A little run-down, but lovely."

"We have stripped out the murals and statues. And the altar. Everything of value. The building is no longer safe. It was allowed to grow weak from neglect, as was all of Kestonia, under the old regime. I will change that. Beginning with the new cathedral."

She smiled. "You're so ambitious. But you didn't give us any specifics about your enterprise. Just that it would make money for all of us. You'll eventually have to give details to those men, you know. So? Can't you tell me a little about it?"

Vlad shook his head. "The details are irrelevant for now. But I will tell you that my success in this venture will identify Kestonia as a world leader in the advancement of science, as well as ingenuity and vision."

In other words...Teal.

After what she had witnessed over the last few days, she was beginning to suspect that Vlad himself was the real mastermind behind the kidnappings. Allison had been convinced he was just a pawn, but Allison hadn't been in that conference room listening to this man and his "vision."

It would be a mistake for anyone—especially Sasha—to underestimate him.

In contrast to the lack of drinking during the conference beyond a ceremonial toast at the end, the champagne had flowed freely during the private celebration with Vlad and Nikko. Fortunately, Sasha had remembered to take her antiabsorption medication, but she pretended to be inebriated as an excuse for an early retreat. Apparently her performance was convincing because Nikko insisted on holding her elbow as he escorted her back to her room.

It was easy to keep the banter light with him, not only because the meeting had gone so well, but because of Vlad's jokes about his underling's feelings for Sasha. She wasn't sure it was true, but if it was, it was a stroke of luck. Hadn't she been looking for some way to manipulate him? To ensure that he didn't go and check on Vlad after the ball, only to find that someone had drugged him? Flirting with him seemed far preferable to whacking him over the head with a vase, which was the only other solution she had been able to devise for the Nikko problem.

When they reached her doorway, she thanked him

again for the lovely introduction he had given her, then as if on impulse, she kissed his cheek and insisted, "What would I do without you?" Then without giving him a chance to do anything but blush, she slipped into her room and closed the door firmly between them.

Things are going so well, she told herself as she leaned against the door and allowed her heart to slow to a normal rate. *What if you can actually pull this off? Not only rescue Teal, but also get proof that Vlad's the mastermind* and *get your hands on that key card in case your favorite sleepyhead insists on hitting the lab on the way out of town.*

It was too ambitious. Too complicated. She knew that, yet she also knew she was going to try. Which meant she really *did* need to get some sleep, because the beginnings of exhaustion were lurking under her euphoria. Moving toward the armoire, she began to shed her navy-blue silk suit with one hand while flicking the light switch on the wall with her other.

"Well," said a voice from across the room. "Look who finally decided to show up."

Sasha whirled, completely disoriented by the familiar sound. Then she literally squealed Jeff's name and sprinted over to him, wrapping her arms happily around his neck. "You're here! How is this possible? Oh my God, Jeff, tell me I'm not dreaming."

"More like a nightmare, wouldn't you say?" he drawled.

Sasha drew back, surprised by the tone, and suddenly aware that he hadn't made any attempt to participate in the embrace. One look at his expression confirmed that he wasn't happy with her. In fact, there was a quiet sort of anger behind his eyes that she had never seen before, not even on the day the FBI had first inflicted her on him.

"You're angry?" She touched his cheek, and when he flinched, she insisted, "I wanted to tell you, Jeff. I begged them to let me. But they wouldn't." She bit her lip, then admitted, "They had their reasons. And I desperately wanted to do this, so I agreed. You have to forgive me, though, because I'm so glad you're here—"

"You forgot to ask me *why* I'm here," he interrupted coolly. "So I'll just tell you. I came to rescue you. Isn't that a laugh? I was so sure you were in over your head, I put my whole effing career on the line to come to this hellhole and save you. Like you need saving! My God, you already own the place! Zelasko's mistress. Big Frankie's daughter. Jesus Christ, Sasha—" His tone grew almost reverent. "I still can't believe you did all this. I thought I knew you—"

"Is that what this is about? You think I actually *slept* with him? You think I really reconciled with Dad? Because I swear to you—"

"Don't make me laugh. You *swear?* Like that means anything coming from you?" He exhaled sharply. "You swore you thought your father's business was ninety-nine percent legit. And I believed you so much, I actually felt sorry for you! Like *you* were the dupe, when all the time it was me."

"Jeff—"

"Don't worry. I don't think you really reconciled with the big guy. I think you conned him the same way you conned me. The way you made me believe you were naive. Made me want to protect you. Even fall in love with you. All part of your mission for the NSA, right?"

"You need to be careful now," she warned softly. "I can see why you're angry, but I can explain. I really *did* think Dad's business was legitimate. I only found out this week that I've been blind about that. But I had enough information, from the past, and from talking to him on Sunday, to sound convincing today in the conference room. And you were there, right? In the shadows? Oh, Jeff." She took a deep breath, then dared to admit, "If you knew the truth—and if you had any idea how much I needed you to come after me this way—you'd take me in your arms right now and never let me go."

"What are you *doing* to me?" he demanded with a groan. "It's like you're a complete stranger, but I still can't help falling for you."

"I'm the same me I was in Chicago. Kissing you. Calling you Summit. Making love with you." She sandwiched his face between her hands. "I don't work for the NSA. This is a freak, one-time occurrence to help someone from my old high school who's in terrible trouble. They're only using me because I had an entrée into Kestonia. Because of Dad. Don't you see?"

For the first time, a hint of renewed trust began shining behind his emerald eyes. Resting his hands on her hips, he murmured, "You're talking about the kidnapped girl? *That's* what all this is about?"

She nodded in relief. "Yes. And I need your help rescuing her, so I'm so very glad you're here. Plus, I've just missed you so much." She flashed a hopeful smile. "There's so much to tell you, Jeff. But first, believe me that I never lied to you. Not about anything except my plans for these two weeks. And I did sort of reconcile with Dad—it might even stick—but it's not how it seems. I'll still never forgive him for killing Mom—"

"Jesus!" Jeff pulled his hands away from her and glared. "You're goddammed unbelievable, you know that? If I hadn't listened to the goddammed tape I would have fallen for that performance in a minute."

"The tape?"

"Yeah." He pulled the recorder out of his jacket pocket and waved it in her face. "What I don't get is *why?* Are you a compulsive liar or something? Why now, when it doesn't even matter—"

"Jeff!"

He stopped dead at her strident tone. "What?"

Sasha stepped closer to him, her mind trying to make sense of what he had said. "Are you telling me there's something on that tape that *exonerates* my father?"

"Huh?" His face was suddenly the color of ash. "You haven't listened to it yet?"

"No." She held out a trembling hand. "Give it to me now, please."

Chapter 10

"Sasha, baby." Jeff shook his head as though he still didn't quite believe what he had done. "I thought you already heard it. I never would have—"

"*Give it to me!*"

"Right." He placed the recorder on her outstretched palm, but didn't let go of it himself. "Before you listen to this, we need to talk. It gets a little rough—"

"I'm fine." She pulled it away from him, then turned and walked over to the bed. Jeff started to follow, but she waved him away. Then she stripped off her suit until she was down to a lacy slip and underwear, and crawled into the middle of the bed, where she sat cross-legged and tried to take a steadying breath.

Reminding herself that she had already heard the

opening lines, she turned up the volume on the recorder and pushed the play button.

Her father's voice began, soft and sad and filled with love.

"I have protected you from the truth for so long, my darling daughter, the lie has become an old friend. Almost a member of the family. By choice *and* by blood, one might say. I've told myself I was doing it for you, but it has hurt you as much as the truth ever could. So I've decided to confess. But not to your face. I'm making this tape instead, and one day, when you feel strong—when you feel ready—you will listen to it and know the truth. Selfishly, I pray that day never arrives."

Her father's gulp was audible.

"For most of your childhood, Antonio Martino and I had an iron grip on Chicago. I'm sure that's how you remember it. But what you didn't know was how often challengers would arise. Punks who thought they could muscle their way into my territory. Whenever that happened, we dealt with it swiftly, Antonio and I. We jealously guarded our empire, not just for ourselves, but for our children. I had you—the most precious child in the world. Antonio had Carmine, and little Gianna, and above all, his beautiful Vittoria, the light of his life.

"When you had barely left for college, a new

challenger arose. A punk from Los Angeles.
Martino and I decided to deal with him they way
we'd always done. We agreed I would handle the
hit. This punk had a dance club downtown, and I
gave the job to my best guy, Little Jay. Remember
him? The plan was to plant a pipe bomb that
would explode after hours, when the customers
were gone, but when the punk and his two thugs
were still in the back room counting the money
they had ripped off from us. What we didn't
know—what I couldn't have known—was that
the punk had a girl with him that night."

Big Frankie's tone was so guarded—so riddled with
guilt—that Sasha braced herself for the worst. But even
so, when he spoke his next words—when he said, "That
girl was Vittoria Martino"—she gave a sharp, strangled
cry of disbelief.

"No. Not Vittoria… Oh, Dad, not Tori. Please?" Sasha
pressed the pause button on the machine, then pulled her
knees up to her chest and wrapped her arms around them,
trying to ward off the icy chill of disbelief and foreboding. Beautiful Vittoria Martino—not just pretty or
pampered, but truly pure and innocent. And so beloved.

Especially by her father don Antonio Martino.

Sasha vividly remembered Tori's funeral. Everyone
had been weeping. Gianna had literally been wailing.
Even Carmine—the tough guy—had cried like a baby.
And don Antonio had seemed like a ghost. Pale and
drawn. Unable to look Sasha in the eye.

Now she knew why.

"Sasha," Jeff murmured, but she glared and reminded him to stay where he was. Then she started the tape again. Her father's voice became a whisper.

"When I heard Vittoria was dead, I was numb with grief. And with fear. Because I knew how much Antonio loved her. I knew he would blame me. He was right to do so. No one but Antonio, Little Jay and me knew we planted that bomb. I killed Jay myself with my bare hands. He's still rotting at the bottom of the lake. But I knew Martino wouldn't be satisfied with that. I knew exactly what he'd do.

"He'd try to kill *you*. My precious, irreplaceable Sasha. A daughter for a daughter. It's what I would have done in his place, and I knew I couldn't talk him out of it. But I was desperate to save you. To take you away somewhere. But nowhere on earth was safe from that man at that moment. I knew that for a fact.

"And your mother knew it, too. She figured it out, and before I knew what was happening, she went to Antonio in secret and offered a proposition. Instead of you, she would sacrifice herself. True, she wasn't my child, but she was the great love of my life. Losing her would kill me as certainly as if a knife had been thrust into my own chest."

Oh, no...Mom...no...

"Your mother reminded Martino that he had other children. Another beautiful daughter. A strapping son. But you, you were my only child. It would be too harsh to leave me childless because of a gruesome error in judgment. Antonio agreed with her. Then they came to me. I'll never forget it when they stood before me—your mother, Antonio and Antonio's cousin Vincenzo. Before I knew what was happening, they overpowered me. Tied me to a chair. Then they told me their plan."

Her father's voice grew strident.

"I screamed. Cursed. Begged. Cried like a woman. I tried to tear my arms from their sockets to free myself from the ropes, but it was no use."

Oh, Dad... Sasha swiped at the tears streaming down her cheeks.

"Your mother made me promise never to tell you. She said you would hate yourself forever if you knew. Better you should hate *me*. Hate *her*. But never yourself. So we would deceive you. We would make it appear as though she had been unfaithful to me. That I caught her making love in our bed with another man and had them both murdered in a jealous rage.

"The whole world believed that story. But the truth was so much uglier—"

His voice broke, and Sasha hugged her knees with her arms again, terrified to hear the rest.

"There was a man on one of my crews who had always looked at your mother with lust in his eyes. It had bothered her, and had enraged me more than once. But he was a good producer otherwise, so I had allowed him to remain after a stern warning.

"Your mother invited that man to our bedroom."

No, Dad. Oh, please, no.

"I was still tied to the chair, pleading with Antonio for your mother's life. But he wanted his revenge. It was all that mattered. And because he wanted it done with speed and certainty, he asked his cousin Vincenzo to take care of it personally."

"No!" Sasha gasped at the sharp stab of pure terror that had gripped her. "Not the Butcher. Oh Mom…"

"Vincenzo went up to that room and busted down the door. He cut them both to ribbons with a machine gun. No one but Antonio, Vincenzo and I ever knew the truth of that awful day. Everyone believed I had done it myself, and no one blamed me for it. She was in bed with another man when it happened, so everyone believed my actions were justified. Everyone that is, but you."

His tortured voice turned calm at last.

"I promised her I'd never tell you any of this, darling Sasha. But you deserve to know the truth about me, and more important, the truth about her. That she loved you so much she traded her own precious life for yours.

"I've tried to find the right time to tell you in person, but you wouldn't meet with me. Wouldn't speak to me on the phone. And I'm enough of a coward to admit I couldn't imagine saying these things to your face. Watching your beautiful eyes fill with tears. You begged me so often at the beginning to tell you the truth about her death. Now you will wish I had lied to you forever. All I can ask is that you forgive me. Forgive her. And understand that what we did, we did out of love for you."

Oh my God...

Leaving the tape still running but now voiceless where it lay, she crawled away from Jeff, sliding off the other side of the bed. From there she wandered to the corner of the room, where she sank down onto the cold stone floor and huddled, completely disoriented, covering her face with her hands in a useless attempt to blot out the horror of her mother's death.

"Sasha, baby."

"Go away."

Jeff was silent for a moment, then he hunched down in front of her and insisted stubbornly, "You have to let me help you."

"No! Just go back to wherever you came from. Please?" She peeked between her fingers and insisted sadly, "I'm not upset. Just numb. Believe me, I don't need anything from anyone. I just need to be left alone."

"Come on, Sasha. I'm sorry I shot my mouth off the way I did—"

"Basta!" she ordered him, holding up her hand in imperious warning. But when a flash of hurt crossed his face she softened enough to explain, *"Basta* doesn't mean bastard. It means enough."

He grimaced. "What a day, huh? Let's talk about it. About your mom, I mean."

"I need to get past all that. At least for the moment. I need to concentrate on getting Teal out of this awful place. There's so much to do." She eyed him hopefully. "You said you came here to help. That's good, because I need you to be Summit for me one last time."

Jeff struggled to keep his reactions in check as he watched Sasha pace the room. She was describing in minute detail what she thought she needed from him, but he knew better. She needed him to hold her. Caress her. Comfort and make love to her.

But there was no hope of that, so he listened in silence as she outlined their mission. They were going to rescue some kid named Teal who supposedly had been genetically enhanced. Sasha had done a tremendous amount of legwork already, gathering intel and setting up connections they could exploit during the next twenty-four hours.

"The only real variable at this point is Teal's condition. If she's been able to counteract the sedatives, she could be extremely valuable, given her abilities. But if she's still drugged when we make our move—"

"Then I'll carry her. No problem," he promised.

For the first time, Sasha actually smiled at him. "I didn't even think of that. Thanks. So? Are we clear on the plan?"

"Sure. It's a good one, Camper. A little complicated, though. Now that you've got help, there's no need to go to Zelasko's room with him—"

"We need the key card. And I want to search his room for proof that he engineered the kidnapping from the start."

Jeff licked his lips. "You said yourself that you only needed the key card for the eggs. And I agree with your original assessment on that. It's an unnecessary risk. We should just head straight from here to the border."

"Teal won't agree to that. She's terrified Zelasko will use them to father some sort of mutant superchildren. Even if we *could* talk her into leaving them behind, it would haunt her for the rest of her life, Jeff. I can't put that sweet kid through that kind of senseless, terrifying nightmare—" Sasha choked back a sob, and Jeff imagined she was remembering her own misery, these last eight years, knowing that her mother had been gunned down by thugs.

Before he could offer comfort, she rallied and insisted angrily, "I'm going after the eggs. Either you come with me, or you can take Teal to the border and I'll catch up to you."

"We'll all hit the lab together, grab the eggs and head for the border. Piece of cake."

She nodded. "Thanks. Once Teal is in safe hands, you and I will go after the Butcher."

"There's something you don't know, Sasha. My

team hit Palermo yesterday. I'm sure Vincenzo's in custody by now."

"Actually," she drawled, "there's something *you* don't know. He's here. Under Zelasko's protection. In one of the cottages next to the fortress."

As Jeff stared, she explained how she had stumbled upon the Butcher, and how he had confessed his true identity, apparently never suspecting that Sasha had had a hand in his betrayal.

"Remember when I said I can get an escape vehicle? It's his. He arrived in a Hummer. I'm going back for a visit tomorrow morning, and hopefully, I can swipe the keys."

"Negative. You can't take chances where he's concerned. If he suspected for a second it was you who betrayed him—"

"I *want* him to know," Sasha assured him with a grim smile. "I want to look him in the eye and *tell* him it was me. After that, he'll go to prison and I'll go into witness protection. Because we both know my life won't be worth dirt if I don't. But I'm fine with that. Even though…" She sighed. "The idea of never seeing Dad again didn't bother me before. Now that I finally know he didn't kill Mom…" She sighed again, then squared her shoulders. "I can't afford to care about any of that. All that matters is making Dante pay for the terrible things he's done."

"We'll find another way," Jeff told her. "You're not going into witness protection. That's nuts." Stepping closer, he added firmly, "You've had a helluva day. And I didn't make it any easier. But I'm not going to let you throw your life away—"

"Basta!" she repeated forcefully, and this time, he was pretty sure she *did* mean bastard.

And he wholeheartedly agreed. He was a first-class jerk who didn't deserve to breathe the same air she did. But for the moment, he was all she had, and he was determined to do his best for her. "You're exhausted," he noted in his most soothing voice. "Come and sit with me on the bed for a minute."

"I hope you're kidding," she muttered.

"I didn't mean it like that. Although I've gotta admit—" he paused to flash a hopeful smile "—I haven't been able to get you out of my mind. I think I'm falling in love with you."

"Think again. And do it someplace else. If they find you in my room—" She paused to wince. "How did you get into Kestonia anyway?"

"I'm translating for a Polish mob boss. Long story."

"So? You *were* there today? In the shadows?"

"While you taught Racketeering 101?" He grinned. "Yeah, you put on quite a show."

When she shrugged, he stepped closer again. "I came here to rescue you. Then I saw that performance, and I realized you didn't need me. Which wouldn't have been so bad if you and Zelasko hadn't been so chummy. I was jealous. Not because I thought you were doing anything wrong, but because I thought you didn't need me. That you *never* needed me. That you'd been playing me the way you played that roomful of thugs—like a pro."

She bit her lip. "You said earlier that you put your whole career on the line for me. Does that mean you came here without permission?"

"Against orders. I went crazy thinking of you here alone. I didn't think you could handle it. Not without me. But I was wrong. You've done a great job."

"But I *did* need you," she insisted. "When I saw you here tonight, I knew for the first time that Teal was really going to make it out of this nightmare alive. I'll make sure your superiors realize that. Plus, you'll be the one who brings in the Butcher. That alone should redeem you in their eyes."

"And in your eyes?" he murmured, adding quickly, "Never mind. We'll hash that out once the superkid is safe. For now, get some rest. Do you want me to stay until you fall asleep?"

"No, thanks. I'll be out like a light the minute my head hits the pillow."

He doubted that, given the terrible thoughts he knew would be swirling around in her brain. Still, he nodded encouragingly. "Try not to think about the tape, okay? Or my *many,* many screwups. We need you in perfect shape tomorrow if we're gonna pull this off. Right?"

"Right."

"So…" He stepped forward and brushed his lips across hers. "Good night, beautiful."

"Good night," she replied quietly, as though the kiss hadn't taken place. "Get some rest. I'll meet you and Teal at the rendezvous point tomorrow night at ten, just like we planned. And, Jeff?"

"Yeah, baby?"

"Thanks for coming."

"My pleasure." He gave her a wistful smile, then crossed to the door, reminding her over his shoulder, "Lock up behind me and get some rest. You're gonna need it."

* * *

As soon as the door was closed, Sasha walked back to the bed and picked up the tape recorder, which had finally shut itself off. She placed it in her overnight bag as though it were simply a toiletry, then she dug through her belongings until she found the capsules of knockout powder that Allison had given her.

She felt as though she was teetering on the edge of insanity, forcing herself *not* to think about her mother, *not* to think about her father, *not* to think about Jeff….

Instead she thought about Teal. And about Allison's careful, detailed instructions, specifically her instructions regarding the knockout powder.

It will work almost instantaneously. The victim will go completely limp, so make sure he's someplace out of the way when he conks out. There are no long-term effects, but for four to six hours he'll be dead to the world.

Dead to the world.

It sounded pretty good to Sasha. So good that she carefully broke open one of the capsules and poured the contents into the empty glass on her bedside table. Then she opened a new bottle of water, added it to the drug and climbed into bed with it.

And just as Allison Gracelyn had promised, she was blessedly unconscious within seconds.

"Your mother was the prettiest woman I ever laid eyes on. And the bravest, too," Vincenzo Martino declared solemnly the next morning as he and Sasha visited in the parlor of his Kestonian cottage. "We all worshipped Julia. Like a goddess! And now here you sit, just as pretty, and according to General Zelasko, every bit as spirited. I'm proud of you, and when Big Frankie hears about your performance at the conference table, he'll be proud, too."

Sasha looked down at her hands, desperate to hide her revulsion at the sight and sound of the monster who had butchered her mother. She wanted to throttle him. To riddle him with bullets the way he'd done to the beloved body of a brave, innocent, selfless woman. But instead she was sitting and sipping cappuccino with him as though they were the dearest of friends.

She had awakened that morning with her body eerily refreshed thanks to the knockout potion. Her mind, however, had been instantly wary, as if it knew a sea of pain awaited it. She hadn't dared think—not about anything. Not her father, her mother, the Butcher, not even Jeff.

Smile, she reminded herself now. *You may not be a very good daughter. Or even a good operative. But you're one helluva talented mole. Worth your weight in secrets and lies. So do what you do best. Charm this creep, get the keys from him somehow, then get out of here. Once Teal is safe, you'll have your revenge. I promise you that.*

"I love hearing you talk about Mom," she lied sweetly. "You so obviously adored her. You don't really believe she cheated on my father, do you?"

Dante pursed his lips, then used a blunt tone to declare, "Yes. I sincerely believe it. And I believe her death was necessary for the sake of everyone involved. For the sake of your family's honor. But still—" he paused for a hearty sigh "—her death was a tragedy. For me as well as for your father."

When Sasha looked down at her hands again, he scolded her. "You've been feuding with Big Frankie about it, but the truth is, he had no choice. There's a code that guides our actions, Sasha, and that code demanded her death. Your father took no pleasure in it. But if she hadn't died, someone else would have. Perhaps even a war would have begun. That's why our families have put stringent rules into place. So that order can be quickly restored when mistakes occur."

"Mistakes?" She stood and walked around the living room, pretending to be restless while actually scanning each tabletop and ledge for the Hummer keys. She had already checked the vehicle itself on her way up to the cottage and had confirmed that the keys weren't in the ignition. Now it seemed that the driver might be carrying them around with him, frustrating Sasha's plan. "That's an odd word, isn't it? I mean, if she cheated on Dad, that wasn't just a mistake. It was a betrayal of his trust."

"Exactly. It was a betrayal that needed to be swiftly avenged," Dante agreed, and Sasha knew he was really referring to Vittoria's accidental death in the pipe bomb explosion. "With Julia's death, balance was restored. *She* understood that better than anyone. So while you can grieve her, you must also understand that your father grieves, too. He loved her as much as you did. And *she* loved *him,* even at the end. She loved him, and she understood why he did what he did."

"Because she believed in the code, too?" Sasha murmured.

"Exactly! For most of her life, she prospered because of it. As Franco Bracciali's wife, she had wealth and privilege. The code protected her. Protected her husband. Protected *you,* her beloved child. It has served you well, Sasha. And it always will. Isn't that what you told the conference members yesterday?"

Sasha grimaced, then nodded. "I told them how safe I felt when I was a little girl. Because of Dad's status and power. That's what you mean, right?"

"Yes. His enemies—and even his closest friends—know that if they make a mistake, they will pay dearly. So they try not to make mistakes."

"I'm finally beginning to understand," she admitted. "I just wish the code was protecting *you* better. Every time I think about the traitor who gave the police information about your new face—" She arched a stern eyebrow. "Did you talk to Carmine about those thugs that were guarding the door to zio Antonio's study?"

"Not yet. It's sweet of you to be so concerned." He gave her a fond smile. "Come back here and sit with me in front of the fire. This godforsaken place is like an iceberg."

"It's freezing," she agreed. "Let me get you a blanket." Before he could protest, she dashed into the cottage's only bedroom and quickly checked the bureau and nightstand, but again there was no sign of the keys. Grabbing an afghan, she hurried back to Dante and spread it over his lap. "There, that's better."

"You're too good to me."

She backed away from him and smiled. "I wish I could

stay, but I need to get ready for the ball. I want to make a good impression on Vlad—I mean, General Zelasko."

"He's bewitched by you," Dante assured her. "If anything, his interest is a little too intense. I'm not sure your father would approve."

"Vlad's scary," she agreed. "But that's all part of his sexy dictator appeal. You didn't say anything to discourage him, did you?"

Dante laughed. "I didn't need to. He's heard enough about me to know what I'd do if he hurt someone I loved."

Sasha forced herself to smile again. "I feel so much safer knowing you're in Kestonia, *zio*. If Vlad gets too rough I'll remind him that I've got powerful friends."

"If he gets too rough, report it to me and *I'll* remind him."

Sasha nodded, intrigued by the idea of pitting the monster Zelasko against the butcher Dante. That would be almost as much fun as taking this creep down herself—a reward she had promised herself if she managed to stay on task for the next twelve hours. She had even fantasized about commandeering a machine gun from one of the border guards and blasting her way into the cottage. Not that Jeff would allow that sort of tactic. But maybe she'd ditch him at the border and come back alone.

"Have fun at the ball tonight, Sasha," Dante was insisting from his seat in front of the fire. "You'll be the most beautiful woman there, I'm sure. Come back soon and tell me all about it."

"Don't worry, uncle," she said, waving cheerfully from the doorway. "I'm already looking forward to our next visit."

* * *

She knew she should return to her room immediately and prepare for the ball. So much of her plan rested on her ability to charm and manipulate Vlad, and for that, she truly did have to be the most beautiful woman in the room, at least in his eyes. He wanted a Kestonian princess, and the gold brocade dress was a good start. Add to that the traditional hairstyle she had seen in the portraits along the walls, where the women's hair was elaborately braided with jewels and then wrapped around their heads like crowns. It would take hours—and her beloved string of lapis beads—for Sasha to achieve that effect on her own. But it would be worth it.

Still, she wasn't quite ready to go back. Not just yet. The icy wind that was stinging her cheeks made her feel alive for the first time since she'd learned the truth about her mother's death. It was dangerous to dwell on that truth for too long—there would be time enough for that later. But her soul needed to acknowledge the amazing sacrifice Julia Bracciali had made for her, and almost without thinking, Sasha turned her steps away from the fortress and along the path that led to the dilapidated church on the mountainside.

It seemed like a fitting place to say thank you, given the fact that Julia had been devoutly religious. Of course, that piety had always seemed a bit hypocritical to Sasha in light of the barbaric underworld code that had touched their lives so subtly yet completely.

Even in death…

Seating herself in a humble wooden pew, Sasha looked around wistfully, confirming that the church had indeed been stripped of everything of material value. Still, the building itself with its rough walls and hand-hewn vaulted ceiling had a priceless quality that offered comfort to her aching heart.

And there was good news in all this misery, wasn't there? Her father was innocent. Not only had he *not* killed her mother, he had actually tried to stop it!

Maybe that butcher Dante was right. Maybe in a strange way, Mom did benefit from their stupid code all those years. You never believed in it, but maybe she did....

Sasha scowled, knowing that Dante's claim simply wasn't true. Julia Bracciali couldn't possibly have believed in that code. If she had, would she have sent Sasha to Athena Academy, a thousand miles away from Big Frankie's territory? A school where Sasha's eyes would be opened? Where she would be exposed to another, truer set of principles—

She sent you away to school so you wouldn't buy into Dad's twisted values. She knew it was too late for herself, but she was hoping you'd never be victimized by it.

Then Vittoria Martino had been killed, and the code had demanded Sasha's life in payment. That was the second time Julia saved her little girl. She was so brave! Yet so trapped. Dependent on men who dared to claim that they loved her—that they "worshipped" her beauty, bravery and innocence—yet could still strafe her with a machine gun, all in the name of honor. They were worse than hypocrites, they were cultural sociopaths! And even though Dante was the most evil of them all, Sasha needed to accept the truth: that her father was almost as bad.

Her first reaction to the tape—that Big Frankie was innocent of her mother's murder—wasn't really true at all. His lifestyle had all but assured that his wife and daughter would be touched by violence eventually. Vittoria Martino's death had been the result of Big Frankie's cold-blooded murder of a rival—not an "accident." Not a "mistake." And that chain of events had led to Julia Bracciali's brutal murder. Her father might not have pulled the trigger—and he surely wept like a baby while he was tied to that chair—but he had set the murderous sequence into motion.

What if Julia hadn't stepped up to save their daughter? Sasha suspected that her father might have allowed Antonio and Vincenzo to exact their vengeance, taking a daughter's life for a daughter's life. Maybe not with a machine gun. Perhaps a faulty gas line in Sasha's dormitory.

"Wow," she said to the crumbling rafters. "Did you really tell Jeff that your father believed in honor and justice? No wonder he was so worried about working with you. He knew the truth—that you weren't ready yet. You thought you knew your father—thought you understood his world—but you were still thinking like a daughter. Still making excuses."

Wiping a tear from her cheek, she gazed around the church again, wondering what the Kestonian people thought of Vlad's plan to raze it. Did they honestly believe they didn't need humility and spirituality anymore? That their faith in Vlad was enough of a foundation on which to build a lasting culture? If so, they were in for a rude awakening.

With a weary smile, she stood and walked toward the door, where she almost tripped over a crate filled with sticks of dynamite. Her first thought was to hide it so that the church would get a reprieve. Then she laughed at herself, remembering Allison's instructions that Sasha would need to find weapons in Kestonia.

This seemed a little extreme, but if she failed to locate the key card that night, dynamite could come in handy for breaking into the lab. She took a few sticks, then shuffled the rest so that the box still appeared full. The side pockets of her wool coat were just deep enough to hold the explosives, along with a blasting cap and a spool of fusing from a second crate.

Walking back into the open, she considered advancing their timetable. They could grab Teal now, blow the door to the lab, get the eggs and speed down the mountain on snowmobiles. Then they could toss another stick of dynamite at the guard tower and blast their way across the border. No hours of braiding her hair. No fancy ball. No seduction. Just a good old-fashioned shoot-out!

So much for your subtle, sophisticated plan, she mocked herself. *It's probably a good thing you can't get in touch with Summit. He'd think you were nuts!*

She laughed at the thought, allowing herself to enjoy, just for a moment, the fact that her handler was in Kestonia. His mere presence practically guaranteed that Teal would be safely returned to her family and friends, even if Jeff had to toss her drugged body over his shoulder and carry her across the border. He even knew how to work the dammed video feed cyclers! And even though she had forgotten to ask, she was pretty sure he had "armed himself" upon arrival in Kestonia.

Most importantly, he was there to ground her. To play Summit to her Camper. Because of him, she would stick to the plan. And even when she deviated from it, she would do so with confidence, knowing that he was out there—less than a hundred yards away—backing her up emotionally as well as physically.

Which brought her back to the question she had been asking herself since their unexpected kiss in her apartment. If she had to choose between having Jeff as her handler or as her lover, which would it be?

The answer was now clear. He had to be her handler until Teal was safe and Dante was dead or behind bars. Once they brought Dante down, the issue would become moot, because Sasha would have to go into hiding. There would be a contract the size of Chicago on her head, and the first thing the hungry hit men would do would be to track the movements of the man who had helped her betray them. Which meant that even if Jeff wanted to visit Sasha, and even if she wanted to allow it, it simply couldn't happen.

But if you had the choice, which would it be? Handler or lover?

She smiled in wistful defeat. Jeff would always be Summit to her, and while she would love to have him as a boyfriend, too, there would always be a sense of loss, knowing that he was handling cases but that she wasn't one of them. Jeff as just a lover? No, to be honest, she probably wouldn't want that.

Lucky thing, too, because you can't have it. So stop

daydreaming about your handsome prince, Cinderella. Time to get ready for the ball.

Standing on the perimeter of the grand Kestonian ballroom, Jeff Crossman tried to appear detached as he scanned the crowd for some sign, any sign, of his price-less asset. There were so many females in elaborate gowns and glittering tiaras—some with fans that par-tially hid their faces—that it was a struggle to keep track of them all.

By contrast, tracking Vlados Zelasko was a piece of cake. As much as Jeff despised him, he had to admit, the jerk was a natural attention grabber. The dictator was wearing a black tuxedo like dozens of other men in the room, including Jeff, but while *they* all looked like penguins, Zelasko looked like a movie star. Taller than most of the others, he had an air of power and impor-tance that simply couldn't be ignored. Hated? Sure. But never ignored.

The room itself was almost as impressive, from the fifteen-foot chandelier blazing overhead to the ten-piece orchestra filling the air with sounds of Tchaikovsky and Strauss. Most of the couples were still mingling, their conversations blending into a chattering roar of hilarity and gossip. But a dozen or so had taken to the dance floor, looking like something out of a period piece—the kind of scene Jeff usually wouldn't watch even if his life depended on it.

But for Teal's life, and for Sasha's, he was willing to make the sacrifice.

As he had done several times since his arrival at the

gala, Jeff eyeballed the various flunkies standing around
the perimeter of the room. Interpreters like himself. As-
sistants to dignitaries. Bodyguards. The last category
was the one that interested him because he suspected
they were armed despite the strict no-weapons rule announced by Zelasko. Of course, Jeff was armed, too, but
he still didn't like the idea that anyone else in the
vicinity might be carrying.

He was just about to change positions, to watch
from the other side of the room, when the chattering
died down to a hush, accompanied by a few muted
gasps. Even the musicians seemed to notice, and their
playing grew soft until it faded into complete silence.
Intrigued, Jeff turned toward the grand entrance in
time to see a stunningly beautiful Kestonian princess
arrive on the arm of Zelasko's second in command,
who, unlike his superior, was wearing his dress
uniform, complete with white gloves and gleaming
sword. And looking as proud as a father on his
daughter's wedding day as he led Sasha Bracciali to
the middle of the room, where Vlad Zelasko was
waiting for her.

Jeff shook his head in slow disbelief, wondering if he
hadn't somehow dozed off and was now dreaming. Not
that Sasha didn't always look great. And not that he hadn't
seen her all decked out before. But here, at this moment,
in her flowing golden dress…with her braided hair
forming a jewel-laden crown…her blue eyes glowing
with anticipation as she gracefully walked up to Zelasko
then curtsied with a blend of elegance and mischief…

Man, just look at her. Like something out of an effing fairy tale.

It was okay to stare. Everyone in the room was staring. He knew they were enraptured by the romance of the moment—the stunningly beautiful maiden being courted by a dashing ruler. But Jeff saw something else, something that made his gut twist. A brave, innocent young woman at the mercy of a megalomaniacal monster.

Sure Zelasko was infatuated for the moment. But he wasn't a noble prince. He was a ruthless gangster incapable of love, and definitely incapable of respect, especially for a woman. Beneath the thin facade of romance, Vlados Zelasko wanted to subjugate everyone and everything in his path.

And there in his path stood Sasha.

You're doing it again, Jeff warned himself harshly. *Underestimating her. Wanting to rescue her. Get over it, will you? Think about yesterday when she conned a roomful of underworld leaders. Hell, forget the meeting. Think about last night! That effing tape would have annihilated anyone else, but not Sasha. She pulled herself together and started plotting this mission like a seasoned professional. Because that's what she is. So get over yourself, will you?*

He didn't dare try to catch her eye. It wasn't necessary anyway. This was their signal, wasn't it? In the absence of micro-mikes and earbuds, they had decided that Jeff would arrive first at the ball. He would scope out the situation, then wait for Sasha's arrival. When it was clear that she had gotten Zelasko's undivided attention, Jeff would proceed with stage one of the op.

And she's definitely got that jerk in her sights, he told himself with a grim smile. *So why don't you get cracking, too? Time to go rescue the superkid.*

Chapter 11

"Of all the women in the world, you are the only one worthy of being with me tonight," Vlad told Sasha as they waltzed among the throng of dancers, all of whom seemed to be paying more attention to the commanding figure of Kestonia's leader than to their own partners.

"You honor me," Sasha replied with a coquettish smile, but inside, she was all business. This was the signal, wasn't it? Vlad's stare was fixed on her, which meant Jeff would now commence the op. If she dared glance toward the entryway, she'd see him leaving the gala. But of course, she didn't dare take her eyes off Vlad, even for a moment. His ego—always inflated—had swelled to even grander proportions with the attention he and Sasha were receiving, and while he seemed to acknowledge her supporting role in this romantic display, he clearly believed himself to be the focus of all adulation.

If you only knew, she told him as she beamed into his arrogant face. *My thoughts are so completely elsewhere right now. Cheering Jeff on as he changes into his Kestonian uniform and plants the video cyclers. Maybe he'll even manage to get his hands on a pistol! He just needs to keep his eye on the clock. To get to the tunnel before the gate closes at nine. And then...*

She felt her heart pound, knowing that he would be whisking Teal to freedom within minutes. Hopefully the teen would be traveling under her own power, but if Jeff had to carry her, he would. With his muscular, well-trained build, it probably wouldn't even slow him down! Her ambitious plan was actually going to succeed thanks to his involvement.

The only foreseeable problem was Vlad's lack of lust for Sasha. She had assumed he'd be anxious to take her to his room and ravish her as soon as good manners allowed him to abandon his guests, but he was so in love with the attention he was receiving, making love to a mere woman simply didn't seem to be on his agenda.

Then he surprised her by murmuring, "You said you fantasized about this evening for months. Has it met your every expectation?"

"It's more than I dared to dream," she assured him. "The music, the dancers, the gowns, the pageantry. And *you.* Every woman's fantasy, a dashing, fearless prince among men. I only hope," she added, her voice throaty with anticipation, "when the time comes for the rest of the fantasy, it will be half as amazing as this."

"The rest of it?"

"I've planned every detail," she said breathlessly. "We'll sneak away from the others and go to your suite. You'll kiss me as I've never been kissed before. Then I'll pour you a glass of champagne, and you'll sit back on the bed and watch me while I undress for you." She paused for a long, amorous sigh. "You won't be able to take your eyes off me, even when you're sipping your drink. I'll mesmerize you, peeling off layer after layer until I'm only wearing a wisp of panty."

She smiled shyly. "I bought special lingerie especially for tonight, and it's so beautiful. So lacy. Then I'll come to the bed and pleasure you. You won't need to do a thing. Just lie back and relax. Only when I've satisfied you like you've never been satisfied before will you start making love to me. And for the rest of the night, we'll be lost in one another's passion. *That*," she finished with another sigh, "is my fantasy."

He had been staring at her, his face expressionless. Now he came to a dead stop, heedless of the other couples dancing around them, and declared, "We are leaving now." Before Sasha could say another word, he waved his hand in an imperious gesture and called out, "Nikko!"

"Are you sure we should leave?" she asked with feigned confusion. "Your guests—"

"I have honored them long enough with my presence. Now it is time to honor you. And your fantasy."

"I wish Nikko could stay and dance with someone. He needs some romance in his life, too."

Vlad chuckled. "He could be dancing at this very moment if he would choose an acceptable partner. But he is in love with a servant. It was impossible to invite her tonight. She works for my sister. Perhaps you have seen her—"

"You mean Niski?" Sasha smiled with delight. "She told me she was engaged. What a perfect match! He's so wonderful, and so is she. She made this gown, you know."

"Did she?" Vlad pursed his lips, then turned to his second in command, who was waiting patiently a few feet away for instructions. Then the dictator began speaking rapidly in Kestonian.

Nikko's eyes grew huge, and to Sasha's amazement, he grabbed her hand and kissed it. Then with a final word to Vlad, he spun on his heels and half ran toward the entry hall.

"What did you say to him?" Sasha demanded.

"I have given them permission to marry." Vlad flashed a mischievous grin. "He has been loyal. And this gown pleases me greatly. Why should they not be rewarded?"

"Oh, Vlad!"

"I imagine he will lose no time finding a *pralat* to perform the ceremony. He will have his night of love, and so will I." The dictator's eyes were shining with lust as he took Sasha by the elbow and suggested softly, "Shall we go?"

Jeff had stolen a Kestonian officer's uniform earlier that day, along with a long wool military overcoat, boots and a hat. Striding now toward the tunnel that led from the living quarters to the offices, he tried not to think about Sasha's impending seduction of Zelasko. She would handle it well, he was sure. But he would have felt better if he could hear what was going on, the way he'd always done for their ops. And he wished he could be in closer proximity, too, in case something went wrong.

Well, at least you're in Kestonia, he reminded himself. *Not that it was such a thrill for her, all things considered.*

He was still kicking himself for the fiasco with the tape recording, but knew he had to get past that. He was a colonel in the Kestonian army, for now, and from what he had seen, those guys were virtual robots, emotionwise. It was time he embraced that role.

Arriving at the tunnel, he discovered that the gate had already descended—almost thirty minutes ahead of schedule—barring his path. Without a key card, he couldn't gain entry this way. Fortunately, he had scoped out the exterior door earlier that afternoon to see what sort of resistance he and Teal might encounter when they exited the office hall.

He had liked what he'd seen. Two bored-looking guards seated on either side of the door. This entry also had a key card panel, but it had apparently been deactivated, because the light at the bottom had been green, and Jeff had seen the guards spring to attention and open the door whenever authorized personnel approached.

Without missing a step he continued down the hall that led from the gate to an exterior door. Stepping outside, he found that it was snowing heavily, giving him even more of a reason to adopt a no-nonsense, impatient demeanor as he hurried down the path. He had mastered a little Kestonian, which was very similar to Polish, so as soon as he reached the manned doorway, he barked at the two guards in their native tongue, "Do your jobs! You are a disgrace to your uniforms!"

As they bolted out of their stupors and fought over the honor of opening the door, Jeff saw one of them tuck a small metal flask into a coat pocket.

They've been drinking? Perfect.

His only thanks to them was a disgusted grunt. Then he was inside the fortress again, headed for the office where Sasha had located Teal. If the kid was still there, this part of the op would be a complete success, especially if the anti-absorption drug had protected her from being sedated.

He had installed one of the NSA's video cyclers on the feed for this hallway just a few hours earlier, so presumably no one was observing him. Still, he was careful to hide his movements as he affixed Svetlina Zelasko's palm print to his own left hand. Then he set his briefcase onto the floor outside Teal's doorway, activated the scanner, and when the light turned from red to green, he pushed open the door, grabbed his briefcase and strode inside.

One glance at the slender figure on the cot told him he might have his first serious problem. The kid's eyes were open but vacant, and she barely moved an inch despite the shock of having a male visitor at this hour of the evening.

So carry her, he reminded himself with a shrug. *It's gonna attract a lot of attention, but that was bound to happen eventually anyway, so just get to it.*

Kneeling next to the cot, he whispered her name in

as gentle a voice as he could manage, trying not to alarm her. But he apparently didn't succeed, because her fist shot out, slamming him in the chest, then she scampered out of the bed and positioned herself in the middle of the floor, assuming a martial arts stance and glaring at him through eyes that were now clear and cool.

"Stay back," she warned him angrily.

"Look who's wide awake." He grinned. "I take it Sasha's pills worked?"

"Sasha?"

"Yeah. I'm a friend of hers. She was afraid I'd have to carry you out of here. Now—" he paused to rub his chest where Teal had punched him "—it looks like *you* might have to carry *me*."

"Oh!" The girl flushed. "Did I hurt you?"

"It's gonna leave a mark," he teased her. "But I'm fine. Are you okay?"

"You're Sasha's friend?" she asked, as though the information was finally sinking in.

Then she surprised him again, this time by crossing to him and wrapping her arms around his waist. "Thank you. Thank you. I was so scared."

"Hey." He pried her face away from his chest and gave her a reassuring smile. "Everything's fine. We're gonna get you out of here. All you have to do is change into the clothes I brought for you. Okay?" Patting her hair, he added warmly, "It's almost over, kid. I promise."

Teal stepped back and bit her lip, her blue eyes shining with hope. "We're leaving right now? Where's Sasha?"

"She's stealing a key card so we can get into that lab. We're meeting her up there."

"The lab?" Teal's face lit up even more. "To get my eggs?"

"You bet. So here." He flipped open his briefcase and pulled out jeans, tennis shoes and a long-sleeved knit shirt. "These are Sasha's. Put 'em on. We'll steal you a coat once we get outside."

"Real clothes," she murmured. "It's been so long…."

"Yeah, I'll bet it seemed like a lifetime. But it's over now," he promised, turning so that she could change out of her white hospital gown.

After a minute, Teal said softly, "I'm ready. What do we do now?"

"We're gonna walk right out of here and down the hall to a door to the outside. It's guarded by two men, but they shouldn't be much of a problem. We'll have the element of surprise. Plus, they've been drinking. You'll take the small one on our left, I'll take the big one."

"You mean, fight him?"

"Yeah. You need to knock him out. Should be a walk in the park for you," he assured her with a laugh. "Just try not to hit him in the nose, okay? We're gonna prop them against the wall, like they're punchy from all the booze. It'll be better if their faces aren't bleeding. Use that left hook of yours to crack him on the side of the head, like this." He touched his fist to her right ear. "Then slam him in the jaw or the upper chest."

"What if I kill him?"

Jeff laughed again. "That's okay as long as his face isn't bleeding. Plus, you're gonna wear his coat, so you don't want it to have blood all over it, right?"

He could see the confusion in her eyes, and added

reassuringly, "If it all goes south, just yell my name then jump back. I'll step in. I promise."

"Your name?"

Jeff winced. "Sorry, I should have introduced myself. Jeff Crossman, FBI."

She gave a shy smile. "Thanks for coming after me."

He patted her arm. "Let's get going. We need to walk fast. Like we own the place. There shouldn't be anyone in the hall, but if there is, just keep walking. I've got a pistol," he added. "A shot will attract attention, so I don't want to use it if we can avoid it. But one way or another, you're leaving this place right now. And you'll be out of Kestonia by midnight. So?" He walked over to the door and rested his hand on the knob. "Ready?"

When she nodded, he pulled open the door and stepped into the hall, checking to be sure it was deserted. Then he motioned for her to follow him and without another word, he headed toward the exit.

He knew she would have trouble keeping up with his long strides, but he maintained his pace for two reasons. The first was to get her blood pumping, so she'd be physically ready for the fight ahead of them.

The second reason was an emotional one. If Jeff hesitated, he might start focusing on what a sweetheart Teal was, and he'd offer to take out both of the guards himself. He could undoubtedly handle them, but he had no idea how many adversaries they'd encounter at the lab or at the border. He might really need her then, and this preliminary bout would give her some practice while also bolstering her confidence.

They reached the exit in less than ten seconds, and he gave her an encouraging grin. "Ready?"

She exhaled then nodded, and Jeff pulled open the door. Then he winked and motioned for her to precede him.

She didn't hesitate. Instead, she strode up to the smaller guard, who had jumped to his feet, and she struck him so hard on the side of his head Jeff could actually hear bones crunch. Grinning, he grabbed his own victim by the lapels and slammed the guy against the stone wall of the fortress, then watched in satisfaction as he slid down to the ground.

Turning back to Teal, he saw that she was already pulling the wool overcoat off her unconscious prey, and he couldn't blame her. Not only had the temperature been plummeting, but an icy wind was roaring down the mountain, striking them full in the face.

"Here." He shoved a stocking hat into her hands. "Hide your hair under this, and make sure your ears are protected."

"Okay." She put it on quickly.

"Hey, Teal?" He touched her cheek. "Nice job."

"Thanks."

Jeff put the guards back in their chairs on either side of the door, then propped them up against the wall. "We'll head up to the lab now, okay? There may be more guards, so be ready. Just follow my lead. Right?"

"Right." Teal stuffed her hands into the pocket of the oversize coat, then gave him a dazzling smile. "I'm ready."

"Yeah, I can see that." He took her by the arm and led her into the shadows as he scanned the twisty mountain path to the lab. There wasn't a soul in sight, so he nodded with satisfaction, then turned to his super-partner and suggested briskly, "Let's get it done, shall we?"

"Jeff?"

"Yeah?"

"You're sure Sasha's okay? You said she's stealing a key card. That sounds dangerous. Especially if it's from…" Teal winced expressively. "She's with Zelasko, isn't she?"

"Yeah, but don't worry about her. She's got him wrapped around her little finger. Believe me, I know the feeling."

"Because you're in love with her, too?" Teal's eyes were suddenly shining. "I sense it every time you say her name. No wonder she didn't think Zelasko was handsome. She was too busy thinking about you."

Jeff cleared his throat. "At the moment, she's pretty mad at me. And she's gonna be *really* pissed if we're late to the party, so…" He urged the teen onto the snow-covered path.

"Okay, okay." Teal glanced back at the fortress with concern. "He's such a scary man. Nice one minute, mean the next."

"Hey." Jeff shook his head in warning. "Don't do this to me. I'm jonesing to rescue her as it is. But we've got a plan and it's a good one. Plus, I've got complete faith in Sasha. So we're gonna head up to the lab. Got it?"

"Got it." Teal gave another, longer sigh. "It's soooo romantic."

"I'm glad someone thinks so," he said with a rueful

chuckle. For a brief moment he wondered if it would
be so bad for him to burst into Zelasko's suite, knock
the jerk out cold, grab Sasha and the key card, and just
head for the border with Teal in tow. Wasn't that what
his instincts were telling him to do? Hadn't his gut been
warning him for hours that a vicious animal like
Zelasko could never really be seduced by a woman,
even one as charming and clever as Sasha Bracciali?

"You're a rotten influence," he muttered to Teal. "Are
we gonna stick to Sasha's plan or aren't we?"

The teenager glanced at the fortress again, her blue
eyes clouded with concern. Then she turned back to Jeff
and told him with a wistful smile, "I want to go home
as soon as possible. But not without Sasha. So let's do
what's best for *her,* okay?"

Chapter 12

"Vlad! *Wait!*"

"I cannot wait. You are too beautiful," the dictator declared, clawing at the front of Sasha's gown while his body pinned her hips to the wall of his bedroom.

She fought to maintain some shred of control. "I want this as much as you do. Maybe even more! But you're scaring me—"

"I am impatient. It is my only flaw." He gave her a lascivious grin. "It is also the quality that made Kestonia great overnight. I am certain you will enjoy it if you relax—"

"Fine, but first…" Sasha wriggled free and reminded him, "I've been planning this for weeks, remember? It's the reason I traveled all this way. To seduce you." With an offended pout, she added unhappily, "At least allow me that illusion."

She could see he was annoyed, but she forged ahead anyway, flashing a hopeful smile. "I spent fifteen hundred dollars on the sexy lingerie I'm wearing under this gown. All for you. So I could dance for you. Undress for you. Drive you wild with desire. Is that so wrong?"

Vlad eyed her for a moment, then gave a defeated laugh. "You have intrigued me with this talk. And so you may indulge your fantasy. But do not keep me waiting forever."

"Five minutes," she promised, stepping up to him and running her finger under the satin lapel of his tuxedo jacket. She didn't need to feign the purr in her voice as she fingered the fabric. It was simply the most stunning men's wear she had ever seen, let alone touched, in her life. Finely tailored, of jet-black supersoft wool, it fit Vlad's broad chest and shoulders perfectly, and she suspected that his pleated shirt of white silk would be equally exquisite.

Sasha credited this tuxedo with the romantic performance she had been able to give at the gala. Even though most of her brain had been focused on Teal's rescue, the designer in her had mentally drooled over Vlad because of his outfit. And he had seemed equally enchanted by her traditional gown, so much so that as they strolled from the ballroom to his suite, she had been certain she had the situation under control.

Right up to the moment when he had rammed her against the wall!

Determined not to make any more miscalculations, she carefully removed his jacket and laid it on a bench at the foot of the bed. Then she unfastened the pearl buttons of his shirt, sighing with every glimpse of his strong, hairy chest. Finally, she pushed him back until he was seated on the mattress, then she knelt and unlaced his shoes and pulled them off.

"Now sit back and watch me," she ordered him playfully, backing away until she had reached a built-in wet bar along the side of the room, where she switched on a sound system that began playing one of the waltzes that had filled the air at the gala. Delighted, she turned back to him, and as he watched, his eyes dark with fascination, she ran her fingers over her bodice and around to the back of her gown, then slowly unzipped it, all the while eyeing him with exaggerated innocence.

When she allowed the gown to slip to the floor, revealing a ruffled black petticoat and sexy strapless corset, she could see Vlad was about to jump off the bed and attack her again, so she held up her hand to stop him.

"Silly me. I almost forgot your drink! No wonder you're so impatient." Turning to the bar, she swayed her hips to the music, hoping that her movements would hold his interest as she covertly retrieved a capsule from her evening bag and broke it open over a crystal flute— one of a pair that had been set out, presumably for their tryst. Filling both from the champagne bottle chilling nearby in a bucket, she brought the one laced with knockout powder to Vlad.

Retreating quickly again for fear he'd make another grab for her, she winced when he set his drink on the nightstand without taking even one sip. She didn't dare make a fuss about it for fear of arousing his suspicions, so she forced herself to smile and continue dancing while also taking a small sip of her own drink to set a good example. But her date clearly wasn't interested in anything except Sasha's half-naked body.

Chagrined but still smiling, she unhooked her petticoat and let it float to the floor, uncovering black panties, a lacy garter belt and sheer stockings. She removed the stockings slowly, her gaze always fixed on her prey, willing him silently to take a taste of his champagne.

Make him drink it! she ordered herself nervously. *You're going to run out of clothes pretty soon. Then what?*

She was grateful at least that he seemed to finally be relaxing, settling back against the pillows, signaling that he wasn't going to pounce on her, at least for the moment. Still, she didn't dare drag this out too long.

It occurred to her that she could just grab the champagne bottle and clobber him with it. Given his relaxed attitude, she might actually be able to execute such a move. But she couldn't be sure. He hadn't gotten to this point in his career by being careless or unwary, had he?

Seduction still seemed like her best weapon, so she began to loosen the hairpins that held her braid in place. Unwinding the long tresses as she danced, she sifted her fingers through them until the locks draped softly over her chest all the way to her waist. Then she let out a quick breath, flashed another, more provocative smile and unlaced the corset, which she removed and let drop to the floor.

Her hair partially concealed her bare breasts, although the tips of her nipples were visible, and Vlad's stare was so focused on them, she was surprised they didn't melt from the heat. Nervous but hopeful, she took her champagne glass from the sideboard and danced over to him, then held the flute forward in a toasting gesture and murmured, "To us. May tonight be filled with magic."

To Sasha's relief, Vlad retrieved his glass from the nightstand and touched it to hers, but when she took a long sip, he turned his attention back to her breasts. His breath was so ragged she could hear it, and she knew she was out of time, so she held up her glass in toast again and exclaimed, "To the passion of a thousand stallions!" Then she gulped the rest of her drink and hurled the flute against the bedroom wall where it shattered wildly.

A huge grin spread across Vlad's face and he drained his glass as Sasha had done, then flung it against the same wall. Even as it crashed, he grabbed Sasha and threw her onto the bed, then mounted her while crowing, "You will now see why my people both love and fear me!"

Sasha screamed out loud, terrified and disoriented by the fact that he was unaffected by the powder. Should she have used two capsules? He was so much larger than she—why had she assumed that the dose that had knocked her out would do the same to a muscular, six-foot-two warrior?

His hands were pawing her bare breasts while his mouth covered hers. Dominated hers. Then without warning his body went completely limp, crushing her under its lifeless weight.

For a moment, she just lay there, struggling to catch a breath. To gather her thoughts. To reassure herself that it had really worked. Then she rolled him off her and tried to remember what she was supposed to do next.

The key card...

Still shaky, she crawled to the foot of the bed and grabbed his jacket. No longer enchanted by the fine garment, she rifled through it. There was no key card, but she did find a pill bottle in the inside pocket. According to the label, it was a prescription for Nikko.

For an erectile dysfunction drug.

Well, that explains the urgency. Not to mention, the guided missile, she complained to the sleeping man. *I wonder if the knockout powder will get rid of that, too. Otherwise, you might still have it when you wake up.*

Genuinely smiling for the first time since they'd reached the bedroom, she rolled him over and checked his pants pockets, amused by the persistent bulge that was impossible to ignore. Unfortunately, the key card wasn't there, so she moved to his dresser, and then into the small office that adjoined the bedroom.

His computer was there, and while the screen was black, she thought she heard a soft whir from the processor unit so she touched the keyboard and an e-mail display appeared before her.

No password? That's the kind of impatience that's going to destroy Kestonia overnight, she warned Vlad with a laugh, although she knew that security for his room was usually so tight, the computer simply wasn't at risk.

But tonight was different. Nikko was off somewhere marrying Niski, and Vlad had ordered his men not to disturb him until dawn, when he needed to be awakened for the demolition of the old church.

Even if Vlad had lied to her and there was actually a guard at the door, Sasha knew she could use her final knockout capsule on him, offering him a glass of champagne then moving his collapsed body into the room for the night. The idea of humiliating poor Nikko hadn't appealed to her, but drugging a strange guard was different. It would be a gentle fate compared to the one that she and her associates would inflict on anyone else who tried to stop them at the lab or at the border.

Even if Jeff had to carry Teal, they're probably at the lab by now, so get back to work, she ordered herself, pawing through the desk drawer in search of the key card. To her relief, it was there, and she was about to go back to the bedroom to get dressed and then get out of there when a dinging sound from the computer told her Vlad had just received an e-mail.

"At this hour? On the night of the gala?" Sasha sat at the desk and clicked the mouse, opening a message from an address composed completely of numbers. But the body of the message was in English, and its contents were disconcerting at best.

Be warned. One of your guests—the one named Sasha Bracciali—is working for the NSA. She has come to rescue the girl. Stop her, or all of our hard work will be for naught.—A

"Tattletale," Sasha scolded the sender. Then she reached over to turn on a nearby printer, but before she could make a copy of the message, tiny virtual spiders began crawling all over it, erasing the words as they moved until nothing was left.

"Cute trick, A. I guess there's no point in looking for

other messages from you. It doesn't matter anyway. I *am* going to rescue the girl. And all of your hard work *will* be for naught. So you lose. Buh-bye."

Jumping to her feet, she returned to the bedroom and located a sheet of latex in her evening bag. After making an impression of Zelasko's palm, she used the NSA pen to transfer the code sequence from the key card to her credit card, then she returned the card to his desk. Finally, she dressed herself in the gold brocade gown without bothering with any underwear. Instead, she scooped up her expensive lingerie and sprinkled it all over the bed and its occupant.

You look like you had a great night, Generalissimo. Maybe when they wake you up at dawn, you'll actually think you had wild sex with me! Unless the ED drug is still working, in which case, you'll just be in terrible pain. What a shame.

Laughing, she patted his cheek, then she moved to the wet bar to prepare the final glass of knockout champagne.

There was no guard at the door, but Sasha carried the glass with her back to her room just in case she ran into anyone suspicious. Fortunately, the halls were relatively empty. That is, until she ran into Svetlina and two gentlemen admirers, all of whom had clearly had too much to drink.

"I am so perfect in this gown," Vlad's sister told Sasha. "I was the most beautiful woman at the gala."

"I agree."

"I am grateful to you."

Sasha smiled. "The perfect dress for the perfect

woman. A designer's dream come true." When Svetlina frowned, Sasha added quickly, "That was a compliment."

"To you? Or to me?" the major demanded.

"To you, of course."

"Good." She frowned again. "Where is my brother? I did not know he would allow you away from his sights."

"He enjoyed attacking me in this gown. Now I'm going to change into something sexier for him." Sasha gave her a conspiratorial smile. "He's so impatient, though. I'd better hurry or he'll send his soldiers after me to drag me back to his bed."

"He is impatient," Svetlina agreed. Then she reached for the arms of her two escorts and said with a sly laugh, "It is our family curse to have this appetite. We must all have sex right away. We will see you again. At midnight."

"Midnight? I don't think Vlad and I will be done by then."

Svetlina's hand flew to her mouth. "I have forgotten. It is your surprise."

"Pardon?"

"To see the church burst away. Vlad has decided that midnight is more— What is the word? Dramatical? Yes, more dramatical than dawn. Do not tell him I have spoken of it to you. He believed you would be pleased by the lights and the noise."

"I won't say a word," Sasha promised. "You and your friends better get busy if you only have two hours. See you at midnight."

She hurried down the hall to her room, chagrined to know that Vlad's men would come for him at midnight rather than at dawn. Surely they would realize that their leader had been drugged, and they'd sound an alarm that would extend to the border.

The plan called for you to get Teal out of Kestonia by midnight anyway, she reminded herself. *But it would be nice to have some wiggle room. Plus, it'll make it more challenging when you come back for the Butcher.*

She couldn't afford to worry about that yet, so she concentrated on changing into black jeans and a heather-gray Henley top. She had sent her only pair of tennis shoes with Jeff, so she stuffed her sturdy Kestonian oxfords into the pockets of her long wool coat along with her passport, then put on a pair of black high heels that were so sexy, anyone who saw her would assume she was returning to Vlad for more lovemaking. Once she reached the door to the garden she could ditch the heels in favor of the oxfords.

And now for the weapons, she reminded herself, grabbing the dynamite from its hiding place behind the room's small refrigerator. *Even though you won't need to blow anything up now because*—she pulled out her credit card and admired it proudly—*you've got this!*

She had never felt so confident during an op, and forced herself to remember that there were still things that could go wrong. Not to mention, things that may have already gone wrong on Jeff's end.

But that seemed unlikely. He was too careful, too methodical, to leave anything to chance. He and Teal were awaiting her at the lab—she just knew it—and that knowledge fueled another burst of confidence as she strode out of her bedroom and back into the hall.

* * *

Sasha's bravado took a blow as she battled her way up the mountain with the icy wind stinging her eyes, making her gasp aloud again and again. The hail-like snow combined with the darkness had lowered visibility nearly to zero despite the full moon that was trying to be of assistance.

Then Sasha heard shouting from the direction of the lab door. The sound was moving toward her, and she realized someone was running down the path, calling out in Kestonian. All she could think was that a guard must have spotted Jeff and Teal.

You were supposed to find a safe hiding place and wait for me, she rebuked them. Then she stepped directly into the man's path. He drew up short and fumbled with his machine gun, but Sasha was ready for him and kicked it cleanly out of his hands. Then she advanced on him, swinging her right fist as though aiming for his face. As she had hoped, he erroneously assumed she was right-handed, and he tried to block the blow with his own right arm, allowing her to grab him above the wrist with her left hand, shift her weight, then flip him onto his back. Diving for the machine gun, she used the butt of the weapon to bash his skull soundly.

He didn't move after that, even when she poked him with her foot, so she dropped to her knees and gagged him. Then she tied his hands behind him with his belt, bound his ankles with his wool scarf, and shoved him into the brush that lined the path.

Where there's one, there could be more, she reminded herself. Concern for Teal and Jeff bubbled through her adrenaline-laced high. Jumping to her feet, she reached for the machine gun, turned, then gasped at the sight of her two accomplices standing right there on the path, wide grins on both of their faces.

"Nice work, Camper," Jeff said, his green eyes twinkling.

"Teal!" Sasha strode up to the teenager and gave her a hearty embrace. "Are you okay?"

"She's amazing," Jeff said reverently.

"Except I punched Jeff by mistake," Teal told Sasha. "But he's okay, I think."

Sasha gave Jeff a smile. "So far so good?"

"Yeah. Did you get the key card?"

Sasha nodded. "And some dynamite, just in case. Now we have a machine gun, too."

"We have a whole pile of them up by the lab," Teal told her proudly. "Come and see."

Intrigued, Sasha followed them to a cache of six guards who were gagged and trussed just like the one Sasha had overpowered. "You were supposed to wait for me!" she reminded her companions with a frustrated laugh.

"If there had been a lot of them, we would have," Teal explained. "But six? It was so easy."

"Definitely helps to have a superkid on our side," Jeff added with a wink.

"He fought four of them. I only did two. He's been so wonderful, Sasha," Teal gushed.

"Really? Well, from now on, he and I will do all the fighting. Understand?"

"You have to let me help!"

Sasha pretended to glare. "Those are my favorite jeans you're wearing, and I want them back in perfect condition. *No* bloodstains."

Teal sighed. "We were so worried about you, we almost came to get you. But Jeff said you could handle Zelasko, and he was right."

Sasha flashed him a grateful smile. "Thanks for sticking to the plan. It's working, right?"

"Definitely. But we've still got a couple of hurdles to clear," Jeff reminded her. "For one thing, we don't know how many guards are inside the lab, or what other security measures they're using in there."

"And we have to be across the border by midnight for sure," Sasha added, explaining rapidly about the change in the timing of the demolition.

"That's a bad break," Jeff murmured. "We can't afford to spend much time up here."

"I'm not leaving without my eggs," Teal countered stubbornly.

Jeff scowled, but didn't protest. "Let's get moving then. Camper? We saw a camera over the lab door. I doubt if the feed goes back to the fortress—it's probably dedicated to the lab. And at this hour, I'm ninety-nine percent sure the monitor isn't manned. Still, we can't just waltz up to it. We've got to assume we're being watched."

"I agree."

"There's a palm print device up there as well as the slot for the key card," Jeff continued. "If someone's monitoring from inside, they'll see that the print doesn't match the card."

"I got Zelasko's palm print, so we're okay on that front. But the video camera—"

"Don't worry. Jeff has a plan," Teal assured her, and Sasha had to smile at the adoration in the girl's tone. Not that she blamed her. Sasha had felt that way about Jeff herself, hadn't she? The more she saw him in action, the more she watched him plan his ops, the more impressed she had become.

Jeff cleared his throat. "I figure Zelasko's men have all heard about your romance with him by now. So you're gonna play you, Teal's gonna play Teal. And I'm gonna be Zelasko. Think I can pull it off?"

Sasha nodded, then reached up to straighten his cap so that it completely hid his blond hair. "You're only slightly taller. And your coat is just like his. Don't look at the camera. Like you said, when they see *me,* they'll think you're him. And when you use his key card, that'll confirm it. If I seem enthralled, and you seem confident, and—Teal? You need to act loopy, like you were the other day." She paused, then nodded emphatically. "Absolutely. We can pull it off."

As they approached the arched door imbedded in the mountain, Sasha forced herself to smile and talk to Jeff as though she were flirting with Zelasko. He had one arm around her waist and nuzzled her a little as they walked, but his attention was partly on Teal, who was trudging ahead of them like a zombie. They had tied her hands, and "Zelasko" had a gun trained on her, but it hardly seemed necessary, since she didn't appear to have the presence of mind to mount an escape attempt.

Jeff's idea was that anyone monitoring the situation would think the dictator was trying to impress his American mistress by putting on a demonstration of Teal's powers. If their performance was convincing, the onlookers would be confused enough to hesitate, and that moment of hesitation would give Jeff a chance to swipe the key card and use the palm print. Then the threesome would storm the lab, overpowering any resistance before word could be sent to the fortress.

When they reached the door, Jeff pulled Sasha against himself and kissed her.

She gladly wrapped her arms around his neck and returned the kiss. She was so grateful to him, and she suspected that after tonight she would never see him again. It was a shame, because there was so much to say. So many loose ends to wrap up. But at least they had rescued Teal together, and if they managed to take down Dante, also, that would have to be enough to last them the rest of their lives.

She knew his thoughts were quite the opposite. His was the thorough, adoring kiss of a man who believed he was *beginning* a long, sexy affair, not ending one. In fact, he was *so* loving, so tender, she wanted to warn him that in this one sense, his impression of Vlados Zelasko was completely and utterly unconvincing.

But it was over before she could bring herself to say anything. Then as they had planned, she turned her face up toward the camera, pretending to admire the height of the arched door frame. At the same moment, Jeff slid the card in the slot, then placed the palm print over the scanner.

A loud click announced that the lock had been

released, and Jeff grabbed the door handle and pushed, then motioned for the females to precede him into the lab. There were two guards, both at attention, neither of whom had drawn a weapon. There were also two men in lab coats. All four were staring at the newcomers, and it was clear they were too afraid to be vigilant or suspicious.

Sasha walked right up to the two soldiers and began babbling as though she had been drinking. Teal distracted the two civilians by pretending to be so unsteady on her feet that they rushed to her assistance. Meanwhile, Jeff strode right past the entire group and down the only hallway. When he finally turned back to them, he was pointing the pistol and barking orders in Kestonian, the signal that he had checked the entry and hall for additional cameras and hadn't found any.

The soldiers and lab workers fell to their knees, and while Jeff kept the pistol on the guards, Sasha and Teal tied up and gagged the civilians, who seemed relieved that they were going to survive the assault. Then Jeff ordered one guard to tie up the other. When that was done, Jeff cracked the butt of his pistol onto the skull of the unbound guard, who slumped to the ground. Sasha then tied up that one, as well.

"Come on." Jeff led Sasha and Teal down the hall, narrating as they walked. "Office, office, laboratory, restrooms, a small kitchen and…" He sent Sasha a warning glance before saying, "That room at the end looks like a containment facility."

"Like a refrigeration room?" Teal asked. "Maybe that's where my eggs are!"

"I'll check it out," he told her gruffly. "You said you're good with computers, right? Try to hack into the records in one of those offices, will you? Sasha? You help her."

Teal shook her head. "But—"

"Just do it," Jeff interrupted. "Until we find out what's in the containment lab, no one goes in there but me. Got it?"

Teal pouted. "Okay, okay."

Sasha touched her shoulder. "It makes sense, honey. If you can find records of their experiments, we'll know *where* the eggs are, we'll know how many and we'll know what's been done to them. Plus, you might find more information about the people behind all this. We need that, right? So we can stop them. Otherwise, you'll spend the rest of your life looking over your shoulder, wondering if they'll come after you again."

"I didn't think of that," Teal admitted. "Sorry, Jeff. I didn't mean to be a pain."

He grinned. "You're like the bratty kid sister I never had. But I forgive you. Just get going."

Teal walked back toward the closest office, then turned to Sasha and murmured, "Are you coming?"

"In a sec. I've got to ask Jeff something first."

The teenager nodded then disappeared into the room.

"Okay," Sasha said quietly. "Tell me what's wrong."

Jeff cleared his throat. "It's not a refrigeration unit, it's a Level Four biosafety lab. Which means they're storing a lot more than eggs in here."

"You mean, viruses? Biological weapons? In Vlad Zelasko's hands?" Sasha groaned. "He's so power hungry, Jeff. I think he really wants to take over the world. Or at least, Europe. But I thought it was just megalomania."

"Teal can't go in there, that's for sure. You and I have to minimize exposure, too. Which means I go, you stay out here. That's an order." Stepping closer, he added with a warm smile, "Just for the record, that's the last order I'll ever give you. You have my word on that."

Sasha scanned his expression warily. "What do you mean?"

"Remember when you told me to find a way to be your handler *and* your boyfriend?"

"Jeff—"

"Wait. Let me say this." His words came out in a torrent. "As your handler, I'd be your superior. I couldn't ethically pursue a sexual relationship with you. And trust me, I'm going to pursue one."

"Jeff—"

"Ten more seconds," he insisted. "You're mad at me. I don't blame you. But I'm going to make things up to you. From now on, we're partners. Equals. And in my book, partners can get away with a lot more, relationship-wise. So—" he gave her a proud smile "—that's the new plan."

"It's soooo romantic," Teal announced from behind them, her tone breathless. "Sasha, you *have* to say yes."

Chapter 13

Sasha sent Teal a warning glare. "Aren't you supposed to be hacking into the computer?"

"I already found my records. And guess what? The surgery to remove my eggs is scheduled for next Wednesday." The girl's blue eyes danced with happiness. "You rescued me before they got them."

"You're not rescued yet," Sasha reminded her. "We need to get you to the border before midnight. And before then, Jeff needs to check out the containment lab, and I need to search for records about A. Are you going to help me?"

Teal nodded, subdued.

Sasha turned to Jeff. "We'll talk later. Okay?"

"Sure." He gave Teal a reassuring smile. "We're almost out of here, kid. Just give me a few minutes."

Sasha watched him push a metal release button next to the containment door, which then slowly opened with a hissing sound. It closed just as slowly behind him.

"He loves you," Teal murmured.

"Or at least he thinks he does." Sasha grimaced. "I'm sorry I snapped at you, honey. But things between me and Jeff are complicated—not to mention hopeless. So don't encourage him, okay?"

"I can sense things about people. About their feelings. Jeff doesn't just *think* he loves you. He honestly does. The weird part is—" Teal took a deep breath "—I can't tell how you feel about *him.*"

"It's moot. Once we leave here, I'm going into a witness protection program and I'll never see him again."

"Oh, no." Teal bit her lip. "Will you see *me?*"

Touched, Sasha admitted, "Probably not. But Allison will make sure we always know the other is happy and healthy. That has to be enough." Resting her hands on the girl's shoulders, she explained simply, "I dedicated myself to helping you. Because you deserve it. Because you're a sweet, wonderful, innocent person. And once you're safe, I'm going to dedicate myself to punishing the man who butchered my mother. Because *she* was sweet and innocent, too. I hope you understand that."

"I used to be sweet," Teal said, her voice suddenly choked with emotion. "But I've been awful to you and Jeff. Talking back and complaining, when you both risked your lives for me."

"Hey!" Sasha pulled her into an amused embrace. "What are you talking about?"

"I pouted, too."

"You call that a pout?" Sasha scoffed. "Remind me to give you a quick lesson after we get out of here."

"You don't understand. I used to be an angel. That's what everyone said."

"Even angels get cranky when they're kidnapped and tormented," Sasha told her fondly. "I like you this way, anyway. Brave and fun and flawed. That makes you perfect in my book." She draped her arm around Teal's shoulders. "Come on. Let's go find those files on A— and on Zelasko's bioweapons, too—so we can go home."

Teal pulled free and glanced at the pressurized door. "I can find the files myself. You should help Jeff."

Sasha gave a grateful nod. "We'll be out as quick as we can. Pound on the door if there's trouble, but *don't* come in. No matter what."

The instructions for suiting up were prominently displayed on the wall in both English and Kestonian, complete with detailed diagrams, and as Sasha diligently checked the thick outfit, helmet and breathing hose for leaks, she realized that Jeff was right about this place. The very fact that such elaborate precautions were needed told her something awful was taking place inside.

Once she was secure in her suit, she walked through a second pressurized door and over to Jeff, who said through the speaker built into his helmet, "Big surprise. Even when I was your handler, you disobeyed me. Now that we're partners, it's just gonna get worse. Right?"

"Did you find anything?"

He nodded. "The usual suspects, plus two real scary ones. Then the worst—an unknown. I think this nutcase

developed his own bioweapon. He calls it aero-filovirus. I have no idea what it does, but it's Level Four, and
that's bad."

"Can we destroy it? Or take it with us?"

"No way can we take it with us. We don't know
what's going to happen on our way out of Kestonia. But
we can't just leave it, either. So destroying it, and all
the records, is the only option. Problem is…" He
pointed to the equipment surrounding them. "How do
we do it? It looks like they deal with spills with a
chemical disinfectant so bleach is a good bet. But they
also have a high-tech furnace over there. Some kind of
incinerator, I think."

"So we do both," Sasha suggested.

He nodded. "That's my best guess, too. I'll load the
specimens into the furnace. We'll pour the bleach in,
then set it to the highest temperature. It could take hours,
so we'll use the dynamite to blow the doors to the lab
once we've left. That way no one can interfere. I'll set
the charge on delay to give us a chance to reach the
border before alerting them to what we've done up
here."

"That sounds right. Let's get going."

She followed him into a refrigeration unit lined with
shelves, and groaned at the labels that confronted her,
including anthrax, Ebola, and two other forms of hem-
orrhagic fever as well as the feared aero-filovirus, also
labeled AFV.

When Sasha reached for the AFV specimen, Jeff
protested with a sharp, "Negative, Camper!"

She arched a stern eyebrow. "I thought we were

partners. Just grab that Ebola, please. We've got to get this done quickly."

He growled but did as she suggested, and they gingerly transported the specimens to the incinerator. When all of the bioweapons were accounted for, Jeff poured the bleach solution over them. Then he closed the oven securely and set it for maximum heat.

"That's all we can do," he announced. "Let's get cleaned up and out of these suits. I'll help you first. That's nonnegotiable."

"You're such a gentleman." Sasha followed him into the first decontamination chamber where they were bathed by a spray of disinfectant. When the residue had drained away, they proceeded to the second chamber, where they removed and discarded their suits and helmets and donned goggles for a second round of spraying. Finally they returned to the room that held their clothing, where they squeezed together into the only shower stall, facing away from one another as they scrubbed with regular soap and water.

Then Jeff turned and murmured into her ear, "You've still got disinfectant on your back. Let me get it for you."

She lifted her hair and allowed herself to enjoy his firm touch between her shoulder blades.

Finally she said, "You, too," and he turned again so that she could wash the green residue from his strong, muscled back.

"Okay, you're clean. Let's get dressed."

It seemed silly to turn her back to him in the dressing room as she toweled off and began putting her clothes back on. After all, he had just seen her naked, up close and personal, and not for the first time. Still, she felt irrationally shy, and appreciated the fact that he didn't try to make any more physical contact with her.

But apparently, he still couldn't resist talking to her as they dressed, because he asked her carefully, "How are you doing, Sasha? With the news about your mother, I mean."

"The big revelation? Once it really sank in, it was sort of anticlimactic."

"What do you mean?"

She sighed. "In the old days, I was horrified and upset, obviously. But at least the idea of a jealous man killing his unfaithful wife in a rage was kind of understandable. But that's not how it happened. My father murdered a rival in cold blood, and that murder led to the death of a sweet girl like Vittoria and then to the slaughter of my innocent mother. That actually makes Dad *more* of a monster, not less." She finished dressing and turned to find Jeff looking at her with warm, understanding eyes. "Do you know what I mean?"

He patted her arm. "Yeah, it's rough all around. Especially because he's a victim, too, in a really twisted sense. Not an innocent victim, but still… I can't imagine he finds much joy in life, knowing that the woman he loved was braver than he was, and was gunned down for that bravery."

"That's true," she admitted. "This mess has more layers than an onion, doesn't it?"

His tone grew wistful. "I was so sure that when the day came for you to face your demons, you wouldn't be able to handle them. But look at you. You're just like your mother. Stronger and more fearless than any ten guys I know."

She felt her cheeks redden. "Thanks, Jeff. That means a lot. I'll never forget how much you helped me—"

"Hey!" He caught her in a loose embrace, then told her bluntly, "You're not going into witness protection. We'll find another way. I promise."

She gazed up at him, her heart aching for what they could have been to one another. "It has to be tonight. If we don't grab Dante now, he'll disappear for good. And when we *do* grab him, he and his men will know I'm the one who fingered him. If I don't disappear, I'll be dead in a week. And after that, they'll watch *you*. Hoping you'll lead them to me. You'll have to stay away from me, or you'll be signing my death warrant."

His green eyes blazed. "I know you don't believe that I love you—"

"Actually, I do believe it. And I know something else." Her throat tightened to hold back a sob. "If I let myself feel what my heart wants to feel..." A tear trickled down her cheek, and she slipped her hands behind his neck, then pulled his head down and kissed his mouth with unrestrained hunger.

But only for a moment, and then, even though his kiss told her how great things could be with him in her life, she stepped back and repeated sadly, "If we don't get him tonight, he'll get away. I can't risk that. Not for anything. Not even for you. So set the charge. Please? We've got to get Teal out of here."

* * *

As they descended the mountain toward the parking lot, Sasha carefully explained her new transportation plan to Jeff. She would go to Dante in tears, telling him that Zelasko had made improper advances—violent ones—and then she'd beg her "uncle" to get her out of Kestonia right away. Dante would love playing the role of protector, and would order his driver to take Sasha across the border in the Hummer immediately. Once they were away from the cottage, Sasha would use Jeff's pistol to make the driver pull over. Teal and Jeff would get in, and voilà—foolproof transportation. After that, even if the border guards dared to try and stop Dante's Hummer, the vehicle could almost certainly withstand their bullets.

"You can't pull a gun on the driver while you're still in Kestonia. If you're dead set on getting the Hummer, okay. But wait until you're safely across the border before you make your move."

Sasha bit back an argument, surprised he was accepting any part of this plan. She had expected him to insist they all grab machine guns and snowmobiles and head for the border, blasting their way across if they couldn't find a way to sneak out of the country.

"I don't like the idea of you seeing Dante at all, not in your present state of mind," he explained. "But once we get across the border, we're going to need long-term transportation. The snowmobiles won't cut it for long distance. Once Zelasko realizes we grabbed Teal, he'll send his goons after us. So that Hummer is looking pretty danged good."

"But how are you and I going to get *into* the Hummer?" Teal asked.

"Easy. We snowmobile to the border. It'll be fun, I promise. Sasha rides in style in the Hummer. Once the driver takes her safely across the border—once we're absolutely sure nothing can go wrong—*then* she pulls the pistol. She makes the driver stop and get out. The guards will be watching, but they won't interfere because it's not their jurisdiction. So it'll be the perfect distraction, especially if Sasha puts on the kind of show I know she's capable of. You and I will sneak over during the show, make our way a few hundred yards down the road, and she'll pick us up in the Hummer."

They had reached the last wooded spot before the fortress, and Sasha stopped, turned around and told Jeff coolly, "That's the worst plan I've ever heard."

"Fine. Then all three of us take snowmobiles. I like it better that way, anyway."

"No, no. We need the Hummer."

He looked down at her, his expression grim. "Too many things can go wrong on this side of the border. The gun could go off accidentally. The driver could have one, too. He could be in secret communication with Dante. The last thing we want is for you to get stuck inside Kestonia. So—" He took a deep breath, then insisted, "I want your word you'll wait till you're safely across."

"I promise," she grumbled.

"And I want your word you won't engage with Dante. No matter what he says. Just play the grateful, helpless niece. We'll get him later. I promise. This isn't the time. Not till Teal's safe. Right?"

"Right." Sasha nodded, then turned and gave the teenager a hug. "Do whatever Jeff says."

"I will. Be careful, Sasha."

When Sasha began walking toward the cottage, Teal called after her, "Sasha? Aren't you going to kiss Jeff goodbye?"

Sasha looked into the girl's hopeful eyes and told her with a sad smile, "Don't worry, honey. He and I already took care of that back at the lab."

Once Teal and Jeff were out of sight, Sasha continued toward Dante's cottage, but not before glancing wistfully at the castle. It had suddenly hit her that she was leaving some of her favorite belongings behind, and while she was more anxious than ever to get out of Kestonia, she mourned the loss of her tango shoes, her soft black boots and her navy-blue silk suit. She had tried to bring things she didn't care about losing, but in order to impress Zelasko, she had needed some heavy artillery, fashionwise, not to mention hundreds of dollars worth of makeup and jewelry in her carry-on bag—

And the tape recorder!

She had completely forgotten about that little item, tucked neatly under her makeup kit. Now she knew she'd have to enter Zelasko's stronghold one last time. There was simply no way she could leave that taped confession behind, knowing it could fall into the hands of her father's enemies.

Just make it quick. Jeff and Teal are already speeding toward the border! she reminded herself as she sneaked into the garden and changed into the black heels that she had hidden there. Then she covered her wet hair more completely with her stocking cap, stuffed the Kestonian oxfords into her deep pockets and reentered the fortress. The hall, which had been almost deserted when she left, was now teeming with finely dressed partygoers, some of whom sent curious looks in Sasha's direction. But for the most part, they seemed distracted, whether by fatigue, inebriation, or upcoming romantic trysts.

Passing them confidently, she reached her room without incident, and immediately rushed over to the armoire where she had stowed her carry-on bag. Pulling it out, she transferred Jeff's heavy pistol to it, then reached for her tango shoes. Anything else would be greedy, she warned herself, trying not to glance up at her favorite silk blouse and the black cocktail dress that could probably be squished into the bag.

"Looking for something?" a male voice demanded from behind her.

Instantly terrified, she whirled around just as the bedroom door slammed shut, imprisoning her with her uninvited guest.

Chapter 14

"Carmine?" Sasha barely managed to croak his name. "What are you doing here?"

His hazel eyes gleamed with fury. "You're surprised? Our fathers sent me to take care of you after reports that the barbarian's interest might be too intense for a delicate flower like you."

He was obviously still upset over the way she had backed out of their bet and humiliated him by calling his father at her apartment. It was a complication, but Sasha didn't mind. She was simply relieved that her gentleman caller wasn't Vlad or one of his cohorts. She wouldn't know how to deal with that, but she had always been able to handle Carmine.

Unfortunately, she was running out of time. Teal and Jeff needed her to stay on schedule, which meant she needed to soothe this hothead's ruffled feathers right away—lull him a bit, with seductive flattery so that he'd let his guard down. Then she'd get Jeff's pistol from the bag and order him to tie himself up.

"It was sweet of you to come all this way. And it's true. Zelasko's an animal. I'm so glad you're here to protect me from him."

"Yeah? The way I hear it, you've been his slut since the minute you got here."

She winced. "I flirted with him, but I never slept with him—"

"Liar!" Carmine stepped closer, his face contorted with rage. "You're a fucking liar, just like your father. And now you're going to pay for those lies."

"What are you talking about?" she demanded. "What lies did my father ever— *Oh!*"

"Yeah." He pulled the tape recorder from his pocket and waved it in her face, not with confusion, as Jeff had done, but with menace.

Déjà-screwed! Sasha told herself unhappily. *Why didn't you destroy that stupid thing last night?*

Backing away, she considered diving for Jeff's gun, but she quickly rejected the thought. There was no way of knowing if Carmine had a pistol of his own, but she knew for a fact that he had his knife. He *always* had it. One suspicious move on her part and he'd probably slit her throat.

Meanwhile, his rant continued. "No one was *ever* going to tell me the truth about my sister. Just let me believe a fucking lie forever. All to protect a spoiled, stuck-up bitch like you."

"I'm so sorry you had to find out about it this way,

Carmine. I just learned the truth myself yesterday, and it almost destroyed me." She took a step toward him. "I'm truly sorry about Vittoria—"

"Shut up! You're not worthy to speak her name! She was a saint."

"Really? Then what was she doing in a nightclub with your father's rival in the middle of the night?" Sasha backed away, fearful, yet also knowing she had to bring this situation to a head, once and for all, if she was going to reach Jeff and Teal in time. "Be reasonable, Carmine. Suppose you manage to kill me. Would that bring your sister back? She and my mother died because of the twisted code that rules our lives. Isn't that enough?"

"My father lost a *daughter.* If he was a real man instead of a sentimental fool, he would've demanded the life of a daughter in return. Luckily, *I'm* not a fool. But it'll hurt me to kill you, because I loved you once. Wanted to marry you even. Now that can never be."

"Love?" Sasha's throat tightened with disgust. "My father loved my mother, and what did it get her? Butchered, that's what! Men like you don't have any idea what real love is."

"Watch your mouth! Big Frankie and my father aren't here to protect you anymore. Neither is my uncle. It's just you and me, slut."

Your uncle? In other words, you don't know Dante's in Kestonia?

A glimmer of hope at last! All she had to do was tell this angry bull that the Butcher was in Kestonia, and he'd rethink his plan for vengeance.

But it was too late. Carmine was already lunging

at her, and although she managed to sidestep the impact, he grabbed a handful of long, wet hair and dragged her to the floor. Then he straddled her body, pinned down her wrists, and grinned at her, insisting, "First things first. You owe me something, and I'm going to collect."

He leaned down, clearly intending to kiss her, and she used the opportunity to crash her forehead into his the way she'd seen in the movies. Nothing could have prepared her for the blinding pain she inflicted on herself, and even though Carmine yelped and released his grip, she was so dazed, she could barely manage to roll free in time to see him pull his stiletto, his expression literally murderous.

Think! she pleaded with herself. *You've gone over these moves a million times with sensei Hakira.*

Unfortunately, the knives at the dojo had been made of wood. This one was gleaming steel. The technique for disarming would be the same, of course. It was just the consequences of failure that differed so greatly.

So don't fail! she ordered herself, and when Carmine made his move, aiming the point of the weapon at her heart then lunging straight at her again, she followed her training by slamming her right forearm against his right wrist, hoping at least to ruin his aim. And thanks to the strength and precision of her movement, the impact actually sent the knife flying out of Carmine's hand.

"Bitch!" He tried again, his empty hands grasping for Sasha's neck. She was able roll away and spring to her feet, but her right arm had been damaged so severely, she knew she couldn't hold off another attack unless she managed to get the stiletto, which was lying on the floor several yards away.

With pain radiating from her wrist to her shoulder, she dived for the weapon with her left hand, but Carmine anticipated her move and kicked the blade away, then threw his full weight onto her, flattening her to the floor again, then crowing lustfully as he yanked her around to face him.

"Bastardo!" she yelled, punching him full in the face, drawing an instant gush of blood from his nose. Undeterred, Carmine slammed his fist down toward her, but she managed to deflect it with her semi-useless right forearm while her left hand grabbed his shirtfront and she butted foreheads with him again.

She was almost unconscious now, but could sense that he was even worse off than she, at least for this instant, so she propelled her upper body against his, sending him careening backward. Then she jumped onto him, sandwiched his head between her hands, and bashed it against the stone floor, not once, but twice. His eyes rolled back and his mouth gaped open, appearing to signal complete incapacitation.

But Sasha wasn't taking any chances. She retrieved the stiletto, fully prepared to impale him with it if necessary. Then she pressed her fingertips to his neck and learned that her instincts had been accurate.

Carmine Martino—her childhood playmate, longtime suitor, and occasional assailant—was dead.

She still had need of the stiletto, though. Almost without thinking, she used it to slice her father's taped confession to shreds.

* * *

The cottage was only a few feet away, yet as Sasha stumbled toward it, she wondered if she shouldn't just succumb to the hazy incoherence that was trying to overtake her. Surely she couldn't be useful to Jeff and Teal in this condition. Better to slump to the snow-covered ground and get some rest. Or pull the pistol from the bag slung over her shoulder and enter the cottage in a blaze of glory, cutting Vincenzo to ribbons as he'd done to her mother so many years ago.

Jeff needs the Hummer. And you can deliver Dante at the same time. It's perfect, so just suck it up, she told herself groggily. *It's almost over. Almost over... Think of Teal... Think of Mom...*

"Stop! Identify yourself!" a voice commanded, and two burly shapes appeared between her and the cottage porch.

"I need my uncle," Sasha told them. "Please, please help me."

"It's Big Frankie's kid," one of the men announced, and then the larger of the pair of them grabbed her, bolstering her steps, guiding her toward the cottage.

"My arm!"

"Scusi, scusi," the man murmured, shifting his grip so that he was almost carrying her up the porch steps.

Dante appeared in the doorway and asked with alarm, "Sasha? What happened to you?" Then his face contorted with disgust. "The barbarian will pay for this!"

"No, no, *zio.*" She nestled herself against his chest and began to weep. "It wasn't Vlad. It was Carmine. He—he went crazy. Tried to rape me. Tried to kill me."

"Carmine?" Dante pushed her back enough to stare into her eyes. "What are you saying?"

"He broke my arm!" she wailed. "He was talking crazy. About you. And his father. And *my* father. And Vittoria and my mother! Some sort of insane conspiracy theory that made no sense. He scared me to death."

"It's fine," Dante assured her, pulling her into another embrace. "You're safe here."

"No! You don't understand. It's not safe at all. Carmine called the FBI. He told them where you were. He hates you, *zio*. You should have heard the things he said about you and Dad. He kept calling you a coward. It was so awful." She stared into Dante's dark eyes. "At first I thought he was angry because you protected me at the wedding. But it's something else. Something about Mom and Tori. It made no sense, but that's not the point. You're in danger. We need to get out of Kestonia right away."

Dante led her to a chair. "Sit. You need some brandy." He motioned to one of his men, who responded instantly.

Sasha accepted the snifter and cradled it in her left hand inhaling the fumes from her drink, hoping they might clear her aching head. Then she repeated, "Just before he attacked me, Carmine said he had called the FBI and reported your location. They're on their way— with Interpol, I suppose—but it will take them hours. We have to go now, or you'll never be safe again. Please, I'm begging you."

"Where would I go?"

"I have friends in Provence. They'll shelter us, no questions asked. But we need to leave right away."

"I must deal with my nephew first," Dante reminded her.

"I think he's dead. I pushed him—I was so scared!—and he fell backward. Tripped over my suitcase. And he hit his head on the stone floor." Sasha gulped at the brandy, then added unhappily, "I didn't mean to kill him. I just wanted to make him stop."

"He deserved to die, the traitor. He dared to cross me? To attack you? He's lower than an animal. But we need to be sure—"

"I checked his pulse. There wasn't any. Then I dragged him over to an armoire and hid him in it. I didn't know what else to do. I just knew I had to warn you."

"You did good," Dante assured her. "You're brave, like your mother."

Sasha set the snifter down and buried her face in her good hand. "I don't feel brave. I feel scared. And I'm sure my arm is broken."

"Let's take a look—"

"*No!*" She pulled away, honestly fearful of having her arm touched. But she also didn't want them to discover Carmine's stiletto hidden in the right sleeve of her wool coat. "It hurts so much, *zio*. Just take me to a hospital once we leave Kestonia. Please?"

The Butcher hesitated, then nodded and turned to his two men who were hovering nearby. "Get the bags. Now! Don't alert anyone yet. We'll call the barbarian from the Hummer and make sure we don't encounter any interference at the border. Sasha's right," he added with another, more emphatic nod. "We need to get out of here before the cops can mobilize."

One of the men strode into the bedroom while the other scooped Sasha's carry-on bag off the floor near her feet.

"Wait!" She grimaced, then explained, "I have to keep that with me. My face is a mess from crying."

"Put it with the other bags," Dante countermanded, adding to Sasha, "This is no time for vanity. You shouldn't be carrying anything. Not with that arm."

"You're so good to me," she murmured, but inside, she was more miserable than ever. She had counted on access to Jeff's pistol, knowing that the stiletto, while dramatic, wouldn't be enough for the plan she was trying to piece together. Assuming the driver and the bodyguard sat in the front of the Hummer, she could probably get the knife against Dante's throat, but then what? Without a gun in her other hand to keep them all at bay, these professional killers could undoubtedly overpower her before long.

"Sasha? Are you ready?"

She glanced up, taking full advantage of the haziness filling her brain. "Hmm?"

Dante shook his head, then instructed his driver to carry her to the Hummer. To her shame, she appreciated the help, and took the opportunity to nestle against the strange man's chest, trying not to think about anything but reaching Jeff—and safety—soon.

"Hey, boss?" The bodyguard turned around to look at Dante, who was sitting on the left side of the bench-style rear seat of the Hummer with his arm around Sasha's shoulders. "This Kestonian guy says we've gotta stop at the border for a routine check."

"Fools!" Vincenzo Martino growled. "Tell them I want to speak to Zelasko."

"He's asleep, and they've got orders not to disturb him. And standing orders to stop every vehicle at the border, no matter who's in it."

"Tell them to wake him up!"

"No, no, uncle," Sasha whispered. "That won't work. I heard Vlad threaten to kill anyone who dared disturb him." Licking her lips, she goaded her escort carefully. "I just hope it's not as bad as when I arrived. They were so thorough, it took forever. We don't have that kind of time if we want to be far away before the feds get here."

"It's not like they can stop us, boss," the driver interrupted cheerfully. "We added fifty-thousand dollars' worth of armor plating and bulletproof glass to this bad boy. Unless they've got a bazooka set up down there, we can barrel right through."

Yes, yes, Sasha urged silently. *Listen to him, Butcher. Make a huge scene at the border. That's just the diversion Jeff and Teal need to sneak across.*

Dante pursed his lips, then instructed his bodyguard, "Tell the barbarians we will cooperate. That way they won't be ready for us. Then do as Johnny says, barrel through. Let them try to stop us."

"What if they shoot the tires?" Sasha asked.

The driver grinned at her in the rearview mirror. "These babies have special inserts. Solid rubber. We'll make it across that border. Don't you worry about that."

"What a relief." She cuddled against Dante again, trying to ignore the throbbing in her forehead. At least the pain in her forearm had subsided, replaced with an eerie numbness and stiffening that made the limb essentially useless, except for the key role it played in keeping the stiletto hidden.

It's going well, she assured herself miserably. *In less than ten minutes, Teal will be safe, and Dante will be dead or in custody.*

And Sasha would be dead. She had no more illusions about that. Without the pistol, she couldn't really make three powerful men do anything for long. But at least she could make them stop this vehicle before they killed her, and that was all Jeff needed from her. He'd have to do the rest himself.

With a sigh, she went over her revamped plan one last time, reminding herself that the most crucial element was timing. As much as she needed to get this over with once and for all, Jeff had been correct about waiting to make her move until the Hummer crossed the Kestonian border. If she tried to attack Dante now, she'd be dead within seconds, and then they'd turn around and go back to the fortress.

But the instant the Hummer cleared the border, the Kestonian soldiers would break off their fire. Jeff was right about that, too. They had no jurisdiction outside their country, and they wouldn't risk an international incident and an underworld shoot-out on the night of Zelasko's fancy gala.

So she'd wait for that precise moment to pull the stiletto. She'd press it to Dante's throat and order the driver to stop. Surely he'd do so, if only to enable himself to pull his own pistol from his shoulder holster. At that point, if Jeff could get to her quickly, she might survive. But she suspected it would be otherwise. Dante would resist, and with her arm out of commission, she'd run out of time. But she'd use those last seconds to kill the Butcher. At least then she'd know she had avenged her mother before dying.

The driver and bodyguard would be in shock. They'd shoot Sasha, probably multiple times, then they'd get out of the Hummer and try to save Dante's life. That would give Jeff the chance he needed. With Teal's help, he'd overpower Dante's men, or maybe he'd be lucky enough to get a clear shot at each of them from a distance. Then he'd drive Teal to safety.

He'd be so unhappy. He'd blame himself. And Teal would carry the weight of Sasha's death with her for the rest of her life. Sasha's heart ached for the poor girl— the way she imagined her own mother's heart had ached. But like her mother, Sasha knew that the only thing that mattered now was to save the life that had been entrusted to her care.

And at least Dante would be dead. That also mattered.

She could almost hear Summit's voice saying, *Don't do it, Camper. We'll find another way.*

But it wasn't true. He needed the Hummer to get himself and Teal far from Kestonia. The instant Zelasko realized Teal was missing, he wouldn't hesitate to send troops across that border in pursuit, jurisdiction be damned. Teal was too valuable a prize to let slip away. He had sent his soldiers out of Kestonia for her once, hadn't he, recovering her during the first rescue attempt? Jeff and Teal needed to be far away before the dictator knew what was going on, and for that, they needed the Hummer.

"You're trembling," Dante whispered, stroking Sasha's damp hair. "Don't you realize how safe you are with me?"

"I know. I'm so grateful."

"Are you?" Pressing his lips to her ear, he asked, "How grateful?"

"What?"

"You're so beautiful. Just like your mother. But—" his hand moved to cover her left breast "—I could never touch her like this."

"Oh, God!" Sasha recoiled in absolute horror, then begged him instantly, "I'm sorry! Please forgive me? It's my arm. It hurts so much."

Dante's face had hardened into expressionless stone, but she persisted shakily. "I'm so sorry. I've wondered myself, ever since this morning at your cottage, if you and I—well, what it might be like to be with a man like you. It would be my honor to…to make love with you in Provence. Especially after spending time with a crude man like Zelasko, I crave someone like you. But my arm…" She covered her mouth with her right hand as though stifling a sob.

His gaze warmed. "That's fine, Sasha. I can see you're in pain. I'll wait for Provence."

Bile rose in her throat, burning it, threatening to spill over, and while she knew she should go back to him— nestle against him again, her stiletto at the ready—she backed away until she was pressed against the door, then she curled into a ball.

She couldn't help herself. The thought of his touch disgusted her so completely, she couldn't pretend otherwise anymore. Even during the worst of it with Zelasko, she had never felt her stomach twist with such pure and utter revulsion.

And Dante could sense it. She saw that in his narrowing eyes, so she explained in a tremulous voice, "How can you even *look* at me? I'm such a hideous mess. You compare me to Mom, but I'm *nothing* like her. I'm nauseous, and injured, and exhausted. Puffy eyes, no makeup, crying. Just when I want to look my most beautiful. For you."

"You're being too hard on yourself."

"You said she was brave. Look at me. I'm shaking with fear! We'll be at the border any minute, and Zelasko's guards will start shooting at us—"

"Sasha!" Dante reached over to pat her hand. "You really are exhausted, aren't you, poor child? There's no danger here. What Johnny said is true. This vehicle cannot be stopped. And if those guards have any brains, they won't try too hard. It'll be over in no time."

"Really?"

He smiled fondly. "Try to sleep. That's what I intend to do. We'll be driving for hours. Then we'll get that arm looked at. And after that…" His tone grew husky again. "I assure you, you are the most beautiful woman in the world to me at this moment. As soon as we can get you some painkillers, I'll find a way to prove that to you."

"You're so good to me."

"You saved my life, didn't you? I was a sitting duck

there in Kestonia. Thanks to you, the authorities will be too late. Again."

I don't need the authorities. I'm going to take you down personally, she promised him as she huddled in her corner.

All that stood between Sasha and revenge was the challenge of wielding the stiletto with her injured arm. She didn't have much strength at her command, but if Carmine had kept the implement perfectly sharpened— as she absolutely *knew* he had—it would glide into Dante's neck as though he were made of butter.

Her muddled thoughts drifted to a spring afternoon just before her fifteenth birthday. She had come home from Arizona, and was helping seventeen-year-old Vittoria Martino perform emergency surgery on the neckline of an ugly prom dress she was supposed to wear that night.

Eighteen-year-old Carmine had burst into the room. Cocky. Handsome. Anxious to show off a brand-new stiletto. He had had knives before, but this was something special. A gift from his uncle Vincenzo.

Taking Sasha aside, he had explained to her that if he kept the blade in top condition, it would puncture an enemy with barely any pressure. Then he had added huskily, "Now I can protect you from anyone, anytime."

Seduced by his sexy swagger and declarations of love, she had tumbled onto the sofa with him, but their make-out session been quickly interrupted by Tori, who threatened to tell Big Frankie if Carmine didn't go away and leave them to their dressmaking.

Now as she remembered that innocent day, a tear slid down Sasha's cheek.

If you're crying for Carmine Martino, you really are a basket case, she taunted herself. *Try to focus, Bracciali.*

"Hey, boss!" Johnny announced. "There's the border. And it looks like they're ready for us. Or at least, they think they are. The chumps."

Sasha scooted back toward Dante, pretending to be scared, but really just wanting a better view. There in the distance was the Kestonian border, where four guards with machine guns had positioned themselves across the road in front of the control gate's mechanical arm.

The soldiers clearly expected the Hummer to stop. But it did not. In fact, it increased its speed. The Kestonians dived out of the way, all the while shouting and spraying the Hummer with bullets—bullets that bounced harmlessly off the armored plating and bullet-proof windows.

"Woo-hoo!" Johnny yelled, like a cowboy at a rodeo, flipping off the guards with a series of colorful hand gestures.

Sasha had a hand gesture of her own in mind as she took a deep breath, then allowed the stiletto to slip down into her palm.

Chapter 15

"Suck-ers!" Johnny shouted as they cleared the border, then he rolled down the window of the Hummer and repeated the taunt at the top of his lungs, clearly hepped up on adrenaline. It seemed like a fool-hardy move, but no gunfire erupted, and Sasha realized that the Kestonian guards had indeed chosen the prudent course and retreated behind their now-shattered gate.

Which meant it was time for Sasha's own personal attack, and she was more than ready. No more visions of her mother's riddled body, or Carmine's leering expression or Vittoria Martino's fragile smile. In Sasha's world, only two people existed now—Teal and Jeff, sprinting across the border, relying on her to provide them with a vehicle.

And thanks to the blade in her hand, she would do just that.

Then the roadway before them lit up like a scorching desert at high noon, and the Hummer skidded wildly to a stop as a man's voice over a bullhorn roared out instructions.

"Vincenzo Martino! You're under arrest! Exit the vehicle immediately."

Sasha stared in shocked fascination as a dozen armed men in black outfits scrambled into view. A row of vehicles that blocked the road provided them with ample cover.

"The goddamn feds," Johnny muttered, twisting to look at Dante. "What now, boss?"

"Are you an idiot? Drive through them!" the Butcher told him between gritted teeth. "We've got a fucking armored car, don't we?"

"Sorry, boss, but this time, well—" The driver pointed. "They actually *do* have a bazooka. See over there?"

"Yeah, boss," the bodyguard echoed. "We'll be blown to bits."

Confused, Sasha used her palm to force the stiletto back up into her sleeve. It was too soon to know, but either she and Dante were about to be annihilated together, or she was going to get out of this alive.

The agent on the bullhorn had an American accent. She wasn't sure what that meant, but was fairly certain Jeff was behind it. All she could hope was that he had gotten across the border in time to enjoy this scene from a safe hiding place with Teal.

"Exit the vehicle with your hands in the air," the official voice was instructing confidently. "You're under arrest. No sudden movements, and we'll all get out of this alive. Use your heads."

"Boss?"

Dante gave his driver an exhausted scowl. "Go ahead. It looks like it's over."

Johnny nodded, then opened his door slowly and got out of the Hummer with his hands above his shoulders. The man with the bullhorn instructed him to walk toward the lights, and a swarm of men descended on him, cuffing him and leading him behind the barricade.

The bodyguard didn't follow suit, at least for the moment. Instead, he turned and gave Dante a tearful look. "Wanna go out blasting, boss?"

"No, it's fine. Do exactly what they say," Dante murmured. "Your loyalty will be repaid, I promise you that."

The bodyguard nodded. Then he opened the front passenger door, exited the vehicle and walked over to the agents who immediately took him into custody.

Sasha gave Dante a mournful sigh. "After all this…"

"I know." His voice was surprisingly calm. "My only regret is that you killed Carmine by accident. He should have died slowly and with great suffering."

She nodded, struggling to control her expression. "I guess they'll arrest me, too. For being your accomplice. And do you know what? I've never been prouder of anything in my life."

"Let's do it then." He motioned toward the door on her side of the backseat. "Shall we?"

Thrilled beyond belief, Sasha opened the door and set her feet on the ground. Then she stood, raising one hand above her head, prepared to walk over to the agents.

Over to safety.

But Dante grabbed her from behind, shoving a pistol against her neck as he imprisoned her against his body. Then he shouted victoriously toward the barricade. "Do you want this girl's blood on your hands?"

"Let her go, Martino," the agent with the bullhorn responded, his voice still confident. But Sasha knew he was beginning to panic. His carefully executed arrest had just become a hostage situation, and if it wasn't handled properly, Vincenzo the Butcher was going to get away.

She didn't need to feign a frightened tone when she demanded of Dante, "What are you *doing?* I've been loyal to you! I tried to save you—"

"You'll be fine. Just follow my lead."

"They'll kill me!"

"Shut up! Stupid bitch," he muttered. "Just like your mother. Brave, sure. Until you see the gun. Then you beg like a helpless whore."

An icy shudder ran down Sasha's spine as she imagined that moment—the moment when Julia Bracciali had actually looked into the barrel of the Butcher's machine gun.

"Bastardo," she whispered.

Dante chuckled. "That's just what *she* said."

"Let her go, Martino," the agent repeated over the bullhorn.

"I'm giving the orders here," Dante shouted back at

him. "If you want to save this girl, put down your weapons and move those vehicles. Then get out of our way. We're driving out of here, and if I catch even a glimpse of you in my rearview mirror, I'll drill a hole in her throat."

Glancing at Dante's wristwatch, Sasha noted that it was thirty seconds until midnight. There would be an explosion soon, one that would distract the Butcher. She needed to be ready to make her move then. So she edged the stiletto back down her sleeve and into her right hand. Her arm was still numb, but somehow she would find the strength to ram that blade into this evil man's torso.

Because there was simply no way she was going to allow him to escape. Not now. Not ever again.

"Let her go!" the agent repeated, but Sasha could see his team mobilizing again. Getting ready to move their vehicles. They were going to cave. Or at least, that's what they thought was about to happen.

"Do you want me to blow her ear off, just to prove I mean business?" Dante taunted them.

"No! Don't harm her. We'll let you go, but you have to release her first."

"Bullshit. Clear those cars away. Sasha and I are getting into my Hummer now. One false move by you or your men and she's a dead woman."

As Sasha watched, the digital display on Dante's watch turned from 11:59:59 to midnight.

But nothing happened on the mountain above the fortress, and she realized that the demolition of the church had been delayed.

Probably because they can't wake up their fearless leader, she told herself grimly. *So? What are you waiting for? Just do it, will you? Before you lose your nerve!*

With a silent apology to Jeff and Teal for making them witness this, Sasha grabbed Dante's wrist with her good hand, forcing the pistol away from her throat. As the weapon fired wildly into the air, she buried the stiletto's blade between the gangster's ribs, hissing as she did so, "*Bastardo!* This is for Julia Bracciali."

As the Butcher's eyes widened with shock, a single shot rang out from the distance, exploding his skull into a thousand bloody pieces.

And Sasha couldn't help but notice that the shot hadn't come from the barricade, but rather, from the direction of the Kestonian border.

Whirling, she saw Jeff standing there, a rifle in his hand, a grim expression on his handsome face. She would have run to him—or at least, she imagined that her legs might have been able to do that—but he made a gesture that stopped her, a gesture he had taught her for their ops. With his open palm by his hip, he pressed downward, signaling her not to react.

Then she understood. He didn't want the world to know—or more specifically, he didn't want Dante's men to know—that he and Sasha were connected.

"Miss? Are you okay?"

She turned toward the voice, recognizing it as the man with the bullhorn, even though he was now standing before her with nothing in his hands but a blanket, which he draped around her shoulders.

"Thanks." She pulled it tighter. "Am I under arrest?"

"Yes. You have the right to remain silent. I suggest you exercise it."

"How dare you treat her this way!" a female voice interrupted. Sasha spun, concerned that it might be Teal. Then she saw Shannon Conner, and had to bite her bottom lip hard to keep from laughing with exhausted hilarity.

"I'm Shannon Conner of ABS news. You've been through an ordeal, Ms. Bracciali, but my viewers need to hear your story in your own words. What just happened here?"

"Leave her alone, she's hurt," the agent warned, but Sasha waved him away, saying, "She's an old schoolmate of mine. I *want* to talk to her. Unless it's against the law."

He winced. "Just for a minute, then."

Sasha turned back to Shannon and embraced her. "It's so good to see a friendly face! This has been such a nightmare!"

Shannon patted her shoulder awkwardly. "I can imagine. Are you really okay? They probably have doctors—"

"My arm's broken," Sasha agreed. "But it's practically numb, so I can talk for a minute. It's the least I can do for you."

"For me?"

"You're so amazing! I can't *believe* you really stayed here all this time! Vlad told me you threatened to do that, but it's so cold out." With a smile, Sasha added softly, "I tried to convince him to let you into Kestonia, but he wouldn't."

"You tried to help me? Why?"

Sasha shrugged. "We have so much in common. We both went to Athena Academy. And neither of us fit in. Right? You left, I stayed. But both of us were black sheep in our own way."

"Well…" Shannon cleared her throat. "What just happened here, Ms. Bracciali?"

"Call me Sasha. I came to Kestonia for the ball. I'm a fashion designer, so it was more or less the mother ship for me. I ran into my uncle up there, and he needed to leave quickly. So I left with him. Out of loyalty. But the next thing I knew…"

Shannon cocked her head to the side. "The next thing you knew, he was holding a gun to your head?"

Sasha choked back a sob. "I thought he loved me, but… Well, I guess he just didn't want to be taken alive."

"What about Teal Arnett?"

"The Athena student who was kidnapped? Is there news?" Sasha demanded. When Shannon just stared, Sasha continued blithely. "I haven't seen a TV broadcast in almost a week, but after what *I* just went through, I can imagine how she felt, being kidnapped and all. Poor kid. *Please* tell me she's safe?"

"That's it," Jeff's gruff voice interrupted. "The interview is over. Ms. Bracciali? The medic wants to take a look at you."

Sasha turned to him and sniffed. "Let me say goodbye to my schoolmate first, please." Embracing Shannon again, she whispered, "He saved my life, but puh-leeze. Some manners would be appreciated."

Shannon laughed. "Can I call you when we're all back in the States? I'd love a full-fledged interview."

"I'd love that, too. Take care."

The newswoman walked over to a Volvo SUV that was parked along the side of the road, where two young men were waiting for her. Meanwhile, Jeff rested his hands on Sasha's shoulders. "If you're okay, we should get going."

She nodded.

"Wait a minute." A man in a black parka stepped up to them and flashed his credentials in Jeff's face. "You're Crossman? I'm Cole Stringer, NSA. Any chance you have a package for me?"

"I don't have it on me. But come on," Jeff said, his green eyes twinkling. "We'll go pick it up." He led Sasha and Stringer to one of the FBI's vehicles and motioned for them to get into the backseat. Then he drove a short distance, pulling up next to a stand of black-barked trees. "I've got to take a leak. Wait here."

Sasha smiled and opened the back passenger door. "I'd like to stretch my legs, too. Will you excuse me, Agent Stringer?"

The NSA operative grinned. "Maybe *I* should drive from here on out so Crossman can debrief you." He exited the vehicle and walked around to the driver's side just as Jeff hustled Teal out of the trees and into the backseat through Sasha's door.

"I thought that creep was going to kill you!" Teal squealed, embracing Sasha heartily. "You were so brave!"

"Just like her mom," Jeff said quietly.

Agent Stringer pulled the SUV back onto the road and headed away from Kestonia. "Nice work, folks."

"I'll ride up front with you," Teal told him. "These two have issues to work out."

Before Sasha could stop her, the teen had scrambled up to the front passenger seat, turning to beam in the direction of Sasha and Jeff. "*Kiss* her."

"Turn around and I will, brat," Jeff said with a chuckle. Then he turned to Sasha, his eyes shining with relief and love. "You had me worried for a minute. But I should have known. You were unbelievable, as usual."

Sasha wanted to pour her heart out to him, but instead all she said was, "Nice shot."

"Thanks." He cupped her chin in his hand. Then with a wary glance in Stringer's direction, he murmured, "We make a good team, right? Equal partners. Et cetera."

"Especially the et cetera," she agreed, trying not to notice that Teal was giggling at the romantic double entendre. Then she arched an accusatory eyebrow at Jeff. "How exactly did those agents know Dante was coming across the border tonight?"

"They didn't know about Dante. They just knew about his car. He was a helluva bonus, wasn't he? After all these years, you got revenge against your mom's killer. That must feel good."

"Don't try to change the subject," she warned. "You called them, didn't you? Arranged for them to stop the Hummer and pretend they were executing an arrest warrant for Dante, even though you couldn't have known he'd actually be with me. Why?"

Jeff flushed, then admitted, "They were supposed to take *you* into custody."

Sasha cocked her head to the side. "Pardon?"

"You were hell-bent on going back after the Butcher.

It was nuts, but you wouldn't listen to reason. No way was I going to let you throw your life away in some stupid witness protection program. We needed time to come up with a new plan. Meanwhile, I did what I had to do."

Sasha pretended to scowl. "So much for being partners."

"Actually," he told her with a confident smile, "that's exactly what real partners do. Watch each other's backs."

"Did you say 'watch'? Or 'wash'?" she asked teasingly.

"In our case, I hope it's both," he admitted. Then with a quick instruction to Teal to, "Face front!" he pulled his new partner into a long, loving embrace.

Epilogue

"And no matter what happened, he never panicked. Even when that awful man was threatening to shoot Sasha, Jeff was so cool. He just raised that rifle and pow! Perfect shot."

Allison Gracelyn struggled not to laugh at Teal Arnett's blatant hero worship as the teenager described her twenty-four hours with Jeff Crossman. "He sounds very brave. Of course, Sasha was brave, too."

"She's so lucky. After he saved her, he waited to kiss her until we were driving away. And at that very moment, the lab blew up in the background. Ka-*pow!* I think Jeff timed it that way—with the kiss, I mean— just to make it more romantic."

"Teal?" Allison murmured. "You remember that's all classified information, right?"

"Oh, right." Teal looked around at the other students and alumni at the impromptu celebration in the Athena Academy dining hall. "Sorry, I'll be more careful. Look! There's Sasha!"

Allison turned in time to see Sasha Bracciali entering the dining hall. True to form, the designer made a dramatic entrance in her sassy red sundress. A coordinating shawl was draped around her bare shoulders, partially obscuring a cast and sling on her right arm. Otherwise, she was dressed as though it were the middle of summer rather than the end of February, apparently making the most of the warm Arizona evening after the freezing world of Kestonia.

But it was Sasha's radiant smile that provided the real warmth as she rushed over to embrace Teal and Allison. "Did I miss anything? My flight was delayed for some ridiculous reason, and I was so anxious, I almost threatened to hijack it."

"We're just getting started," Allison promised. "How's the arm?"

"Just a hairline crack. I don't think it even needed a cast, but you know how doctors are." Turning to Teal, Sasha smiled fondly. "I hear you got a clean bill of health, thank God. Nothing missing except a few pounds, right? And that buffet table over there should take care of that. Everything looks so yummy, Allison."

"Did Jeff come with you?" Teal asked hopefully.

"He's at the hotel. Do you think he'd miss a chance to see his favorite girl? But he understands this party is no-guys-allowed, so he's being patient. As long as you let him buy you breakfast tomorrow."

Allison smiled. "I take it you and Agent Crossman are officially an item?"

"Definitely. And guess who arranged it? Big Frankie! When he heard that an FBI agent saved my life, he insisted on meeting him. And when he found out Jeff was single, he set us up on our first date. Do you *love* it?"

"That's a good sign. They obviously believe your story—that Carmine betrayed Vincenzo, and you tried to save him."

"Right."

Teal beamed. "So now you and Jeff can work *and* play together?"

Sasha nodded. "But not in Chicago. It's just too awkward. Plus, getting the Butcher was his main objective. So he's going to ditch the organized crime scene. He's hot to work kidnapping cases now. Don't ask me why," she added, arching her eyebrow at Teal.

"He'll be sooo good at that. So will you," the teen added magnanimously. "I can't wait to see him tomorrow morning. Oh, Sasha, by the way, I washed and ironed your jeans. They're in my room, so remind me to give them to you in the morning."

"I was just kidding about that, Teal. You can keep them."

The girl's eyes danced. "I would, but they're too short for me. *Way* too short."

Sasha rolled her eyes, then told Allison, "She used to be such an angel, you know. Too bad she turned evil."

Teal giggled, explaining to Allison, "She's teasing me. Because of something I said in Kestonia. I should have known better than to tell secrets to a snitch, right?"

Allison laughed, noting that the two seemed more like long-lost sisters than rescuer-rescuee.

The ringing of her NSA cell phone interrupted the charming moment, and Allison glanced at the screen, then winced to see the caller was Morgan Rush, a colleague who had reportedly been making a nuisance of himself trying to learn the classified details of the Kestonian incident.

"Sorry, I have to take this. We'll catch up more in a bit, Sasha, okay?"

"Sure. Teal can introduce me to Lena. Plus, we can hit the buffet table."

"Thanks." Allison flipped open the phone as she strode toward the doors that led to the terrace. "Morgan? This is a bad time. I'm at an important school function. Can I call you in the morning?"

"This won't take long," he promised, adding in a drawl, "And since you haven't returned my last three calls, I'd like to do this while I have you on the line."

"It's been a circus," she assured him, "but I was going to call you back. Really. So? What's up?"

"That scene at the Kestonian border—I get why the Bureau had agents there to advise and assist Interpol. They've been hunting Martino forever. But why was Stringer there? And why are the files so sensitive that I can't access them? It's not like I don't have clearance—"

"It's complicated. And quite frankly, I can't discuss it over the phone, even on a secure line. Maybe when I get back to headquarters—"

"Right," he said sarcastically. "Come on, Allison.

We both know you're evading me. What I want to know is, why? What the hell happened in Kestonia? It's got something to do with your missing student, obviously. My question is, what? And I'm not going to stop asking until I get an answer."

Allison paused for dramatic effect. Then she informed him coolly, "It's strictly need-to-know, Morgan. And quite frankly, curiosity is not the same as need. So I suggest you back off for now. If and when the situation changes, I'll be glad to share the details with you. Until then, this conversation is over. Have a nice evening."

As she closed the phone, she pictured Morgan's usually handsome face twisted with annoyance and frustration. He was an arrogant, stubborn man who didn't like to hear the word *no*—not even from a superior and *definitely* not from a woman.

Which meant Allison Gracelyn had a big problem on her hands.

At that same moment in the Athena Academy office, principal Christine Evans was discovering an even more serious problem in the form of a fax that had come from an unknown—and undoubtedly untraceable—source.

It read:

You have won the battle. Be smart now and let it go. I am the enemy of all things Athena, and if you do not abandon your search for me, no one—not

your students, not your graduates—will ever
know a moment's safety or peace.

The warning was signed simply and chillingly:
Arachne.

* * * * *

Don't miss the next exciting
ATHENA FORCE ADVENTURE
VENDETTA by Meredith Fletcher
Available November 2007

Silhouette®

Romantic
SUSPENSE

Sparked by Danger,
Fueled by Passion.

When evidence is found that Mallory Dawes
intends to sell the personal financial information
of government employees to "the Russian,"
OMEGA engages undercover agent Cutter Smith.
Tailing her all the way to France, Cutter is
fighting a growing attraction to Mallory while at
the same time having to determine her connection
to "the Russian." Is Mallory really the mouse in
this game of cat and mouse?

Look for

Stranded with a Spy

by *USA TODAY* bestselling author

Merline Lovelace

October 2007.

Also available October wherever you buy books:

BULLETPROOF MARRIAGE *(Mission: Impassioned)*
by Karen Whiddon

A HERO'S REDEMPTION *(Haven)* by Suzanne McMinn

TOUCHED BY FIRE by Elizabeth Sinclair

nocturne™

Look for
NIGHT MISCHIEF
by
NINA BRUHNS

Lady Dawn Maybank's worst nightmare
is realized when she accidentally conjures
a demon of vengeance, Galen McManus. What
she doesn't realize is that Galen plans to teach
her a lesson in love—one she'll never forget....

DARK
ENCHANTMENTS

Available October wherever you buy books.

Don't miss the last installment of Dark Enchantments,
SAVING DESTINY by Pat White, available November.

REQUEST YOUR
FREE BOOKS!

2 FREE NOVELS PLUS 2 FREE GIFTS!

Silhouette® Romantic

SUSPENSE

Sparked by Danger, Fueled by Passion!

YES! Please send me 2 FREE Silhouette® Romantic Suspense novels and my 2 FREE gifts. After receiving them, if I don't wish to receive any more books, I can return the shipping statement marked "cancel." If I don't cancel, I will receive 4 brand-new novels every month and be billed just $4.24 per book in the U.S., or $4.99 per book in Canada, plus 25¢ shipping and handling per book plus applicable taxes, if any*. That's a savings of at least 15% off the cover price! I understand that accepting the 2 free books and gifts places me under no obligation to buy anything. I can always return a shipment and cancel at any time. Even if I never buy another book from Silhouette, the two free books and gifts are mine to keep forever.

240 SDN EEX6   340 SDN EEYJ

Name	(PLEASE PRINT)
Address	Apt. #
City	State/Prov.	Zip/Postal Code

Signature (if under 18, a parent or guardian must sign)

Mail to the Silhouette Reader Service™:
IN U.S.A.: P.O. Box 1867, Buffalo, NY 14240-1867
IN CANADA: P.O. Box 609, Fort Erie, Ontario L2A 5X3

Not valid to current Silhouette Intimate Moments subscribers.

Want to try two free books from another line?
Call 1-800-873-8635 or visit www.morefreebooks.com.

* Terms and prices subject to change without notice. NY residents add applicable sales tax. Canadian residents will be charged applicable provincial taxes and GST. This offer is limited to one order per household. All orders subject to approval. Credit or debit balances in a customer's account(s) may be offset by any other outstanding balance owed by or to the customer. Please allow 4 to 6 weeks for delivery.

Your Privacy: Silhouette is committed to protecting your privacy. Our Privacy Policy is available online at www.eHarlequin.com or upon request from the Reader Service. From time to time we make our lists of customers available to reputable firms who may have a product or service of interest to you. If you would prefer we not share your name and address, please check here. ☐

SRS07

Silhouette®
Desire

**There was only one man for the job—
an impossible-to-resist maverick
she knew she didn't dare fall for.**

MAVERICK
(#1827)

BY *NEW YORK TIMES*
BESTSELLING AUTHOR
JOAN HOHL

"Will You Do It for One Million Dollars?"

Any other time, Tanner Wolfe would have balked at being
hired by a woman. Yet Brianna Stewart was desperate to
engage the infamous bounty hunter. The price was just
high enough to gain Tanner's interest…Brianna's beauty
definitely strong enough to keep it. But he wasn't about
to allow her to tag along on his mission. He worked
alone. Always had. Always would. However, he'd never
confronted a more determined client than Brianna. She
wasn't taking no for an answer—not about anything.

Perhaps a million-dollar bounty was not the only thing
this maverick was about to gain….

Look for MAVERICK

Available October 2007 wherever you buy books.

HARLEQUIN®

Mediterranean NIGHTS™

Sail aboard the luxurious Alexandra's Dream and experience glamour, romance, mystery and revenge!

Coming in October 2007...

AN AFFAIR TO REMEMBER

by
Karen Kendall

When Captain Nikolas Pappas first fell in love with Helena Stamos, he was a penniless deckhand and she was the daughter of a shipping magnate. But he's never forgiven himself for the way he left her—and fifteen years later, he's determined to win her back.

Though the attraction is still there, Helena is hesitant to get involved. Nick left her once...what's to stop him from doing it again?

HARLEQUIN
Romance

New York Times bestselling author

DIANA PALMER

Handsome, eligible ranch owner Stuart York knew
Ivy Conley was too young for him, so he closed his heart
to her and sent her away—despite the fireworks between
them. Now, years later, Ivy is determined not to be
treated like a little girl anymore…but for some reason,
Stuart is always fighting her battles for her. And safe in
Stuart's arms makes Ivy feel like a woman…his woman.

Winter Roses

Available November.